■ ■ ■

Papers rustled, and Day turned to see some unused tags flutter off the registration table. Hilda made no move to retrieve them. "What's wrong?" Day asked sharply, advancing toward the table between the regally lifted heads of roses. Then she halted in combined relief and chagrin as she realized the face regarding her from under the rakish hat brim was that of the mannequin. Some practical joker had set it at the table. The vibrations must have been jarring, however, for even as Day watched, the plastic figure listed sideways and fell to the floor, the hat tumbling free to reveal a bald head beneath. From that position, the face looked up at her with the same serene smile.

But if the dummy was at the table, then who…

A dragging dread slowed Day's steps as she proceeded around the table and stood looking down at the crumpled form of Hilda Graveston, who lay facedown on the dais.…On the floor under her outstretched hand lay a white rose, its petals splotched with blood.

■ ■ ■

A "THYME WILL TELL" MYSTERY

# ROSES FOR REGRET

## AUDREY STALLSMITH

WATERBROOK
PRESS

ROSES FOR REGRET
PUBLISHED BY WATERBROOK PRESS
5446 North Academy Boulevard, Suite 200
Colorado Springs, Colorado 80918
*A division of Random House, Inc.*

The characters and events in this book are fictional, and any resemblance
to actual persons or events is coincidental.

Quotes opening chapters are from *King Henry the Sixth*, Part 1, 2.4, Part 3, 2.5,
and *The Tragedy of King Richard the Third*, 5.5, by William Shakespeare.

Two stanzas from "The Aristocrat" by G. K. Chesterton, published in *The
Collected Poems of G. K. Chesterton,* by Dodd, Mead & Co., New York, 1980,
are used by permission of A. P. Watt on behalf of the Royal Literary Fund.

ISBN 1-57856-145-0

Library of Congress Cataloging-in-Publication Data

Stallsmith, Audrey.
 Roses for regret / Audrey Stallsmith.—1st ed.
  p. cm.—(A "thyme will tell" mystery ; bk. 3)
 ISBN 1-57856-145-0 (pbk.)
 I. Title. II. Series: Stallsmith, Audrey. Thyme will tell mysteries ; bk. 3.
PS3569.T3216R64 1999
813'.54—dc21          99-11299
                   CIP

Printed in the United States of America
1999—First Edition

10 9 8 7 6 5 4 3 2 1

*To Brett, Karen, Aleta, Loren, and Carter,*
*my singular siblings who made me what I am today*
*(Aren't you ashamed of yourselves?)*
*With love from Audball*

## THE THYME WILL TELL MYSTERIES

Book I: Rosemary for Remembrance

Book II: Marigolds for Mourning

Book III: Roses for Regret

# CHAPTER 1
■ ■ ■

*Then for the truth and plainness of the case,*
*I pluck this pale and maiden blossom here,*
*Giving my verdict on the white rose side.*

The bedroom had pivoted during the night. Damia Day's feet pointed at a wall that had withdrawn itself. Besides, it was the wrong wall, and she felt cold.

Turning her aching head, she discovered she was lying on top of the covers, across her bed rather than lengthwise in it. That explained the chill and her disorientation. The room glowed with sunlight.

She squinted groggily at the alarm clock. She must be reading it wrong. Pushing herself to a sitting position, she focused on the numbers until the blur around them dissolved. It couldn't be nine. She never slept until nine.

She never slept in her clothes either. Damia, better known simply as Day, stood, staggered, and grabbed the back of a chair. Her body, leaden and detached, was not keeping up with her startled mind.

Releasing the chair, she tottered toward the door and fell. Her body scarcely registered the impact. She crawled through the doorway and across the living-room floor into the kitchen, fuzzily noting dust and cobwebs under furniture she had thought reasonably clean. *Foul underneath like you, Day, dear.* High on the table above her loomed the glass from which she had drunk milk the night before.

Day reached up for the end of the counter, dragged herself erect to lean against it, and fumbled with the lock on the back door. Cool, fresh air surged into her face. She raised her eyes from dewy, verdant grass to—black. The roses, unresponsive to the coaxing caress of sunlight, were black, drooping, burnt, lifeless.

"Falco," she said.

Her voice rang in the quiet. Only then did she recognize that quiet. Her head turned, compelled, toward the small barn to the rear of the property.

"Oh, dear God, he wouldn't!" She couldn't even run in a straight line. She veered erratically, fell, pushed up, reeled, and crumpled again into the soft May grass.

Her breath heaving in dry sobs, she crept on hands and knees the last few yards. By then, she knew. She had no hope left as she put her hand to the sliding door and pushed at it from her knees.

The neat rows of boxes and cages had been tumbled, wrenched apart, stomped. The bodies of animals, songbirds, squirrels, and possums lay dead in the debris like victims of a peculiarly localized cyclone. All of the animals people had brought to her to heal, to make whole—unstirring and lax.

She sank forward and lay facedown and as still as the animals, the gentle sunlight on her back and the breeze whispering in the straw. Then something banged, flailed against metal, screeched. She bolted to her feet. The hawk glared at

her defiantly through th...
was its temporary cage. T...
of this bird.

"Oh, Ivan," she whisper...
hate saved you." With a scra...
tempt to spread one splinted ...
still managed to hop up onto th...

Day leaned to snatch up a tow...
less. The bird succeeded in landing...
before she straightened to toss the ... and
grab at his legs just above the ankles.

"That's right," she whispered, sta... at something that
glittered in the straw. "Hate me, Ivan, hate me." Either the
killer had been frightened or had some fellow feeling.

*Falco*. Latin for "falcon."

"Hate will keep you alive."

■ ■ ■

*Dear Regan,*

*I hope you will be able to read this. My hands are
shaking so much that I can scarcely write. Day came
to my door this morning with blood running down
her face from where that awful bird had bit her.
She would insist on keeping him with her though—
probably because he is the only animal she has
left alive.*

*Most horrible was her quietness, her passiveness.
You know Day isn't like that.*

*She woke from a drugged sleep this morning to
find her rosebushes poisoned and her animals
killed. All but the hawk she calls Ivan, because it is*

*probably only left it because a*
*company symbol. As a signature to his*
*other words. He's her neighbor on the other*

Day thinks somebody must have crept into her house and put something in her milk carton. Perhaps one of those new date-rape drugs, though she says she wasn't hurt herself. Fortunately, I've always insisted that she lock her doors at night.

A couple of women who do volunteer work for her are over there now, cleaning out the cages and crying. But Day won't cry. She's lying here on my couch, staring at nothing, as she's been doing all day. The police chief said that the drug will probably keep her wiped out for a while.

But I know this isn't over, Regan. We have no proof that Falco did it, and his fertilizer company is the main industry in this town. There's no way he is going to be arrested. He has set out systematically to destroy Day. She's already lost her job as secretary to our local lawyer. Everybody knows why. She has always spent more on her animals than she has on herself. She and her volunteers even scavenge in Dumpsters for old vegetables and outdated meat. I call it a thankless job, too, because when the animals recover, she just lets them go.

You may wonder why I'm telling you all this. Falco is worming his way into NORA. He has some impressive gardens, granted, but he also has a gardener who does all the work—and he is very chemi-

*cally oriented. I know we have no rule about that, but most of us have followed your mother's example.*

*One of the reasons for pushing old roses, after all, is that they don't require unnatural pampering. As you know, we had two open places on the board. I can understand your turning us down. I know how busy you are. But, Regan, for your mother's sake, I beg you to reconsider. You could help to counterbalance Falco, whom Day and I have been outvoted on. The others want him. He has offered to host our meetings, and he can certainly afford it. It will save us money, but I hate to think what it will cost us.*

*Day is ascetic, solitary, and sometimes prickly, but she is the closest thing to a daughter that I have ever had. This blank look of hers is frightening me.*

*Right now, I am as afraid of what she might do as of what might be done to her. And that horrible bird is banging at his cage like something evil trying to get out. Please, Regan, say you'll come in June.*

*Love,*
*Millicent*

Having finished reading the letter aloud at the breakfast table, Regan Culver said, "Millie is the emotional type, granted, but I'm afraid this time she probably does have something to worry about."

"NORA is the rose society your mother founded?" Agatha,

Regan's half sister, was elegant, abrupt, and in her fifties. She liked to have everything clear.

"Yes, the Northeastern Old Roses Association. Its base has moved over the years, though, from here in Massachusetts to Pennsylvania. I've been asked to join the board several times. Largely, I imagine, because of the members' respect for my mother. But I've always declined. It's a long way to drive for meetings. I have kept up my membership and try to attend the conference every fall, but I didn't make it last year."

"This Falco was running for the Senate down there, and this Day woman accused him of polluting a river, if I remember correctly." Agatha also had a way of returning to the point.

"That's right." Regan dropped the letter on the table, stirred honey into her rosemary tea and, rising, carried it with her to a window overlooking the kitchen garden. "Day is a wildlife rehabilitator, and she was concerned about ducks dying on the Renova River. Falco owns a fertilizer company. Some other manufacturers routinely dispose of dangerous refuse by paying fertilizer makers to mix it into their product. Surprisingly enough, it seems to be legal. Another good reason not to buy chemical fertilizers."

She turned back to Agatha. "Day took samples of the water where it flows by Falco's plant and had it tested. The lab found some arsenic. In the primary, it was enough to drop Falco from a narrow lead to an also-ran. Of course, he claimed that his company had never included waste products in its fertilizer and that Ms. Day must have planted the arsenic herself. Apparently the public didn't believe him. Apparently he is also a sore loser."

"Which is why I think you should stay out of the whole mess," Agatha said. "You may only succeed in deflecting his fire to yourself."

Regan smiled. "That's an idea. *Garrets and Gardens* has been wanting me to do an essay for them. Suppose I concentrate on this fertilizer issue, maybe mention Falco by name?"

"Suppose you get smacked with a libel suit?" Agatha pushed back impatiently from the table. "Be reasonable, Regan. It's all very well to root for the underdog, but you don't know that Falco killed those animals. It seems unlikely to me. He must realize it would ruin his chances of running for office again. The only thing you do know is, if he is the guilty party, he is not entirely rational when thwarted."

"I don't like Day's going so quiet all of a sudden," Regan said. "She's a small, fragile-looking blond, but her appearance is deceptive. She's always been very outspoken, especially where conservation issues are concerned. Some have even called her strident. She and I, both being single and about the same age, have hung out together at the conferences. And she was very supportive when I was indicted. She wrote me a letter saying that all the cops up here must be imbeciles. Offered to come up and tell them so too."

Regan smiled reminiscently. "Day isn't the type to take something like this lying down."

"I can see her dousing him with weed-killer and striking a match," Agatha conceded. "Which, if she's right about him, is no more than he deserves. But I suppose you would say that she should forgive."

"I never said that was easy."

"Exactly what date is this meeting in June?"

"The weekend of the twenty-third."

"On second thought, maybe you should go away then."

"Because it was supposed to be my wedding day?" Regan sounded amused. "A non-anniversary, in fact."

"How long," Agatha asked impatiently, "are you going to keep wearing Matt Olin's ring?"

"I told him I would wait until June. A betrothal is a promise, and I haven't been released from this one yet."

"The man hasn't spoken to you for months. Are you still in love with him?"

"I don't know. I think God would consider that irrelevant."

■　■　■

Bram Falco and his cousin were also talking about a broken engagement. "Did you ever intend to marry Paula?" Gavin Falco asked.

Bram shrugged. "When you're running for office, *fiancée* sounds better than *girlfriend*—more settled. I never asked her to marry me. She knew that was only a courtesy title."

"And now that you're not running for office, you don't need her anymore? You had better be careful, Bram. You're alienating a lot of people. You haven't been yourself since you lost that election."

"Are you so sure what *myself* is?"

Suit coats slung over their shoulders, they were walking up an alley to a parking lot. Bram was a big, swarthy, hairy man in his late thirties with a bullish, thick neck and shoulders. Some had said he looked more like a stevedore than a senatorial candidate—though they had cynically allowed that his harsh features, which had been compared to those of the falcon on his company crest, gave him much more the rapacious, political look.

Gavin was shorter, lighter skinned, and blond. "Little White Falcon," his cousin occasionally called him; it was what the name *Gavin* meant.

Although abrupt and impatient by nature, Bram also had

a certain brash magnetism that usually carried the day for him. Since his defeat, however, he had been downright rude to friends, servants, and political allies alike. Upon being told he was ruining his chances at another run for office, Bram had laughed. "What chances? The public will forgive almost anything but failure."

"What happened to Day's animals has made people sick," Gavin said. "It was a brutal thing for somebody to do." But not something he envisioned his cousin doing. Bram was much more direct than that. If Day had been a man, for instance, Gavin could see Bram punching her.

"So it was," Bram agreed. "How do you know she didn't do it herself?"

They came around a corner just then and saw Damia Day standing knee-deep in a Dumpster behind a grocery store and holding a shriveled eggplant in her hands. She could hardly have helped overhearing. She wore faded jeans and an equally worn chambray shirt. The violently purple vegetable was the only vivid thing about her. Brushing tawny hair out of gray eyes that were beginning to show squint lines at the corners, she dropped the eggplant into a garbage bag held by a frightened looking teenage girl.

"Hello, Day," Gavin said uneasily.

"Hello." She and Bram seemed the least discomposed people present. She bent to her search again.

The teenage girl gathered her courage to address Bram. "That was a horrid thing to say."

He nodded at her politely. "You'll find that life can be horrid sometimes, my dear."

"Let it go, Joan." Day's voice was muffled by her bent posture. "He knows what he did."

Bram jerked his chin at Gavin and walked on.

"The girl's right," Gavin said when they were out of earshot. "It *was* a horrid thing to say. How could you think Day would do something like that?"

"For attention. Planting that arsenic won the wretched woman the only attention she's ever had. And she liked it. I'm sure she's receiving plenty of sympathy without yours."

"Bram, if you don't mind my saying, you're not being rational about this. You don't know that she planted anything. They say arsenic leaches out of treated wood. I'm sure we have some treated wood around the plant somewhere. Or the lab could have made a mistake."

"Oh, it was a mistake all right. On her part."

■ ■ ■

The two men were trotting their horses through an old overgrown orchard a couple of days later when they came upon Damia Day again, this time sitting with her back against an apple tree. A hawk, tethered to her gauntleted wrist by a long, leather cord, lunged futilely upward at the end of its leash. One of its wings wore a contour splint.

High canopies of poplar leaves roofed the aisles between trees and admitted only a stippled, shifting sunlight. The gnarled tree against which Day sat reached toward them with malignant, arthritic fingers. Ferns and May apples ringed it like tiny umbrellas. Even Gavin, not an imaginative type, could see something exaggerated in this setting, as if it were an illuminated illustration from a medieval allegory. From a time when good and evil, battle itself, had been more clearly defined and immediate. Women who lurked along those allegorical trails were usually up to no good.

In the lead, Bram reined in sharply. "Isn't that cruel?"

The horses danced nervously in place, their rolling eyes fascinated by the raptor, their hooves making scarcely any sound on the thick leaf mold. The greens in the picture glowed a shade too bright to be real, and Day looked insubstantial enough to be a spirit. On the hand she stretched toward the bird gleamed a ring, a miniature silver hawk with spread wings, grasping a turquoise sphere in its talons.

"If he doesn't get his exercise, his chest muscles will atrophy," Day said, "and he'll never be able to fly at all. I usually take the hawks to someone else because I don't have the facilities for them. But the woman didn't have space this time. There are just too many hawks these days."

"I'll give you five hundred dollars for him."

Gavin thought it contemptuous the way his cousin threw down that price, as if knowing how much she needed the money.

Day didn't appear perturbed. "He isn't mine to buy or sell."

"He obviously doesn't like you," Bram pointed out.

"He hates me. He thinks I brought him down."

"Didn't you?"

"Of course not." Her voice remained calm, almost detached. "His greediness was his downfall. When a hawk is after something, that's all he sees. He doesn't care about anything else—until he gets run over."

A certain wariness had crept into Bram's narrowed gaze. She was on his property. Gavin was surprised his cousin hadn't mentioned that. "Aren't you afraid that he will hurt you?" Bram asked.

She shrugged. "He already has. But I can wait him out."

"A thousand dollars if you let him go now." Bram's tone was harsh—almost, Gavin thought, desperate.

She shook her head and began relentlessly to reel in the bird. "He can't fly this way."

"He would prefer to be free of you even if he is crippled."

"But it wouldn't be best for him."

The meaning of the conversation obviously went deeper than the fate of one hawk. Some understanding, some code existed between these two that Gavin couldn't penetrate. Day pressed her gauntleted hand against the hawk's legs from behind, and as if compelled, the bird stepped backward onto the glove.

Bram whirled his horse away. "If he kills you, it'll be your own fault then!"

The raw hatred in his face took Gavin aback. He found such extreme emotion incomprehensible and embarrassing.

He didn't catch up with his cousin until their galloping horses burst into a field where Bram reined back to a jog again. "Can a hawk really kill a person?" Gavin asked.

Bram looked at him blankly. "What?"

Gavin laughed uneasily. "The way you act, one would think she was a bad fairy or something."

"One of the Furies, more like."

"You're not scared of her?"

"Of course I am." Bram grinned mirthlessly at his cousin's incomprehension. "Take a lesson, kid. You can at least fight another guy straight out. Females have no concept of fair play. That's why they don't deserve gentler treatment. Give a woman a handicap, and she'll bury you."

He rode straight in at the wide door to the stables, and the groom-gardener, who was cleaning stalls, came forward to hold the horses' bridles as both riders dismounted.

They strode between rose beds toward the house. Bram

paused beside the early-blooming Therese Bugnet. "They look soft," he continued, cupping his fingers under the base of one of the blossoms, "but"—he spread those fingers to reveal a trickle of blood—"thorns," he finished succinctly.

■ ■ ■

On a Friday morning in June, Regan pulled her Land Rover into a driveway beside a small white house. A girl appeared in the open doorway of the barn farther back. Advancing to meet her, Regan discovered it was not a girl but Day herself. Almost two years had passed since they had seen each other, and the latter of those two years had been a hard one for both of them. Fine lines were etched in Day's forehead and at the corners of her eyes, the same kind Regan was becoming all too aware of on her own face.

"Regan." Day's smile dispelled any awkwardness. "It was good of you to come." They hugged, and Regan thought that the blond seemed much too slight to have been the cause of all this trouble. Slight and more subdued than Regan remembered her.

"I'm glad you stopped," Day said. "I wanted to say that, even though it was Millie who brought you into all this, you needn't feel obliged to vote on our side."

"Good," Regan replied. "Because I haven't decided how I'm going to vote. I brought you some roses. Do you have another spot that would be good for them?" She inclined her head briefly toward the western slope dotted by blackened stubs. "As you know, roses don't do well where other roses have been. Not to mention that some of that weed-killer is probably still in the ground."

She led the way around to the back of her Rover, cranked down the rear window, and opened the tailgate. All of the available space in the back was crowded with rosebushes in black plastic containers.

Day shook her head dazedly. "I can't possibly accept—"

"Of course you can. These are extras from Thyme Will Tell that we didn't sell this spring. Since we don't have room to propagate many varieties ourselves, we ordered a shipment of heirlooms from Tom Raines's nursery, but we had a few left over. I told Tom that you and I probably would be planting them today, so I won't be surprised if he shows up to help. He's very protective of his roses, says that these should have been set out two months ago. And he's right. Now they're root-bound and stressed. I doubt you'll get much out of them this year. But by next summer, they should be happily settled in. Like people, plants have a strong survival instinct. I brought some rock phosphate and greensand too. I assume you probably have your own composted manure?"

"The pile is out behind the barn," Day said. She was leaning into the Rover to read labels. Tears brimmed in her eyes when she turned back to her visitor, but her voice was steady enough. "A mowed space out there might do for a bed. I'll have to be deserting you from time to time though. I have some baby birds, and they have to be fed every hour during the day. Do you want to see them?"

Regan followed her toward the barn. "How did you ever manage when you were working?"

"I kept them in Millie's garage, and she fed them for me. She would become overly attached though. You can't do that with wild animals. The whole point is to make them independent of you."

The baby birds nestled in berry boxes bedded with facial tissues. Those boxes rested on grates over homemade incubators, which actually were wooden crates with low-wattage light bulbs bolted inside.

As Regan touched the side of one of the boxes, three robin mouths opened and shrieked.

"Why don't you feed those?" Day suggested, crossing to an old refrigerator and bringing back a dish of what looked like raw meat loaf.

"What is that?"

"Hamburger, baby cereal, egg yolk, and milk." Day handed Regan a drinking straw that had been cut on a slant. "You can use this. I had better do the doves. Theirs is cereal pellets with corn and oatmeal. But since they're used to regurgitated food, I have to wet the pellets and stuff them down their throats. Also, they tend to circle when they're begging and have to be held still. In general, it's best not to handle wild animals any more than necessary. You don't want them tame."

"This is great." Regan tentatively poked bits of meat into gaping mouths that were much less tentative about gulping them down. "What do you feed the hawk?"

"Road kill mostly." Day looked up from the dove cradled against her to smile at Regan's expression. "You can't do this wildlife stuff if you're squeamish, and hawks need fur and feathers to clean out their crops. Actually, many rehabilitators feed them live mice, but I'm not really set up for raptors. To do what I do, you can't have a sentimental view of nature. You have to realize that if your patients aren't kept apart they're likely to kill each other. Exercising Ivan on a leash wasn't working. I have him out in the aviary now." She tipped her head toward the east. "On the other side of that wall. It was meant for smaller birds, but at least he can stretch his wings a bit."

After they had finished with the birds, the two women managed to set several rosebushes in place before lunchtime. They had decided to dig planting holes instead of trying to spade up a complete bed.

"You can cover the spaces between the bushes with black plastic," Regan said, spreading out the cloth from the picnic basket she had brought along. "If you want to kill the grass, that is. You could just leave it. I have a friend who does hers that way, just mulches for a few inches around the base of each bush and uses a lawn trimmer on the grass. It requires a steady hand, of course, but it seems to work for her."

She passed a plate of roast chicken to Day. "That's one of the things I like about gardening. Each person can bring his or her peculiar stamp to it. That's why I debate the wisdom of Millie's plan too. In theory it may seem like a good idea to have the society resolve to espouse only organic methods. But it's going to alienate some of your members. And you must admit that roses are one of the hardest flowers to grow by purely natural means."

"I do admit that," Day said. "This is very good, by the way." She waved the drumstick on which she had been munching. "I see the difficulty factor as irrelevant though. I'm the one who has to take care of the birds that are brought in suffering toxic shock. Hummingbirds are the most affected because they take nectar from sprayed flowers. You might not know that they also eat the tiny insects attracted by that nectar. Every little bit hurts. Right is right, no matter how hard it is. You of all people should know that, since you're a Christian."

Regan flushed. "Yes, but I can't compel other people to adopt my beliefs without violating those beliefs myself."

"Neither are we compelling them. We just want the society to make a recommendation. Whether our members follow it or not is up to them. My term has expired, by the way. If I'm kicked out, you won't have to worry; Millie won't have enough votes without me." Day laid her chicken bone aside and wiped her fingers neatly on a napkin.

"Have some more," Regan said. "There's plenty. My sister made it. Her way of sending condolences."

"Tell her thank you. I don't usually eat much for lunch." Day began to pick grapes from a bunch. "Part of belonging to a poor family," she added with a wry smile, nodding toward the modest white house that was little more than a cottage. "After my father left, my mother moved here to take a housekeeping job with Connie Falco. Connie demanded long hours and paid only a pittance. My mother was always afraid to quit though. It was the only job she had ever known; she didn't think she would be able to find another. You know how different organizations collect for the needy at Christmastime? Well, in this town my mother and I were it. We had turkeys and fruit baskets coming in from everybody. We always ate well around the holidays."

"I'm sorry," Regan said.

Day shot her an amused look. "For what? We survived."

"And instead of going to college, you had to stay and take care of your mother when she developed cancer," Regan said. "Millie told me. And you'd had a scholarship."

"I imagine Millie made it sound quite pitiful." Day shook her head. "I have no regrets. After all my mother had sacrificed for me, she deserved some consideration. She died very quickly. So as not to be a bother, I expect."

"You're bitter."

"For myself, no. I'm happy doing what I'm doing. For her, yes. Connie Falco was a sadist. Oh, she looked fragile on the surface, but she got her kicks from ambushing people. Building them up just to cut them down again. But she delivered her deadly jabs so subtly that some people—guys especially—had a hard time believing she had done it on purpose. After a couple of encounters, other females got her measure, all right. Everybody hated her, but the guys, at least, felt guilty about it. In a way I feel sorry for Bram. She's the one who kept him tied to that factory where he really didn't want to be."

Day reached into the basket for a brownie. "Another lesson from my childhood," she continued matter-of-factly. "When the food's available, eat a lot of it."

Regan said, "What did Bram's mother look like?"

Day smiled. "Like me. Better looking, but basically small and blond."

"Do you think—"

"It's kind of hard to miss, isn't it? Yes, it was Bram's mother who kept him pinned down here. And when he finally got his chance to fly, it was another scrawny blond who clipped his wings. That's how he sees it anyway."

She chewed reflectively as she looked over the ranks of rosebushes still to be planted. "It's our apparent weakness, hers and mine, that frustrates him more than anything, I think. There's no way he can settle this as he would be able to with another man. And since he couldn't admit to hating her, I get the full load."

She stood and dusted crumbs from her fingers. "An interesting psychological study, isn't it? None of this would have happened if he had taken me seriously when I asked him to have that water tested. If he had agreed, I wouldn't have insisted that the results be made public. But he just said, 'Don't be silly, Dame.' I suppose it *is* hard to take the daughter of your former housekeeper seriously."

"Are you sure Falco killed your animals?"

"Yes." Day's expression had turned tight and cautious.

"How can you be sure?" Regan persisted. "Does he have a reputation for violence?"

"Meaning, is he a bully? No, not that I've heard. But then, he never had to be. This is probably the first time he hasn't gotten what he wanted. Excuse me." She started back toward the roses.

With her head turned away from the drive, Day had not seen Tom Raines's approach. Even though he was quite tall, Tom was easy to overlook. He had a slightly hunched, bespectacled look that implied he should be squinting into a computer screen. In reality, Tom despised technology. Coming up to Regan, he slipped and slid down beside her with a nonchalance that implied he had done it on purpose. He probably had. Regan suspected Tom's notorious clumsiness was largely for laughs.

"Sounds like the hawks have it," he said, propping himself up on an elbow. "We aren't going to avoid a confrontation. So which side is it going to be for you—Lancaster or York?"

"Pardon?"

He grinned. "The War of the Roses, as I recall, was a down-and-dirty conflict that happened before the English had manufactured any fancy ideas about honor. And from what I've been hearing, this one may well give it a run for the money."

"And which faction will you join?"

"Need you ask? I'm always for environmental righteousness.

Besides, Day ordered most of her bushes from me. A few at a time. It took her years to build up the collection that somebody wiped out in one night. I don't like somebody slaughtering my innocents. So I stand for the white rose, the maiden fair. I have a feeling it's going to be a neat split up the middle and that you will have to cast the deciding vote. 'Judge you, my Lord of Warwick, then between us.'"

"So you believe Falco did kill those animals?"

Tom looked away. "Guys like that can't stand to be crossed." A certain bitterness in his tone was, Regan suspected, more on his own behalf than Day's. It seemed his opinion of Bram Falco might not be objective either. But Tom's evasive answer also implied to Regan that he wasn't positive of the other man's guilt.

Watching Day's slight figure bend to the spade, Regan wondered why the woman had been so forthcoming about her past. She had never mentioned her family before. *These people are all virtual strangers to me*, Regan realized. *We get together for a few days once a year and discuss our shared passion for roses. But how much do I really know about them?*

Granted, sometimes it was easier to talk to someone you didn't know well, but she suspected Day's revelations had been calculated to spark pity and righteous indignation. Even this subtlest of pressures annoyed Regan. "Sweet as molasses most of the time," she had overheard one of her teenage employees comment once, "but push Regan too hard and things get sticky."

Regan wasn't proud of such a passive-aggressive trait. But something more than that had given rise to her sudden resistance. Something veiled and secretive in Day had shown itself at the end of the conversation. If she was telling the truth, she was, Regan suspected, not telling all of it. Wasn't it more likely that Day had retained bitterness toward the family that had treated her mother so shabbily? Had blamed the Falcos for the loss of her own education and career?

Through Regan's mind ran a belated response to Tom's earlier quote: *Between two hawks, which flies the higher pitch?*

# CHAPTER 2

*Prick not your finger as you pluck it off,*
*Lest bleeding you do paint the white rose red*
*And fall on my side so, against your will.*

"I say the girl goes." Hilda Graveston approached Regan with no more greeting than that.

"She's hardly a *girl*," Regan responded mildly. Hilda was in her sixties, her big-boned but shapely figure topped by an incongruously plain face with a bulbous nose and an aggressively square jaw.

"She looks it." Hilda turned to stare disapprovingly at Day. "In white too. Probably trying to appear the wounded innocent. After what she did to Bram, I'm surprised she has the gall to walk into his house."

Regan would have expected the simple, sleeveless, white gown to make Day look more faded than ever. But by contrast, it emphasized a light tan that had scarcely been noticeable before and deepened the fair hair to topaz and the gray eyes to azure. Day could be quite attractive when she chose to be.

"She didn't pick where the meeting was to be held," Regan pointed out.

They were all very civilized, eight well-dressed people chatting over drinks while waiting to go in to dinner. The house was very civilized, quietly luxurious from the gleaming hardwoods to the bouquets of roses in crystal bowls. Regan wondered who had picked the roses. Gavin Falco had apologized nervously to her for any disorder, explaining that their housekeeper had quit a couple of days before. Apparently Bram was antagonizing others in addition to his political allies. There had not been time, though, for disorder to accrue.

Unless it was the disorder in Bram Falco's person. Both his hair and his expensive black suit were rumpled. His tie sagged from his shirt collar, and his muscular shoulders strained at the bonds of his jacket. Though she saw no evidence of it in his bearing or speech, Regan suspected he had been drinking before they arrived. Something hot lurked in his dark eyes. Scarcely listening to the man beside him, Bram openly stared at Day. The stare was not the kind calculated to give a female any demure satisfaction. Conventions were conventions, granted, but a breaking down of concern with them often pointed to a deeper breakdown.

As if sensing Regan's worry, Hilda pushed her advantage. Still watching Bram, the older woman said, "I've known him since he was eight. I think he's done exceptionally well, considering the she-devil who raised him. He didn't kill those animals; take it from me. But he may do much worse before this is over. Gavin tells me that Bram hasn't been back to the factory since he lost the election. He's been drinking heavily, not eating or sleeping, and a couple of days ago he was talking to his lawyer about his will. Do you realize what all those signs point to?"

"Suicide."

"Yes. And maybe not just suicide. A man who is going to kill himself has nothing to lose, you know.

"I hear you're a Chesterton fan. So you may recall Father

Brown saying he would crush all the Gothic arches in the world into powder to save one human soul."

"Yes," Regan admitted cautiously.

"I have the same attitude toward institutions of any kind. I liked your mother, but I'll shatter this society of hers if that is what it takes to save Bram. And I think she would have backed me on that. Tell Day I'll get her on any other board she chooses. I have contacts. But she's off this one. It's for her own good."

Hilda swept back to join her host. Regan had been introduced to him upon arrival. Though Bram Falco had been taking top honors at the society rose show for years, Regan had never met him. She seldom attended the show, and he seldom attended the conference.

Only she and Hilda were staying at the house. The others lived close enough to commute. Coming down from the guest room to which she had been assigned, Regan had found the board members already in two separate clusters: Tom Raines talking to Millie and Day, Paul Sedgwick allied with Hilda and Bram. Reluctant to join either group lest she give the appearance of partiality, Regan had chatted with Bram's cousin instead. Although Gavin had veered off at Hilda's approach, he now drifted back.

"I don't see why this whole thing has to be so charged," he complained. "And Hilda is only making things worse. Granted, she's an old family friend, but how can she presume to say that Bram is cracking up? I admit he hasn't been himself lately, but he'll get over it. Can't people see that they're exaggerating this all out of proportion?"

"Oh, I don't know." Regan swirled the ginger ale in her goblet. "Somebody said that we're at our most natural when we realize the importance of things."

Gavin looked disappointed in her. "You're not saying that the decisions of one little gardening organization have any colossal significance in the cosmic order?"

"Not in the *visible* order of things." Regan watched bubbles rise in her soda. "But if you're a Christian, you have to acknowledge all of life as being a desperate struggle between salvation and damnation. And one never knows where the breaking point will come." She looked seriously up at him.

She was discomfiting the younger man. That wasn't surprising. Most people didn't like the idea that their actions could be as crucial as that.

"And you think my cousin is at that point?"

*I don't know your cousin,* she wanted to say, but found her lips forming an implacable "Yes" instead.

He laughed embarrassedly. "Well, that's direct anyhow. Excuse me." And he drifted across to Day's group.

"Hello, Regan." Paul approached her at once. He was one of those intellectual amateurs who were common at rose shows, amateur only in that he didn't make his living in the gardening business. He was, if Regan remembered rightly, a professor of some kind. He had a handsome, light-skinned face and smooth, shiny, blond hair. He and Gavin, Regan thought, were a good example of how two people could answer to the same description—slim, fair, and fine featured—and yet have an altogether different presence. Paul was collected and watchful, whereas Gavin was uneasy and socially inept. They did have one thing in common though. Either of them would probably be considered better looking than Bram Falco. But when Bram was in the room, they paled in comparison.

"I'm surprised you've taken sides so soon," Regan said to Paul, going on the offensive.

"I can acknowledge common sense," he replied. "Hilda is right. A board cannot survive personal animosities. I see no point in breaking up this organization over one person. And I'm a realist. Bram can do more for us than Day can, so logically she should be the one to go."

"It is expedient that one man die for the people?" Regan suggested sweetly. "Or, in this case, one woman?"

He raised an eyebrow. "That's from Scripture, isn't it?"

"Yes, from the priest who ordered Jesus' arrest."

"Let's not get carried away, Regan. We're not talking about anybody dying here."

*Aren't we?* Regan wanted to snap, wanted to crash her frivolous drink down on the table beside her. *If there's even the slightest chance of that, we had better take it seriously. I've had my fill of murder this past year. It's a sickening waste, and I'm not going to stand around making small talk and pretending it can't happen.* In actuality, her hand trembled only slightly.

"How do you know *what* you're talking about, Paul? Both of them have been under tremendous strain recently. Rationality doesn't hold up well under pressure."

Paul, the quintessence of rationality, looked puzzled but agreeable. "All the more reason to separate them then. Best way to resolve any conflict is to keep the combatants apart."

Millie approached. She was one of those soft, sentimental women who can be roused to fury over unfairness, and she was virtually quivering. "Paul, how could you take that man's side?"

She didn't wait for an answer. "After what he did to Day, who is the sweetest, most self-sacrificing person I know. She's like her name, in fact." Millie seemed much pleased with this comparison. Regan winced inwardly as the other woman embellished it. "She's *day*, and he's *night*. That's much better than

Tom's analogy about the roses. It would take a black rose, not a red one, to represent Bram Falco."

"People are not that simple, Millie," Regan said.

Millie looked disappointed in her. "I'm surprised at you, Regan. I thought you believed in right and wrong. What you're doing is called equivocating."

"What you're doing," Regan responded sharply, "is called judging."

A woman wearing an apron came into the room and said something to Bram. He nodded and addressed the room at large. "All right, people. The caterer tells me dinner is ready. So"—he straightened, flexed his shoulders, sketched a mock bow in Day's direction, and offered his arm—"shall we, Ms. Day?"

■ ■ ■

Settling herself in the chair pulled out for her by Paul Sedgwick, Regan looked across the candlelit table. Day was straight-backed and calm in the seat at Bram Falco's right hand where she had been escorted. With her blond hair elegantly upswept in a French twist, she seemed much more unflappably upper class than he did.

Even Paul had been taken aback by Bram's move. Millie had gasped. But Day had glided forward to take the proffered arm with no show of surprise at all.

*Move* was the right word for it, Regan thought, as in a chess game. Regan had always found chess nerve-racking. One never knew from which direction an attack would come.

"Wine, ladies?" Bram inquired, as the caterer hovered with a bottle.

"No, thank you," Day said, and Regan shook her head.

"Are you a teetotaler, Ms. Culver?" Bram inquired. "Chesterton had, as I recall, a very poor opinion of teetotalers."

27

Regan blinked. The man had heard, apparently, much more than he should have of his guests' conversations. "You're right. Chesterton thought abstainers priggish, I expect, and too careful of their own dignity. I don't like the taste of alcohol myself."

"And you, Ms. Day?"

"It's unnecessary," she said.

"Our local ascetic." Bram swirled the wine in his own goblet, watching her. "So you believe that things should be judged by their necessity?"

"They should when you're on a budget like mine," Day responded dryly. She picked up her salad fork, and her silver hawk ring winked in the flicker of candle flame. It was the only jewelry she wore.

"Are you a Chesterton fan yourself, Mr. Falco?" Regan asked quickly.

"The man is entertaining. Perhaps a bit too romantic. The type who can see glory in common things and common men. The common people are, in my experience, easily fooled."

"But we weren't fools enough to elect you," Tom Raines said.

The suddenness and directness of the attack was staggering to most of them. But Day calmly continued to eat her salad, and Bram grinned ferociously. "Look at whom you did elect. Randall Feebes. Namby-pamby Randy, we used to call him. You think he's going to side with you naturalists? Oh, he'll pretend to, but he's the type who is overawed by power, and you know who has the power—big business. Nothing will change. The truth is, you didn't vote *for* Feebes; you voted *against* me. Isn't that right?"

Raines looked thoughtful. "You may have a point."

"And on the slenderest of evidence."

Bram still seemed to be addressing Tom. Day had stopped eating, though her gaze remained centered on her plate.

"Unfortunately, these days the politician is disbelieved. Whom would you have voted for, Miss Culver, assuming that you lived in our sylvan state?"

Bram had not shifted his attention from Raines, so the question caught Regan by surprise. She flushed. "Probably for you," she said finally. At Millie's accusing look, Regan added defensively, "Mr. Falco is against abortion, and I would not be a true environmentalist if I didn't believe in protecting the most important life-form of all. Besides," she added with an apologetic glance at Day, "I thought the accusations against him were entered too late, when there wasn't time enough to prove or disprove them."

"Thank you, Miss Culver," Bram said. "Unfortunately, the majority of the electorate is, as I pointed out, considerably more gullible than you are."

Day's cheeks had flushed a faint pink, but she did not speak. *A wise move on her part,* Regan thought. *Silence cannot be countered.*

Bram's dark gaze was becoming increasingly frustrated. Regan could see why he was attractive to women. He was extremely masculine with all of the masculine thirst for battle, but his opponent wasn't cooperating. Regan could readily picture Bram at a medieval feast, throwing bones under the table for the dogs, ready to ride off to the Crusades. He had a certain no-holds-barred intensity to him that Chesterton would have liked. Regan was unwillingly inclined to like Bram herself.

*Probably,* she told herself reprovingly, *because he complimented your intelligence. We females are very vulnerable to compliments, and the man knows that. He's no dummy himself. Watch your step.*

And who would Day have been? The saint in one of the stiff, pre-Renaissance paintings with sadly serene face lifted to heaven? Those saints had frequently come to very painful ends.

Regan didn't remember afterward how the conversation had moved on to the subject of names and their meaning, but she seized upon it with relief. She admitted ruefully that *Regan* had originally been a male name—at least up until the time Shakespeare had used it for one of the cruel older daughters in *King Lear.*

*Hilda* appropriately meant "battle woman" and *Millicent* "highborn power." The name *Thomas,* Raines revealed, identified a twin and had gained its popularity not from the doubter in the New Testament but from the twelfth-century martyr, Thomas à Becket.

Another New Testament name, *Paul,* denoted smallness. They discussed whether that was what the apostle had implied when he described his bodily presence as weak.

Bram's certainly was not. Even though he had remained silent during this small talk, Regan suspected that everyone at the table was all too aware of his smoldering attendance.

"My first name means the same as my last," Gavin said. "Falcon. But *Bram* stands for a raven instead."

"Rather a plethora of wild and predatory birds," Tom commented dryly.

"Isn't it?" Bram agreed.

Since this agreed a shade too conveniently with Millie's earlier metaphor of light and dark to describe Day and Bram, Regan wished that Gavin would drop the subject. But, finally receiving some response from his moody cousin, Gavin seemed inclined to persist. "Of course, people are afraid of the raven, too, in some countries. Like Poe, they associate it with death."

The constraint was definitely back now, and even Gavin seemed finally to sense it. He fell silent.

"My father was descended from a titled family," Bram said. He had barely touched his food, and the level of wine in his glass didn't appear to have changed. "The falcon, holding a rose, was on their crest, along with a rather peculiar motto." His gaze still rested, with seeming carelessness, on Day. His tone was almost dreamy. "'Touch me not.' A warning to the family's enemies, I suppose, that interference would prove painful. As Ms. Day could inform us, a hawk's talons can apply a dangerous amount of pressure. You've been too quiet, Ms. Day. What does *Damia* mean?"

She lifted her gaze from her plate to meet his, and a slight smile curved her lips. "To tame," she said.

■　■　■

After dinner, as the others were congregating in the living room again, Regan asked to use a phone. She had promised to check in with Agatha. Bram directed her to his study down the hall. Seated at a large oak desk, Regan dialed her own number.

After she and Agatha had discussed some herb farm business, Agatha said, "Well? Are things as bad there as you were afraid they would be?"

"Worse. This is one of those times I desperately wish my mother were alive. She might have had a chance of resolving this mess. I don't. I have a feeling that man is going to kill himself, Agatha."

"Falco? Well, some guys can't stand to lose."

"I don't think it's entirely that. Besides, what if he decides to take Day with him? Could you find me Reverend Potter's phone number, please?"

"All right. But I want you out of there, Regan. Now."

"No, I don't think he would hurt me." The top of the desk

was bare, and Regan, who had opened a drawer looking for paper and a pencil, caught her breath.

"What is it?" Agatha said sharply.

"A gun. He has a revolver in here. Never mind. That's natural enough. Lots of people have handguns for protection. It just surprised me. Here's some paper. Do you have the number?"

Agatha ground it out in the tone of one exasperated beyond measure. No sooner had she finished than she added, "For once in your life, Regan, listen to me. Even if you're imagining the danger, how long do you think you can stand up under this sort of thing? In one year our father died, you were arrested for his murder, you were almost killed yourself, you became engaged, and you saw that engagement fall apart. Not to mention that you were mixed up in the brouhaha when that Hargrove kid almost died last fall. You're way off the top of the stress charts. What's it going to take for you to see reason? A nervous breakdown?"

"I know, Agatha," Regan said meekly. "But I can't just walk away from all this. I would never forgive myself if—"

"At least check to see if the gun's loaded."

"What?"

"You heard me. If it is, take out the bullets. See if you can find any others and pocket them. I would throw the thing in the deepest pond I could find, but I suppose it's too much to expect you to go that far."

"Unloading," Regan said, "as we speak. I've found a little box of cartridges too. But what do I do with them? I don't have any pockets."

"Stick the box in your bra, and as soon as you have a chance, flush the bullets."

"Thanks, Agatha. You're a very practical person."

"Somebody has to be. Of course, the wretched man could kill himself plenty of other ways. But if you inconvenience him a little, it might be enough. You never know what's going to put off a suicide. With me, it was the mess."

"Agatha!"

"Hey, that was over a year ago, and it was never more than a passing thought. You know me. I can't give up. I have to keep going. So do you. And we were right. Things did get better. But he may know differently about his future. Maybe he's more practical than either of us. Ask him."

"Ask him what?"

"Whether he's going to do it. You might not be as outgoing as your mother was, but people talk to you. I know that asking straight out would be kind of blunt, but is it really more civilized to ignore the issue? Come to think of it, I don't believe you'll be able to reach Potter. Didn't you say he was spending part of the summer in Africa?"

"Yes, I did, didn't I?" Regan thought wistfully for a moment of her astute former pastor, who was now out of reach. "Well, I guess you'll just have to pray for me yourself then, Agatha. I'll call you tomorrow." She hung up before Agatha could raise any objections. Agatha probably would have said she and God weren't on speaking terms.

Regan rose to roam around the room. A man's choices in books and music could reveal a lot about him. One long wall was lined with shelves that included volumes on everything from philosophy and politics to poetry and religion. An expensive stereo system occupied another wall, with a collection of CDs as eclectic as the books. The paintings, which looked like antique originals, were mostly of horses or roses. Perhaps Bram might more correctly be called a Renaissance man than a medieval man.

Regan stopped to look up at a portrait that hung over the fireplace. The person who caught the eye in that picture was a dark-haired, dark-eyed boy of about eight at the lower left who stared defiantly straight-on at the viewer.

The child stood beside a seated woman. That woman, exquisitely blond and blue eyed, gazed into space with a wistful smile. A dark-haired man posed on the other side of her with his hand on the back of her chair. Regan thought he conveyed a rigidity in the set of his shoulders, the immobility of his handsome face, and the watchfulness of his cobalt eyes. To the man's right was a blond, teenage version of himself. That teenager completed the circle with one hand on the boy's shoulder and appeared to be looking affectionately down at the dark head.

Someone rapped on the door, and Bram Falco stuck an adult model of that dark head into the room. "Everybody's going out to look at the roses. Do you want to come?"

His gaze followed hers to the painting. "My family," he explained shortly. "They're all dead."

As if aware of the abruptness of that, he moved his heavy shoulders ruefully, stepped into the room, and shut the door behind him. "Maybe I should take this opportunity to apologize. Usually I'm not so neglectful of a woman as attractive as yourself. But I'm afraid I have other things on my mind these days."

Regan watched him warily, remembering her earlier conviction that he was half-drunk. He stopped where he was and winked at her. "No, unfortunately alcohol doesn't affect me much until I actually fall over. I know exactly how much is required to arrive at that state, and I will refrain from going that far while I have guests."

"Will you also refrain from suicide for your guests' sake?" Regan asked and was surprised at herself.

The silence in the study was broken only by the mellow chime of an old clock striking the half-hour.

Then Bram grinned. "I like you, Miss Culver. I really like you. Under other circumstances…But you are a stranger, and I don't intend to discuss this subject with you."

"That's an answer of sorts itself," Regan said. "A man in an ordinary state of mind would have called me crazy."

"Oh, you're not crazy. Rather unnerving, I would say. And gutsy. I suppose you have to be. From what I've heard, your life hasn't exactly been roses lately."

Regan shifted impatiently. "I went through what had to be gone through. It didn't take any special courage for that."

He continued, as if he hadn't heard. "Yes, you've suffered, and you should thank your God every day for that, Regan Culver. It means you had things you cared about."

He looked around him at the quiet, comfortable room and chanted almost cheerfully, "Oh blind your eyes and break your heart and hack your hand away, / And lose your love and shave your head; but do not go to stay / At the little place in What'sitsname where folks are rich and clever; / The golden and the goodly house, where things grow worse for ever."

He stopped there, but Regan silently finished Chesterton's stanza in her own mind. *There are things you need not know of, though you live and die in vain, / There are souls more sick of pleasure than you are sick of pain; / There is a game of April Fool that's played behind its door, / Where the fool remains for ever and / The April comes no more.*

His attention returning to the portrait, Bram said, as though performing an introduction, "My mother, Connie;

my father, Royce; and my brother, Kurt. That was painted while we were still living in Mexico. My father made his fortune building resorts down there."

"You were an attractive family."

He gave her a crooked smile. "My mother was a mean hypochondriac. My father was dutiful but unhappy. Kurt was a kind, gallant kid who somehow got stuck with the rest of us."

"And you?"

Staring back at the defiant little boy, Bram said, "Oh, I had an attitude. Still do. My father also ran for the Senate, back in the seventies. Kurt died in a car accident just before that election. My father was really too idealistic for his own good. That the voters didn't trust him with a second term is what finished him off, I think. Though the cause was an aneurysm. My mother discovered, much too late and probably to her surprise, that she actually did have a heart problem."

"Why didn't the voters trust your father?"

Bram looked surprised. "Dame Day hasn't told you about her father running against mine? Nobody gave Henry Day a prayer to begin with, but strangely enough, he caught on. People were tired of the Vietnam War and politics as usual. They wanted a change. And Henry was not your typical, well-heeled candidate. He purported to be down-home and grassroots, vaguely hippieish, but not enough so to offend the older set. A people person and poor enough," Bram added dryly, "to satisfy anybody. But basically weak. After the accident, Henry inexplicably forfeited the election and left town. Of course people whispered that the Falcos must have either paid him off or forced him out. So, although my father won the election by default, he didn't achieve a second term. I would advise you not to take everything that Dame Day says at face value. She isn't exactly objective where my family is concerned."

"Are you calling her a liar?"

"Of course."

"Then you didn't kill those animals?"

Bram Falco's gaze didn't flicker. Neither did he answer her question. "But of course you've already realized it wouldn't be wise to trust anything I say either. I've never made any secret of despising Henry. Don't you think it's time we joined the others in the garden?"

For a few minutes, among the roses, all differences seemed to be forgotten in the common passion they shared. Day looked up eagerly, as Bram and Regan joined the others, to demand of her host, "What is this?" She was bending over a bush whose pale pink blossoms were like crumpled silk.

"That's Celsiana," he answered. "Almost luminous, isn't she?"

"Yes," Day answered, stepping back. "She does seem to glow."

For an instant the two enemies stood side by side, contemplating the flowers with equal pleasure. When Bram turned down the path, identifying his roses as he went, Day was the first to follow. The others trailed along.

"This, of course," Bram said, when he came to the end of the first path and turned a sardonic eye on them, "is the ancient Apothecary Rose or red rose of Lancaster." He could not have missed the group's sudden discomfort as each of them looked steadfastly at the large, semidouble blooms to avoid looking at one another. To Day he added, "So, Plantagenet, the bigger bush with the smaller blossoms behind it would be...?" He seemed to know his Shakespeare as well as Tom did.

"*Alba semi-plena,*" Day responded calmly. "Or the white rose of York." At least she didn't call him Somerset in return.

"Very good," he said, as to a bright student, but when he moved on, Day stayed behind.

"I have never seen so much silverware in my life," she commented to Regan, who stopped to join her. "You probably noticed I was watching you to see what I was supposed to do with it all."

"No, I didn't notice." Regan stooped to admire the dark, velvety-wine hues of Tuscany blooms, all too aware of the weight of the cartridges against her breastbone. "I thought you seemed amazingly composed under the circumstances. Are you frightened of him?"

"Should I be?"

"Everybody else seems to think so. Do you know something that would reassure them?"

"No. Rather the opposite." Day cupped a hand under one of the Tuscany flowers and stroked the petals with her thumb. "Don't you wish they could make fabric that feels like this?"

"You think he's bluffing then?"

"Bram isn't the bluffing type." Day continued to study the rose with her head cocked to one side. "Of course I'm afraid, Regan," she added quietly. "But you never show fear around enraged animals. Your fear won't prevent you from getting hurt."

"It might move you out of range," Regan suggested.

Day smiled. "I live next door to the man, Regan. Being out of the club wouldn't mean being out of range. No, I'll see it through. Would you really want me to back down from what I believe is right to save my own skin? If you're any kind of Christian, you'll say no. Millie has been trying to convert me, and I was interested, you know. I've been reading some books…But do you think Millie fully realizes the radicalness of the one she purports to serve?"

Regan didn't answer.

"Because I don't think she does." Day's voice rose. "A Christian must forgive. Isn't that correct?"

"That doesn't mean you should submit to abuse," Regan said. "By doing so, you imply to the abuser that he's not doing anything wrong."

"What abuse?" Day spread her hands. "The man has never struck me, seldom even raised his voice at me. He doesn't have to. Like his mother, he knows where the vulnerable points are. But if I wanted to be a Christian, I would *have* to forgive him." She leaned close. "That's right, isn't it? I would have no choice."

"There's always a choice," Regan said. "A choice for love or against it. God doesn't force anything on you. But there are only two sides. If you choose against love, you choose against God. I'm not saying Bram shouldn't be punished. He should, of course, if he is the guilty one. Punishment acknowledges he also had a choice. But even if the crime could be proven against him, that punishment isn't likely to be very severe. I wish I could make it easier, Day," she added gently as the other woman wheeled away. "I wish I could say that, when the sin against you is so extreme or because you're new at this, an exception might be made for you. But if you don't forgive, you can't be forgiven. There is no other way."

"I know. When I talked to Bram in the woods, I thought I could absolve him. I compared him in my mind to a trapped animal that turns vicious. Animals, you see, are what I have the most experience with. In a way Bram has always been an abstraction to me, a symbol of all self-indulgent types who are only willing to do the right thing when it doesn't cost them anything, who can't tolerate opposition. An abstraction has no soul either. But Bram isn't an animal or a symbol. If he were, it would be much easier to forgive. He's an intelligent man, and he knows all too well what he's doing."

"That man is self-destructing, Day." Regan's tone was urgent, importunate. Darkness was settling in rapidly now, and Day's face was hard to read. "You accuse him of self-indulgence, but are you so sure that he has ever gotten what he wanted?"

"For that I should pity him?" Day turned her back. "I don't get paid for taking care of my animals, you know. Some days I have to choose between feeding them and feeding myself. Oh, I receive a few donations, but people only give when they have extra. And they bring me the dying birds from Falco's polluted river while he shows off his fancy cars and fancy women. You have no idea what it's been like, Regan Culver."

"I know I don't, but that's why you *should* be sorry for him." Regan reached to try to turn the other woman around, but Day's arm was rigid, implacable. "You give until it hurts, and that's the kind of giving that counts. But do you think he has ever cared enough about anything to do that? You have your purpose, but what does he have?"

"I'm all given out." Day's tone was flat and weary. "I'm thirty-seven, and what do I have to show for it? If I don't find another job within the next couple of weeks, I'll have to turn away animals. Maybe it's time for me to quit and start thinking about myself for a change."

"And God can go hang?"

Day gave no answer.

"Well, he did," Regan said, stepping back. "He did. Remember that. He isn't asking anything of you that he hasn't suffered himself. Forgiveness usually takes time, but I'm not sure that we have time. You would have to act by willpower alone, against all your inclinations. I know you have a strong will, Day. Of course, it may be too late to defuse things now. But if I've found out one thing in the last year, it's that one person's change of attitude can make a tremendous difference. Even if he doesn't hurt you, Hilda and I are afraid that Bram may be planning to kill himself. I can't believe you want him dead. You've always been for life. Don't quit now. Please don't quit now!"

Regan turned and ran up the steps to the house, leaving Day standing alone, a small white figure in a dark garden.

# CHAPTER 3

> *If I... for my opinion bleed,*
> *Opinion shall be surgeon to my hurt*
> *And keep me on the side where still I am.*

That evening after Bram and his houseguests had retired to their respective rooms, someone rapped at Regan's door. Having just come out of the bathroom after consigning Bram's ammunition to the septic system, Regan started. If her host had discovered his cartridges missing, he would have no trouble figuring out who had taken them.

When she saw Hilda at the door, Regan breathed more easily. "Come in?" she said, ending on a question mark.

"I can't get him to talk to me," the older woman said. "He seemed to like you. Did he say anything?"

"Nothing much to the purpose. And I asked him."

"You *asked* him if he was suicidal?"

"Yes, it seemed the only thing to do. I unloaded his pistol, by the way, and disposed of the shells. Does he have any other guns?"

Reluctant respect was dawning on Hilda's face. "Not that I know of. He was never much into hunting. I can see I have seriously underestimated you. I can't imagine even your mother doing all that." She dropped into a wicker rocking chair.

Regan perched on the edge of the bed. "You can attribute it to the influence of my half sister, Agatha. She's a very direct person. It's probably easier for a stranger like me, I imagine. Since you're a friend, you won't want to make him angry at you."

"I'd rather have him angry *and* alive. He is my heir, after all, so I'm determined that he outlive me. Where was the gun? Maybe I'd better get it too."

"In his upper right desk drawer. The man will be charging the lot of us with kleptomania. Are you sure we're not exaggerating this danger? Now that I look back on the evening, I think I might have overreacted."

"People's reactions to Bram tend to be extreme." Hilda leaned wearily back in her chair. "It's one of the things I like about the guy. We live in an age that has managed to reduce everything to shades of gray. There's nothing gray about Bram. If he has decided to kill himself, he won't be like those neurotic females who make sure they get caught in time. We won't have a second chance to stop him. I don't think he would do it while we're here though. He would consider that a serious breach of hospitality."

"Bram was adopted, wasn't he?" Regan asked. "In Mexico, I assume?"

Hilda drummed her fingers nervously on the armrest. "How did you find that out? Not that it was ever a secret exactly."

"Two blue-eyed parents can't produce a brown-eyed child. One of the few things I know about genetics. Also, he said that his father was descended from a titled family when it would have been more natural to say that he himself was."

"Yes, Bram was adopted in Mexico. Royce wanted more children, but Connie…" Hilda met Regan's gaze. "Well,

Connie had found her first pregnancy uncomfortable and degrading. So she picked out a child much as she might a puppy from the pound. Actually, Connie and Royce had gone to the orphanage to see a fairer-skinned child, but Bram charmed them into taking him instead. He had his share of impudence even then. I was there."

"You were a friend of Connie's?"

"Yes. She wasn't so bad then. Simply a spoiled southern belle. She liked me, I think, because my plainness served as a foil to her beauty. She might have been okay had they stayed in Mexico. The warm climate and a bevy of servants suited her much better than Pennsylvania did. She hated the cold up here. But she didn't like D.C. either. A lot of beautiful and elegant women lived in the capital. She would have just been a small fish in a big pond. Also, her husband had long since become disillusioned with her. But Royce was an honorable man. Once he had made a choice, he stuck with it. Divorce was not an option for him. But she remained here most of the time he was serving in the Senate."

Lost in her story, Hilda continued automatically. "After my father's death, I had to take over his business interests. One of the side effects was that I finally developed some backbone and was too busy to dance attendance on Connie anymore. She grew increasingly dissatisfied. Realized that she was losing power, I imagine. Her beauty was fading, she no longer had much influence with her husband, and she had to make do with far less staff since labor wasn't as cheap here as in Mexico. Her petty little cruelties were all the control she had left, I suppose."

"And how did Bram respond to all this?"

"One of her cruelties was insisting on keeping him here when he would rather have been with his father. No one has ever induced Bram to complain about Connie though. About either of his parents actually. He knows he would probably still be living in abject poverty today if not for his adoption. And you might say he chose them. He was only about eight at the time, but the *olivados*—street orphans—were old for their years and pragmatic of necessity."

"And they say a child's early life shapes him forever," Regan commented.

"Mexican men have an unfair amount of charm," Hilda said. A reminiscent smile played about her lips as if she were remembering one in particular. "But they don't trust women. Some say that goes all the way back to the conquistadors, who couldn't trust their Indian wives, and to the Indian men, who had their women taken away from them. Latino males also tend to be proud and brooding, with a broad streak of fatalism. Actually, Bram is much more blunt than most of them; south of the border, frankness is considered rude. But I'm afraid he has inherited the whole notion of family honor and pride in appearances."

"And Day blackened his family reputation."

"She certainly did. That isn't anything new either. Considering how that accident with Kurt and her sister affected Royce's good name. And Bram hero-worshiped his father."

"Day's sister?" Regan frowned and leaned forward. "I didn't know she had one. And I wanted to ask you about that accident too. Bram mentioned it briefly, said that his brother died. But what did that have to do with Day's father leaving town?"

"Day hasn't told you? Then I don't intend to. Except to say that her sister also died as a result of the accident. And Bram lost his sense of smell. That's one reason he doesn't eat much. He can barely taste the food. You can look it up. October of

'72." She rose from her chair, as if to imply that the conversation was at an end.

"If Bram didn't kill those animals, who did?" Regan asked quickly.

"Teenagers probably—in search of thrills." Heading for the door, Hilda added, "You see that sort of thing on the news now and then. Though usually the victims are dogs or cats."

Regan wasn't convinced. If it had been teenagers, the police would most likely have discovered them by now. Teenagers liked to brag about what they had done. In a small town like Rosevale, it wouldn't have remained a secret for long.

If, on the other hand, an adult other than Bram Falco killed the animals, that person, too, must have had reason to hate Day—and imagination enough to realize what would hurt her most. Would the murder of some animals satisfy so deep a malice, or was there more to come?

■ ■ ■

The board gathered in the dining room after breakfast the next morning. The table had been cleared for action. Hilda and Millie were setting papers at each place. The others had wandered through the open French doors onto the terrace and were enjoying the freshness of a June morning.

Bram joined Regan. "It's midsummer's eve, isn't it?" he said. "Longest day of the year."

"Yes. It was to have been my wedding day." Again Regan was surprised at herself.

"So spending it at a board meeting is something of a let-down, huh?" Bram glanced at the silver-and-jade puzzle ring that still glimmered on her engagement finger. "At least the guy had some imagination," he said dryly, "or perhaps he was the jealous type. Those things fall apart if you take them off, don't they?"

"Yes, I suppose I should remove it now. He needed some time, and I told him I'd give him until June. I didn't specifically mention this day, but I think that would have been implied."

"You're still in love with him, aren't you?"

"I don't want to take off the ring."

"Then don't. Put up a fight. Is there another woman?"

"Not that I know of."

"So what's the problem? Would you give up so easily on anything else you wanted? You've probably been steering clear of the guy. Big mistake. You have to show the idiot what he's missing. By happy coincidence, you will meet him everywhere, looking your gorgeous self, treating him with just the right hint of courteous kindness. Of course, hanging on the arm of another guy wouldn't hurt. I'd be happy to provide the jealousy angle."

Regan couldn't help laughing. "I must admit I like you too, Bram."

"Only like?" He made a face. "I'm definitely slipping."

"It occurs to me that maybe you're giving up a little too easily also. There's always another election, you know. And if this Feebes wins in November, I'm sure the voters will shortly realize what *they're* missing."

Bram eyed her narrowly and went on as if she hadn't spoken. "Or, if you prefer, I could just beat up this fiancé for you. I wouldn't mind beating up somebody at present."

"Oh, I don't know." Regan looked at him assessingly. "He's a big guy too. It would be a close fight. And he's a cop. It could get you in serious trouble."

"Sounds like fun. When do we start? Oops." Glancing at his watch, he turned her toward the dining room. "Not now, I'm afraid."

They all sat at the table, waiting for Day. Conversation

languished as they watched her slight figure march sturdily up through the gardens. *Like a difficult truth that nobody wants to face,* Regan thought.

"Good morning," Day said as she entered. She slipped into the only open seat, at the foot of the table between Tom and Paul.

*Did my little speech make any impression on her?* Regan wondered.

Day had picked up the schedule and was perusing it, giving no hint of her feelings. This morning she was dressed simply in a white blouse with a straight tan skirt, and her fingers were bare.

"Our first business," Hilda said aggressively, "is confirmation of our new members. I move that we admit Bram Falco to the board. Do I hear a second?"

"Second," Paul said promptly.

"The motion has been moved and seconded. We usually," she explained to Regan, "do an oral vote, member by member, to make sure everyone has a say. You will please vote yes for confirmation, no against." As Hilda's gaze swept the circle, it seemed she was counting. She appeared to falter for an instant before the triumph on Millie's face.

*Hilda realizes now,* Regan thought, *that she should have confirmed me first. What if it is a tie, and they decide I should cast the deciding vote? What do I say? With Bram off, we could re-elect Day. And she certainly seems the more emotionally stable of the two at present. Wait a minute! If Bram can't vote on his own confirmation, there is virtually no possibility of his being elected. Unless, perhaps, Tom...*

She felt rather than saw Bram's amused glance at her. *He has realized this all along. It's going to be very embarrassing if— when we're actually in his house—*

"I vote yes," Hilda said curtly. "Millie?"

"No."

"Tom?"

Raines hesitated, glanced at Day. *Perhaps he's wondering whether he's voting for or against.* "No," he said finally.

"Day?"

"Yes," Day murmured without looking up from her papers.

They all stared at her. "Would you repeat that?" Hilda asked.

Day raised her chin—and her brows. "I said yes."

Hilda closed her eyes, shook her head, and continued weakly, "Paul?"

"Yes."

"The yeas have it then. Welcome to the board, Bram. Would someone make a motion for Regan's confirmation?"

Bram was watching Day. Rather, Regan thought, like a chess player contemplating an unexpected move and trying to determine the reasoning behind it.

By that move, Day appeared to have seriously endangered her own chances of reelection. Of course, chess players were always making calculated sacrifices. And this one might be brilliant. Day had done the genteel thing, and Bram was going to look churlish if he didn't respond in kind.

Regan's own confirmation went through without opposition. Nobody seemed much interested in it; they were all poised for the next item on the agenda. Members up for reelection.

A bewildered-looking Millie proposed Day's reelection. Regan promptly seconded to make it clear which way she would go.

"Millie?" Hilda said, without putting forward her own vote.

"Yes, of course."

"Tom?"

"Yes."

"Paul?"

"No."

"Bram?"

Smiling ruefully, as if he knew that he had been bested, Bram said, "Yes," adding with only the slightest hint of sarcasm and a glance at Millie, "of course."

"Regan?"

"Yes."

"I guess I'll vote yes too, then. Five assenting and one dissenting. Day will serve for another four years."

They all relaxed then, looking a bit dazed, as if not quite believing it had all been that easy.

The society sponsored two events each year, a rose show that was to take place the following weekend and was thus, as far as business went, all but over, and a conference in the fall, around which most of the meeting's discussions revolved.

They made it through the morning with minimal disagreement and approached lunch in a cheerful frame of mind. Bram had dispensed with the caterers for the day by asking them to leave sandwich trays, and he had promised his guests a cookout for the evening meal.

Tom Raines approached Regan with a "whew" gesture, passing the back of his hand across his forehead.

"Tricky, wasn't it?" Regan agreed as Gavin carried in their lunch.

"Not 'alf," Tom said in a fake Cockney accent. "But who would have guessed what the lydy would do? Maybe she thought that losing two elections would send Bram right off the rails."

"Talking about me?" Day had slipped up on them. She added mildly to Regan, "I hope you're happy."

"Ecstatic," Regan answered. "I never thought we would manage to wriggle through that so painlessly. Thanks to you."

"We still have to discuss the recommendation" Day reminded her.

It wasn't reached until late in the afternoon. By that time, though, the meeting had gone so well everyone was in a genial haze of cooperation and good fellowship.

"Well, as long as you call it a recommendation so it's not binding," Hilda said, "I have no objection." Neither, it seemed, did anyone else.

The meeting wound up with a sense of anticlimax. *Leave it to me to make a mountain out of a molehill,* Regan told herself. *The events of the past year have inclined me to see potential tragedy everywhere. By the time the conference rolls around in the fall, everybody will be back to normal and wondering what we made so much fuss about. I'm really going to look stupid trying to explain all of this to Agatha.*

On the following morning, they would all drive out to inspect the site for the rose show and determine if any last-minute adjustments needed to be made. And that would be that.

The air was warm and soft, and the gentle golden sun would be up for hours yet. They all followed Bram out to the terrace.

He shucked his suit coat, tossed it onto the low terrace wall, and impatiently yanked his tie loose before dragging the grill out of the garden shed and positioning it at the outer edge of the paving, just to one side of the steps going down into the gardens.

Sitting on a wooden bench, Regan contemplated her ring. Bram's suggestions, flippant though they might have been, had given her some hope. *I have been something of a wimp about all this. If I had called Matt immediately after the argument instead of waiting for him to call me...*

Bram seemed preoccupied as he dashed lighter fluid over charcoal and groped in his pocket for a packet of matches.

Hilda, who had been chatting to a glumly silent Millie, lifted her head, sniffing like a startled horse. "What smells like gasoline? Bram!" Her voice shrilled. "Don't!"

At her scream, Bram started convulsively and turned his head toward her just as he dropped a lit match onto the briquettes. Flame exploded from that match impossibly high and broad, orange glaring into faces that hadn't even had time to register alarm. The bang echoed back from the verdant hills, and the orange enfolded Bram for a suspended instant before shrinking back to a fierce crackle on the grill, leaving streamers fluttering in his hair and shirt.

After that hot, liquid surge, Bram's chief sensation was the oily aroma of gasoline and a sweeter, nearer stench.

Tom Raines, bent over a rosebush near the foot of the steps, stared, white-faced, up at him. Then Raines took the stairs in a single, ungainly bound, snatching up the discarded coat in passing. Bram wondered vaguely what all the urgency was about as the other man, holding the suit coat like a shield, slammed into him. They both crashed onto the paving.

Smoke and singed cloth mingled with the sharp tang of sweat—or fear. Only then did Bram realize he was experiencing odors. His sense of smell was back. Because he wasn't used to odors, they were overwhelming. All except a soft wistfulness in the background that he finally identified as the scent of roses.

Day was running away, down the terrace to where a hose hung on the outside wall of the house. She turned on the tap, then yanked the coils free, water splaying over her skirt and shoes. Tugging the snaky rubber hose forward, she slipped and stumbled over it and the wet stones. Dropping to her knees beside Bram, she curled a couple of fingers over the nozzle to soften the force of the water, directing the resultant spray over his face and Tom's hands.

She didn't smell at all, except for the clean splash of water and a muskiness of wet leather from her moccasins.

Millie moaned somewhere in the background. Regan, now standing just behind Day, turned. "Is Hilda calling an ambulance?"

Although she spoke sharply enough, she seemed a long way off. They all did. The vividness of one returned sense seemed to overpower, to blunt the others.

"What do we need?" Regan asked, looking over Day's shoulder again. "Ice?" She and Day were very alike in their unshakable self-possession. One could hardly blame the fiancé for being frustrated...

"No. That would send him into shock." Day was speaking now. "Severe burns screw up the body's heating system, and these must be severe. He doesn't seem to be feeling anything. That can only mean that the nerves are damaged. He'll probably start to shiver in a few minutes. You might bring some blankets."

In the background, Paul said almost accusingly to Gavin, "This *is* gasoline. How did it get in here?"

"I don't know." The younger man was pale and shaking. "That's supposed to be regular lighter fluid. Somebody must have changed it."

Bram had no doubt who that somebody was. She had spoken of him as if he were one of her animal patients, efficiently, dispassionately. No wonder she had been so calmly gracious at the meeting. She could afford to be. He should have remembered the female of the species gave no warning before she struck. His right hand felt stiff and strange. He used his left to grab Day's wrist, to bend her toward him in a futile effort to reach, to hurt her. "You won't get away with this." He was surprised that his words slurred.

"That's right, Bram," she said. She was so close that he could feel her breath as she spoke. On the right side of his face. The left side felt nothing. "Hate me. Hate will keep you alive."

■ ■ ■

A half-hour later Regan and Day returned alone to the dining room and dropped into chairs at the still paper-strewn table. Day exhaustedly sank her face in her hands.

"It didn't look that bad," Regan began.

Day raised her head and shook it fiercely, as if amazed at the other's ignorance. "Those were third-degree burns, Regan. They just haven't begun to swell yet. When they do, he'll hardly be recognizable. It will take months—and skin grafts. He's never going to look the same."

"But who would do such a thing? It must have been a mix-up of some kind."

Day shook her head again at this innocence. "I will be high on the list of suspects, I suppose. You haven't asked me if I did it."

"I know you didn't. You wouldn't wish something like that on…" Regan paused.

"My worst enemy," Day finished wryly for her. "After those burns scab over, the doctors will shave them off until they reach the bleeding flesh. Even the movement of air over those raw nerve endings will be agony. They'll give him morphine, but it won't be enough. You're right, Regan. I wouldn't wish that on my worst enemy."

Outside, the local police chief and some of his men were examining the grill and the can labeled charcoal starter. Paul and Tom were driving Hilda and Gavin to the hospital. Regan and Day had been asked to stay behind to answer some questions.

The police chief straightened up from his hunkering position to stand, hand on hips, looking over the gardens. "Nice," he said in a sepulchral tone, as if pronouncing a curse.

The evening remained soft and calm. The low sun gilded his outline as he came in through the open doors, smelling faintly of gasoline, and seated himself at the head of the table. He was lanky and morose. "I'm Bob Newpax," he said to Regan, each word seemingly dredged up from some deep well of world-weariness. "You're…"

"Regan Culver. I'm from Hayden, Massachusetts. I run an herb company there."

His face grew, if possible, longer. "I've heard of you. You were on TV last year." His tone indicated he expected no good from TV.

"Had you known Bram for long?"

"I just met him yesterday. We're all here for a board meeting." She passed him one of the schedules.

"I see." The chief glanced at the paper, folded it listlessly, and stuck it in his notebook. "Day here and Tom went to school with him. How about the others?" Regan looked at Day with raised eyebrows.

"Most of us have known each other for years," Day said, her arms folded tightly across her chest. "Bram was pretty active in the rose world. Bred a couple of varieties of his own. It's kind of ironic, really, considering he has no sense of smell."

"Didn't know that," the chief said, looking interested despite himself. "How many people did?"

Day shrugged, still holding herself. "Most of us, I think."

"So he wouldn't have noticed the odor of the gasoline," Regan said.

"Somebody's been clever all right." Newpax viewed that cleverness with depressed admiration. "The defense attorney will con the jury into believing it was all an accident. He'll say Bram used a handy empty can to put gasoline in and forgot about it. His were the only prints on the can. Then the lawyer will hint that Bram hadn't been himself..."

The two women exchanged a look. "Nobody would choose to kill himself that way," Regan said.

"I wouldn't be so sure of that myself." The chief seemed to cheer up marginally, as if approaching a favorite subject. "Most people don't know how hard it is to die. That's a fact. You can shoot yourself in the head and live, y'know. Seen it happen. This fire thing would be a showy way to go—a blaze of glory."

"No," Day said. "Bram wasn't stupid. If he wanted to die, he would make sure it was quick and painless."

The chief looked down, smoothing the cover of his note-book. "And *did* he want to?"

Silence.

"Guess that answers my question. Bram was not being a good sport about losing the election. In fact, he blamed you, didn't he, Day?"

"Yes," she agreed curtly.

"Most people suspect him of killing your animals. You suspected him too, didn't you?"

"Yes."

"Now that wasn't exactly a rational act. They say he's been drinking a lot, and he was never a heavy drinker before. That'll mess up a guy's mind pretty fast. Seen it happen. So we have a dilemma here. We're likely either talking suicide or—"

"Or me," Day said.

"Or you," Newpax agreed, appearing pleasantly surprised at this ready acquiescence. "So, Day, did you switch the charcoal starter with gasoline? A lot of people wouldn't blame you much. Extreme provocation and all."

Day stared at him coldly. "You know me, Chief Newpax. You've brought me wounded animals many times. I have seen too much injury to be capable of inflicting it."

The chief returned her stare sadly. "I want to believe you, Day. I've known you forever, after all. But in my position, you can't take anybody's innocence for granted. It's a lonely job, you know." After contemplating that loneliness with melancholy enjoyment, he said more briskly, "Can you prove you didn't do it?"

Day shrugged. "How could anybody prove they didn't do it? As far as I know, Frank doesn't keep that shed locked. Frank Younger is the gardener," she explained to Regan.

"That's another question," Newpax said. "I heard Frank was fired. When did that happen? And where did he go?"

Day snorted. "Oh, come off it! You know very well Frank wouldn't hurt a fly! He's helped me with the animals scores of times. And he's just meek enough not to mind cleaning out cages, a task the teenagers aren't too fond of. His stepdaughter has gotten herself in trouble down in Texas somewhere. The girl was always a disappointment to Frank and her late mother. But he considered it his responsibility to fly down there and see if he could straighten things out. Bram agreed to hold the job open. He would be a fool if he didn't. He won't find anyone else like Frank in a hurry. Frank caught a plane Friday morning."

Regan, who had been nursing a small hope that it might be something as simple as a vengeful former employee, felt that hope die.

"I'll still have to talk to him," Newpax said. "Make sure it wasn't he who forgot to relabel that can. People are careless, you know. I hope it turns out that way actually. Frank would feel bad, of course, unless he left it that way on purpose. These quiet ones do snap big-time when they snap. Seen it happen. Whoever made the switch didn't have to do it today, and he doesn't have to be around now. But, human nature being what it is, I think anybody with that much hate inside would want to see the fireworks."

He rose from his chair. "Not that I wouldn't enjoy having a puzzling murder case for a change, but, taking all in all, I do hope it was an accident." His tone didn't hold much expectation of that being the case.

"Is he always so sad?" Regan asked after the chief had gone out.

Day laughed shortly. "Bob enjoys his pessimism. Gets to see his worst forebodings confirmed again and again. He's one of the most pleased-with-himself guys I know. Lazy too. Don't let all that fool you though. He's smart enough when he has to be."

"I would say he's prejudiced on your side anyway."

"He got a look at all those dead animals." Day's folded arms now rested on the table. She pillowed her head on them.

"Do you think we should go to the hospital?" Regan asked.

"I think somebody should stay here. Even in a small town like this, tragedy is an invitation to thieves. And word travels fast."

"You're probably right. We couldn't do much at the hospital anyway. I'll call later. Maybe I could make us some supper." Regan stood and headed for the kitchen. "Do you want anything?"

"I guess so," Day said dully. "Why not? He won't be needing the stuff in his refrigerator for a while. Yes, word travels fast. There will be knowing looks and nudges, I expect. From the kind of people I most dislike. 'I guess *somebody* showed him,' they'll say. And if you thought Bram hated me before…" She lifted her head slightly, managing an imitation of a smile. "I'll probably also be advised to beat it before he is released from the hospital."

Regan had paused in the doorway. "And will you?"

"I doubt that fleeing my particular nemesis would do much good. With his money, he wouldn't have any trouble finding me."

Regan sensed a certain resignation, almost acceptance, in the other woman. "Day, what I said last night…None of that implies you have to accept punishment you don't deserve. Maybe you do need a new life, away from all this. If money is the problem, I can loan you—"

Day was shaking her head. "You can't build a new life on a foundation of cowardice. You run away, you never stop running inside." She finished with a weak smile and a fair imitation of Newpax's laconic voice. "Seen it happen."

■ ■ ■

"Bram said something strange to me in the ambulance," Gavin announced. It was the following morning, and the members of the board had met for breakfast at the Falco house before setting out to inspect the fairground building that was to be used for the rose show.

The doctors had been optimistic about Bram's chances. Because his face had been turned to the side, he had no burns inside his nose or throat. Hilda's scream may have saved his life.

The board members all stopped chewing to look at Gavin. He was addressing Day. "Bram wants to hire you to take care of his gardens and horses until he is released from the hospital. I told him it was out of the question, of course, but he insisted that I ask."

"That's outrageous!" Millie shrilled. "What does he think she is? It's some kind of trick."

"Of course it is," Day agreed calmly. "His way of keeping me on hand until he is ready to deal with me. But practical too. Because I know horses and I know roses. Ten dollars an hour," she said to Gavin.

"What?"

"You heard me. If I'm going to be mucking out stalls and cosseting his prima donna tea roses, I expect to get paid well for it. And I'm not going to use any of his noxious sprays either. I already was weaning Frank off of those things anyway."

"I guess that will be all right," Gavin said dazedly. "I mean, I didn't expect—"

"Her to be that stupid?" Hilda interrupted, red-rimmed eyes fixed implacably on Day's face. "But you're *not* stupid, are you, Ms. Day?"

"Probably," Day responded. "But I need the money."

Hilda glowered around the table. "Don't the rest of you find this the least suspicious?"

"Well, on second thought," Gavin suggested weakly, "Bram does seem to get his way with women." Stopping to look back on his own words, he appeared embarrassed. "I'm sorry. I didn't mean—"

"I think we know what you mean," Tom said. "I swear, every girl in our high school had a crush on the guy. It must have been personality, because, frankly, he was no Adonis."

Paul, who had been eating quietly, said, "Impudent charm. They might be sorry, but they wouldn't be bored."

"Maybe." Tom looked around with raised eyebrows. "Is that the secret, ladies?"

"I, for one, have never been able to stand the man," Millicent said resentfully. "He's as hairy as an animal and brassy to boot. So don't look at me. And Hilda's old enough to be his mother."

Tom turned his head. "Regan?"

Regan felt her cheeks warm, and Day gave her a sympathetic half smile. "It is the confidence, I expect," Regan said finally. "We females are usually kind of shaky in that department. So we admire it elsewhere."

"I agree," Day said. "Though that animal magnetism mentioned by Millie doesn't hurt." At their startled looks, she added with perfect aplomb, "Hey, I'm one of the girls who went to high school with the guy, remember? I had a crush for a while, just like the rest. I would say part of it is the sexiness of success. Failure of any kind tends to have a dampening effect."

Regan glanced nervously at Hilda, afraid that the older woman might be resenting what, under the circumstances, must seem like a flippant discussion.

But Hilda was abstracted. "Sorry," she said, feeling Regan's regard and looking up. "Déjà vu. Something reminded me of something. What were you talking about?"

"Bram's sex appeal," Tom replied.

"He has that all right," Hilda said without resentment. "Had anyway. Were you guys jealous? Because I don't suppose you need to be anymore."

■ ■ ■

That evening, Day went on an inspection tour of Bram's garden, ignoring the full-blown blooms and bending close to inspect the tighter buds. Eventually she entered the garage by a side door and returned to the garden, lugging stakes and what looked like Chinese coolie hats.

Gavin came out onto the terrace to watch her. "What are those?"

"Bud protectors. I usually use plastic milk jugs with the bottoms cut out myself, but Bram has the real thing. If I'm going to enter any of his roses in the show next weekend, they have to be shielded."

Gavin looked dubious. "Are you allowed?"

"I'll enter them under his name, of course. I don't recall any rule that says the grower has to be there to win. He and Frank have done most of the preparation already, the disbudding…" She pointed to where side buds had been pinched off a tea rose's stem. "And the straightening." She touched the pencil that had been affixed to the stem with twist-ties. "I'll just need to feed and water them heavily this last week."

There was, of course, much more to it than that. On Friday evening, Day arrived at the Falco house, prepared for action and relieved that Gavin didn't seem to be around. In the gardening shed, she found a couple of measuring rods, a good pair of pruning shears, and a roll of butcher paper, all of which she dropped into her capacious apron pocket. Then she filled a five-gallon bucket with water from the outside tap and lugged it with her into the garden.

Before cutting each tea rose, she held up a rod to measure twenty inches down from the top of the bloom. After wrapping the cut rose in a cone of wax paper, she plunged it up to its calyx in the water, then thrust the shears into the bucket to resnip the stem end.

Taking the bucket of roses into the gardening shed, Day set an old refrigerator's temperature at thirty-seven degrees, hoisted the bucket inside, and located a shallower pail in which to place the heirloom garden roses, which had much shorter stems. Those exhibitors who had to travel very far would be doing their prepping this evening, but Day could afford to wait until morning.

She arose bright and early to feed her animals and then drove her old station wagon to Bram's house. He had nine-inch bud vases similar to those that would be available at the show. Day had always used detergent bottles for transporting her entries.

She distributed the tea roses, one to a vase, then went over each individually. Most looked fresh and young, only partially unfurled, petals firm with the water they had drawn up overnight. The few that were open completely Day set aside. They would be too far blown to win anything by showtime. Day felt a certain sympathy for them, suspecting that she too was a shade past her prime.

Turning to the first rose she planned to enter, she snipped off the leaves and thorns that would be below water-level in the vase, wedged the stem in place with a piece of green floral foam, and began to dry the remaining leaves with a paper towel.

As her hands moved automatically, her mind returned to its obsessive whys. *That feud between Bram and me must have proved very convenient for somebody. People were expecting me to revenge the death of my animals, so I was the perfect suspect. Would this person have planted the gasoline otherwise? Was it, in a sense, my fault?*

She inspected each leaf axis for side growth, which she delicately removed with an X-Acto knife. Then she used fingernail scissors to trim the overlarge sepals and small imperfections at leaf edges. Finally, she buffed the foliage with a soft cloth and turned her attention to the bloom.

*But who? Others, like Millie and Tom, disliked Bram, but nobody murders over dislike. He may have had political enemies, but why would they bother to attack him after he was defeated? The ex-fiancée maybe? Hell hath no fury…*

Day removed a marred outer petal along with the rest of its layer. The rose wasn't out far enough to suit her, so she wedged Q-Tips between the remaining tiers of petals.

She had left the door of the shed open and looked up from time to time as she worked to watch sunlight strengthen over the garden glittering with dew. Gavin came out to report he was driving into the city to visit his cousin but would try to be back before the show closed in the afternoon. He offered to leave the house open for her, but she refused, saying she had everything she needed. Since the show commenced at ten, she would have to leave shortly herself. The sound of Gavin's car died away, and she began to rack the vases in rose boxes.

*What about Gavin? He is most likely Bram's heir. That would be a substantial motive. I wouldn't have thought him bold enough, but then, it was a sneaky—almost, one might say, a cowardly—crime.*

A door had opened. Day didn't identify the sound until a couple of minutes after she had heard it. Somebody was watching her. Her hands continued to move calmly and efficiently. Behind and to her left. The terrace door then. Opened from the inside because she would have seen anyone who came across the terrace.

But that was impossible. Gavin had gone. No one else was staying at the house. Her hands smelled of attar, the calm air of sun, cut grass, and earth. *No one is there,* she told herself. *You're imagining things. This place just seems peculiarly empty without the force of Bram's personality, so you're reinstating him, so to speak.*

*Maybe he died.* The thought was like a jarring blow. *Burn victims do sometimes die days afterward from sepsis. You know that—all too well. They say sometimes when a person dies, there's a presence...*

A click. Day jerked her head around to look. No one was there. Unless, that is, he had turned back inside.

She forced herself to march across the terrace flagstones, to try the terrace door with a still damp hand. Locked, as she had known it would be.

*If you're this jumpy already...*Day didn't complete the thought but went back to lug the rose box down to her station wagon, to slide it in on the floor in the back. When she had finished loading the boxes, she stood for a moment, regarding the ranks of regal blooms. They were as perfect as money and human ingenuity could make them. But still not flawless. Nothing was ever flawless.

*I'm doing what I can,* she thought angrily, as she drove back to her own place to change her clothes and pick up her picnic baskets full of heating pads and baby animals. *Why isn't that ever enough?*

■　■　■

The rose show was being held in a long exhibition building at the fairgrounds as part of the county's Victorian Days. Day parked the station wagon at the far end of the lot in some shade and walked in, empty-handed, to pick up her tags.

She and the other members of the board had been requested to wear period clothing, so she had donned her grandmother's organdy wedding gown. It was, Day suspected, post-Victorian, but it would have to do.

The registration table was set up at the far end of the building. Hilda stood behind the two seated society members staffing it. On a platform to her rear posed two department-store mannequins dressed to the nines in Victorian clothing. The white-gloved male dummy was very proper in his white shirtfront, black sack suit, bow tie, and derby hat. Half bowing, he presented a nosegay of real roses to the female who smiled demurely. She wore a walking suit of green shantung, which fit snugly at the waist and forearms and puffed out into leg-o'-mutton sleeves and a broad collar above.

The person in front of Day joshed Hilda about how she and the female dummy were both wearing the same outfit. "I've always wanted a face like that on my body," Hilda said dryly, indicating the plastic-perfect features. "This way if my outfit gets stained, I can borrow hers and nobody's the wiser." At that moment the female dummy keeled over, landing with a crash at her suitor's feet. "I would probably faint, too, if a guy gave me flowers," Hilda commented without missing a beat.

Her heart didn't seem in the jest, however, and her expression stiffened when she caught sight of Day. "I didn't think you would have any entries this year."

"I don't," Day said shortly. "I'm entering Bram's roses for him."

She expected a hostile reaction to that news. But Hilda just looked at her and said finally, "That's nice of you," in a flat tone.

Day could feel the surreptitious regard of many others too.

Those in the line behind her studiously avoided her gaze as she turned and walked past them. Sitting in the station wagon, filling out the tags, she had to blink hard to force back the tears blurring her vision. She had never before let other people's opinions of her bother her.

As she carried the boxes in to the staging table, she kept her head up, lips set. All entrants were to use the provided vases, which waited in boxes under the table. Day set to work, transferring roses from Bram's vases to the standard ones. Regan Culver came down the room carrying a few blooms of her own. She was wearing an elaborate, buff-colored dress, tightly fitted above the waist and ruched below, complete with a bustle, a matching hat, and a parasol hooked over one wrist. She looked tired, having driven, Day suspected, for most of the night to arrive in time.

"Good morning," Regan said with an admiring glance at Day's gown. "I suppose that's an original. Mine's reproduction, of course. I can fit into very few vintage dresses without a corset. And, for me, a corset is carrying authenticity just a bit too far. My offering is meager, too, compared with yours. No time to prepare them. I've found it's nearly impossible to run a gardening business and garden at the same time."

Tom Raines, coming up on Day's other side, sported a straw boater. It seemed as if the rest of his outfit had been put together piecemeal from what was already in his closet. He wore a white shirt and black pants held up by garishly red suspenders. A watch on a chain, a polka-dotted bow tie, and a monocle completed the ensemble. "Yes," he said, "it's the amateurs who are the lucky ones, if they only knew it. Speaking of amateurs, I just saw Paul. He's in full Civil War uniform, going to take part in the reenactment. Wool, yet. I bet that thing is hot."

Squinting through his monocle at the roses being ranked under Day's hands, he added, "And then there's Bram, who can't really be called an amateur at anything."

"No, you have to have under one hundred bushes to call yourself an amateur," Regan responded absently. "I do have a very nice Elizabeth Taylor." She regarded it with a certain surprised pleasure. "That was largely luck."

Easing Q-Tips out of one of his own roses, Tom said, "I must admit you're doing a very noble and altruistic thing, Day, but must you? I was looking forward to winning something for once."

"Nobody seems happy to see me, that's for sure," Day agreed. "Though that might be due to reasons other than Bram's roses."

"They think you're either one extremely cold-blooded female or impossibly saintly," Tom said. "Either way, they don't like it. The villains and the virtuous both tend to be widely resented, you know. Most people seem to prefer the middle."

"There is no middle." Regan stepped back to view her entries through half-closed eyes. "Only two sides. If you aren't on one, you're on the other."

"It must be nice to be so positive of things," Tom said. "Is it true that Bram is Hispanic?"

Day looked up in surprise. Regan answered. "Yes, he was adopted in Mexico."

"Then he knows Spanish, I suppose."

"I suppose. I doubt he's had much call to speak it since he was a child."

"Maybe he did deserve what he got then." Tom carried his roses away toward the display tables.

"What was all that about?" Day asked, staring after the tall, rangy figure.

"I don't know. Tom spent several years in the Peace Corps and speaks Spanish himself. And his business partner is Hispanic. Perhaps it has something to do with Inez. Has Bram ever showed any interest in her?"

"Not that I've noticed." Day started for the display tables herself, followed by Regan. "In fact, I doubt that they've met more than once or twice. Mostly at shows like this one. And Bram does seem to stick to one woman at a time. You think Tom was jealous?"

"I think that whoever hurt Bram was not inspired by a cold motive like money. There are surer ways to kill. Somebody wanted to cause a lot of pain. How many people hate that much?"

# CHAPTER 4

■ ■ ■

*Now, Somerset, where is your argument?*

The festival included a crafts show, and the exhibitors' attire varied from colonial to flapper, all of which was apparently considered close enough. Many women had even resurrected their prom gowns, though the shiny synthetics looked tawdry on a sunny morning.

Day returned to the station wagon to feed her wildlife. The exhibition hall would be closed for a couple of hours while the judging took place. When she had finished with the feeding, she stretched out on the car's bench seat and shut her eyes. Spring and summer were her busiest seasons as a rehabilitator, and in the month since the slaughter, she had received many new animals that needed her care.

The real crowds would come in the afternoon. But already the air was filled with a carnival-like chatter of voices and the smells of frying hamburgers and cotton candy. Most of the food appeared to be unabashedly modern.

Someone rapped on the partially open window. Day started, opened her eyes, and scrambled into a sitting position when she saw it was Hilda. "I didn't mean to disturb you," the older woman said. "I wanted to apologize for the way I acted the other day. Implying that you had something to do with what happened to Bram. In my defense, I can only say that he means a lot to me."

"I'm glad," Day said. "That he has someone like you, I mean."

"Someone who really cares about him, as opposed to Gavin, who thinks he should? But he's the one they let in the ward because he's family. Up to a year ago, he barely knew his cousin. But Bram needed someone to look after his company while he was campaigning."

Perhaps, Day thought, Gavin had learned to like being in charge. Maybe he hadn't wanted to give that up after Bram returned, defeated.

Hilda's gaze fell on the basket of animals. "Do you need any help?"

"No thanks. I'm done for now."

"And it's usually easier to do it yourself," Hilda finished for her. "That self-sufficient attitude of yours tends to put people off. Though I'm hardly one to talk, am I, since you and I are very much alike? I've had to make my own way too. I suppose you think I'm turning into the typically silly old spinster, latching onto somebody else's kid. But, knowing what his mother was, I've always felt kind of responsible for Bram. Because I probably could have talked Connie out of the whole adoption idea if I'd tried. Maybe I should have."

"You really think Bram would have been better off poor in Mexico?" Day asked. "I would have to disagree with you there. I'm experienced in poverty, remember, and you're not."

"At least he would still have his looks. Money you can get. You can't get a new face. I'm experienced in ugliness, Day, and you're not. I know the difference appearance can make. No, don't try to argue with me. You're plain because you choose to be, and that's different."

"Why are you apologizing to me anyway?" Day asked. "Clearly you thought me responsible for what happened to Bram."

"I don't anymore. I'd better get back and see how the judges are doing."

After Hilda had gone, Day felt wide awake, and her elbow was aching where she had banged it on the steering wheel. The bologna sandwich she had brought with her appeared unappetizing when compared to all the enticing aromas. She emerged defiantly from her isolation, bought herself a burger, curly fries, and a lemonade, and headed for the ring where a horse show was going on.

But even this unaccustomed splurge didn't affect the dull heaviness that had afflicted her for months. It wasn't anything penetrating enough to be called depression. Perhaps just burnout, as she had insisted to Regan. Perhaps just the realization that things were never going to change.

Leaning on the rail, she watched adolescent girls canter their mounts in a circle. She had often done the same herself when she was that age. The main differences were that the horses she rode weren't hers and the wealthy owners for whom she worked didn't usually bother with events this small.

She had won lots of ribbons for them. She had enjoyed the competition. She smiled nostalgically as she watched a beaming fourteen-year-old ride forward to claim a blue. Clad in a well-cut jacket and jodhpurs, with gleaming boots and hair tucked into a neat chignon, Day, too, had felt like aristocracy, like a winner. Looking back now, she could see that the money spent by her employers on expensive horseflesh, trainers, and tack probably had counted for at least as much as her skill had.

"Did you used to ride too?" Regan asked, having come up quietly beside her.

"Bram and I," Day said. "He was usually my toughest opponent."

"Was he a sore loser?"

"He didn't show it if he was. Judges don't like sore losers, and judges have long memories."

"Don't we all." Paul Sedgwick had come up with Millie. He looked dashing and younger than his years in the dark blue uniform of a Union officer. "I must say that you did a good job of preparing Bram's roses, Day. It was a gutsy move and has caused no end of talk."

Day thought she detected a trace of arrogance in his attitude, as if his approval were to be courted. A uniform did have an aggrandizing effect on some guys.

"Aren't you concerned about leaving your animals alone for so long?" Millie asked snidely. She apparently was still smarting over Day's defection at the board meeting. "What if people bring in some new ones, and you aren't there?"

"Joan is watching things for me," Day replied. "She's one of the few who still come. More for the animals than for me, I imagine. Oddly enough, it isn't what happened to Bram that bothers the teenagers. They don't believe I did that. But they do believe he killed my animals and that I've sold out by taking a job with him."

"I, for one, happen to agree with them," Millie said. "And don't talk to me about forgiveness. Everybody forgives too easily these days. There's no holding people responsible."

"The wealthy are never held responsible anyway," Paul said. "I think Day is just being realistic. Why shouldn't she profit from the man as much as she can? It's the only compensation she's liable to get."

"You weren't so understanding when you voted against her reelection," Millie remarked.

Paul shrugged. "Then I was the one being realistic."

"So you believe he did kill her animals?" Regan asked.

Paul raised his brows. "Doesn't everybody? Those who excuse him do so on the grounds that he probably was drunk at the time."

"That justifies it?"

"No, of course not. You may take satisfaction that, though Bram might not regret his act, I am sure he regrets its consequences."

Day thought she heard more than a hint of satisfaction in Paul's voice. "There's Tom," he said, looking back at the rows of craft booths. "Isn't that his business partner with him?"

"His wife," Regan corrected quietly. "He tells me he and Inez got married a couple of days ago."

"And this is their honeymoon?" Paul asked. "No wonder she looks so sulky."

"They don't look like newlyweds," Millie agreed.

Tom was slouching and glaring at the ground, hands jammed in his pockets, while Inez, partially turned away from him, appeared to be examining, one by one, every item in the booth.

*That's what I do,* Day realized, *when I'm killing time, because I am uncomfortable with my company, as on an unsuccessful blind date.* It seemed a peculiar attitude for someone just married.

The booth was the last one in the line, and when the couple had turned from it, they stopped short, as if uncertain what to do next. Then Tom saw the group by the ring and came across to join them, his wife tagging along to stand quietly in the background.

"I understand congratulations are in order," Paul said, staring at Inez, as well he might. She was a stunningly attractive girl in her mid-twenties and wore a red dress that set off her dark eyes and hair.

"Yeah," Tom muttered. "I think most of you know Inez."

It seemed almost a determinedly gauche performance. His wife's manners were much better. She nodded and smiled all around the group with a touch of hauteur. That stiff-neckedness, however, may simply have been a carefulness not to dislodge the perky little hat that rested on her dark curls. *I have to remember that we're all in costume here,* Day thought, *and as a result, not quite ourselves. Why do long skirts always give me the feeling I should be hanging on some guy's arm? Probably because, without that support, I am all too likely to trip.*

At one o'clock they trooped back to the exhibition hall. Bram's Touch of Class had taken the Queen, the top prize.

"Congratulations, Day," Regan said.

Day shrugged. "It's the only way I'm ever likely to win, as proxy." She didn't need to add that she hadn't the time to nurture show quality roses herself.

The roses and ribbons couldn't be removed until the show closed at six, so Day drove home. The pressure over and under her eyes was turning into a not-quite headache. "You run down to the festival and have some fun," she told Joan. "I'll only have to be gone a half-hour or so to pick up the roses, and I can leave a note on the door then."

■ ■ ■

Regan sat at the microfilm viewer in Rosevale's small library and squinted at the print of a seventies newspaper. The lone librarian on duty had set the outer door open, perhaps as a mute invitation for festival goers to stop in and relieve her isolation. The musty smell of books was sweetened with the hay-scent of mown grass. It reminded Regan of teenage summer afternoons spent curled up with a novel in the porch hammock. It also made her drowsy.

She rubbed her eyes and continued to read the account of a debate between Royce Falco and Dennis Day. It had been a friendly enough debate, as between two men who knew and liked each other. Which meant it was also rather dull. Regan had, as yet, found no mention of Day's sister or Bram's brother.

Yawning, she turned the knob. Someone had come in to chat brightly with the librarian, but Regan remained peacefully distanced with a strong inclination to put her head down and snooze.

*Two Killed, Two Injured After Fiery Crash.* The headline caught Regan's eye because of the reference to fire.

> Kurt Falco, 23, son of senatorial candidate Royce Falco, and an unidentified man were killed in a one-car crash on Plymouth Road last evening. Sondra Day, 19, daughter of senatorial candidate Henry Day, remains in critical condition after suffering severe burns. Falco's brother, Bram, 12, sustained a concussion after being thrown from the vehicle and also remains hospitalized.
>
> Falco, who was driving the car, reportedly lost control on the wet blacktop. The vehicle plunged down an embankment and rolled over twice before coming to rest on its roof and bursting into flames. Falco pulled Sondra Day from the burning car but

was killed when he went back after an unidentified male passenger.

Regan's drowsiness had vanished. She scanned ahead quickly, as if she weren't already sure of the outcome. It appeared in another terse paragraph a few days later.

### Candidate's Daughter Succumbs

Sondra Day died last night as a result of injuries sustained in a one-car crash earlier this week. The male passenger killed in the crash remains unidentified. He is described as dark-haired, about 5 feet 11 inches tall, probably in his thirties. Due to the badly burned state of the body, identification may depend on dental records. Anyone having knowledge of a missing person of this description is asked to notify police.

On the following day,

### Candidate Abdicates

Henry Day, candidate for the U.S. Senate, has withdrawn from the race, citing grief over his daughter's death as the reason for his pulling out. Voters are instructed to disregard Day's name on the ballot.

The voters had also, Regan supposed, been left to draw their own conclusions about all of that. As, she realized, the librarian and her friend were now doing.

"Well, I call it wicked," the librarian was saying, "if she

did that to him just because of what his brother did to her sister. It's unnatural to hold a grudge that long."

"Yes, but look at what he did to her animals," the friend responded hotly. "Don't you call *that* wicked? Maybe she just got tired, like some of the rest of us, of the Falcos always getting their way in this town. Kurt must have been drunk that night. Now they say Bram must have been drunk when he killed those animals. Is that any excuse? If Day had to take the law into her own hands, I say more power to her."

"If that's the way she chose to do it, I say she's as bad as they are," the librarian returned. "Worse, in fact, because she was sober and sneaky. If she had done something right after it happened, in the heat of the moment, okay, I can see that. But to wait until she's a guest in his house—and then to profit from it!"

"He's the one who offered her the job," the friend pointed out, "but she shouldn't have accepted. It's some kind of trap. Mark my words, Day is going to end up like the rest of her family—dead or chased out."

*Not if I can help it,* Regan thought, pushing back from the table and reaching for her parasol.

■  ■  ■

When Day returned to the fairgrounds at about a quarter of six, she found the midway virtually deserted. The vendors were packing their wares, and the wind had picked up, tugging at canopies over the booths. A chatter of gunfire informed her that everybody must be watching the mock Civil War battle being staged in the field behind the exhibition hall.

The plush rope was again strung across the entrance, as it had been during the judging. Day unclipped it and refastened it behind her. Hilda generally closed the show about an hour before pickup time so she could finish her paperwork.

In the hall, the cracking of musket shots sounded dangerously close, a highly incongruous sound effect for the formal ranks of flowers. At every bang the glass vases vibrated faintly, as if shuddering. The place was empty of human life except for Hilda, who was sitting alone at the registration table at the far end of the building. The female dummy behind her had toppled again. Strolling among the heirloom roses, Day thought how some of them harked back to a time when weapons were sharp as thorns and silent except when they rang against chain mail or thudded against bone.

The real War of the Roses had been a brutal series of battles, riddled with cruelty and treachery. When Day had had to do a report on them for school, her research had left her with a sense of oppression for days afterward. It was almost impossible to reconcile history with a belief in humanity's basic goodness.

Perhaps that was when she had begun to suspect that the Christian concept of original sin was right after all. She paused to contemplate Quatre Saisons, probably the oldest rose still available. Wealthy Romans had strewn thousands of dollars worth of rose petals at their bacchanals. Guests were even reported to have smothered in them, a fine example of the wealthy drowning in their own excess. Those guests must have either been very drunk or had help in that smothering. Maybe she was more fortunate to be poor than she knew.

Uneasiness had begun to creep like goose flesh up her spine. She could detect no good reason for it except that Hilda seemed to be sitting peculiarly still. *Perhaps she's changed her mind about me again.*

Papers rustled, and Day turned to see some unused tags flutter off the registration table. Hilda made no move to retrieve them. "What's wrong?" Day asked sharply, advancing toward the table between the regally lifted heads of roses. Then she halted in combined relief and chagrin as she realized the face regarding her from under the rakish hat brim was that of the mannequin. Some practical joker had set it at the table. The vibrations must have been jarring, however, for even as Day watched, the plastic figure listed sideways and fell to the floor, the hat tumbling free to reveal a bald head beneath. From that position, the face looked up at her with the same serene smile.

But if the dummy was at the table, then who…

A dragging dread slowed Day's steps as she proceeded around the table and stood looking down at the crumpled form of Hilda Graveston, who lay facedown on the dais. Outside, soldiers screamed in pseudo-agony, but here the immaculate gentleman still bowed and proffered his flowers. Hilda apparently had accepted one. On the floor under her outstretched hand lay a white rose, its petals splotched with blood.

■   ■   ■

"I've been told that the flower she was holding is a new tea rose," Chief Newpax said to the stiffly silent group of board members. Chairs had been set up hastily for them near the doors, distant from the area where technicians were examining the body. "One called *El Niño*. 'The male child.' Looks like she grabbed it right before she fell. From what you all told me about your dinner party the other night, a white rose would seem to point straight at Day here. Although," he added, taking in her lacy, pristine gown, "anybody seeing her in that getup would never believe it."

Millie bristled. "That's a white *tea* rose Hilda was holding, not the white rose of York. You could just as well say it points to me because my last name is Childs."

"In the plural though," Tom pointed out. "Of course, if Hilda were dying, she probably wouldn't have been picky about semantics."

"We were also discussing the meaning of names the other night," Regan reminded. "Let me be the first to admit that *Culver* means 'dove, a white bird.' And *Regan,* 'son of the small ruler' or 'a male child.'"

"Not to mention that *Gavin* means 'a small white hawk,'" Tom added. "Besides, most people these days associate *El Niño* with storms—or Raines."

The others smiled mechanically, but Tom's face remained stony. Gavin, who had just arrived, looked from one to another of the board members with frightened eyes.

Day was surprised they were all coming to her defense, closing ranks, so to speak. She didn't think it was going to do any good this time.

"I think that may be stretching it a bit," Newpax said. "If I were dying, I think I would be more straightforward than that. And she only had the ones in arm's reach to pick from. Maybe a white tea rose was the best she could do." He looked at Day. "Somebody saw Hilda talking to you this afternoon out in the parking lot. What was that about?"

"She was apologizing," Day said quietly, hands clasped in her lap. "For what she had implied about me the other day. She said she had changed her mind; she no longer thought I was guilty." One of the faces in the crowd after Day had called out for help had been Joan's. Day had looked at her, and the teenager had nodded, wooden faced, and slipped away, going to the animals.

*I hope she'll keep it up somehow if I'm arrested.*

"She was well-off, wasn't she?" the chief said. "Who will inherit? Does anybody know?"

"Bram does," Regan replied. "She told me that the other night."

"The only one who has an alibi," Paul Sedgwick said. "And the one who least needs the money. Provoking, isn't it, Chief?"

Inez sat at the edge of the group, slightly behind her husband, as if distancing herself. "You're Latino, aren't you, ma'am?" Newpax said, looking at her. She inclined her head.

"Neen-yo," Tom said harshly. "As in a male. Inez is neither male nor a child."

"No one here is a child," Newpax said in a mildly rebuking tone that implied some of them were acting the part. "Like I said, the lady may have had to make do with what was close. Or she may just have grabbed at anything as she went down and got the rose by accident. Or the killer might have stuck it in her hand to put us off the track." Viewing his alternatives glumly, he said, "Anybody want to guess which?"

Nobody did.

"No gun either." Newpax added to his litany of woes. "I'd like to take a look at the one you're wearing, Sedgwick."

Paul loosened the flap on his holster to show it was empty. "Sorry, but I'm not quite that authentic," he said. "I don't own a handgun. I just wave a saber around and lead charges."

"The newspapers will have a field day with this," the chief said. "The rose society bit and all. But I'm not so surprised myself. I've never really liked roses. They're pretty, all right, but you'd better be careful how you handle them if you don't want to get hurt."

"You prefer your flowers a little more accessible?" Tom suggested. "Maybe some of us like the challenge."

"Is there any other significance to a white rose I should know about?" Newpax asked, ignoring Tom.

"I am worthy of you," Regan said. "The Victorian meaning. There's also at least one old quote that equates it with femininity. 'Lavender and Rosemary is as woman to man and White Roose to Reede.'"

"Pure woman and bloody man maybe?" the chief said with polite skepticism.

"Well, you must admit men have always been more prone to violence," Regan replied mildly. "Especially violence involving guns. Adolescent girls aren't shooting up schoolyards. Are you sure that a boy in search of thrills couldn't have done this? Another random shooting, in other words?"

The wind banged at the closed door, making them all jump. Drafts prowled the aisles of the long building. The roses shivered.

"Right now I don't mind admitting I'm not sure of anything," Newpax said. "And you people are giving me the creeps in those getups of yours. It's like I've stepped into a time warp or something."

One of his underlings, who had been watching the technicians, approached with a piece of paper and muttered in his chief's ear.

Newpax scanned the sheet and handed it back. "Right. Bag it. What do you all plan to do with the rest of these flowers?"

The board members looked at each other. "I suppose," Paul said finally, "that depends on how long you intend to keep this place closed up. Most of the exhibitors have probably left. We can mail them their ribbons, I suppose. Perhaps we could contribute the roses to a local hospital or nursing home."

"Too bad they won't last until the funeral," the chief said, viewing the display with grim relish. "They would make quite a splash on the casket."

He released them then. "You can go home now. All except you, Miss Culver. You live a little too far away for me to drive. Could you stick around for a couple of days?"

"Day had invited me to stay at her place tonight."

"You're still welcome," Day said. "Unless he's planning to arrest me."

"Not yet," the chief said. "Not yet. I'll have some of the boys walk you to your cars while I chat with the press. I don't want you calling your cousin about this," he added to Gavin. "I'm going to have to drive down there to talk with him tomorrow, and I'd rather he wasn't forewarned."

He went out to meet the reporters, drawing them casually to one side while his officers hurried the board members away.

"What's that?" the policeman with Day said as they approached her station wagon. On the ground near the driver's door something glinted in the long rays of the setting sun. Day regarded the gun with a dull lack of surprise.

The cop hunkered down to scrutinize the pistol without touching it. "Afraid you're going to have to wait here until the chief is done, Ms. Day."

Regan, whose Land Rover was nearby, hurried over to look. "That's Bram's," she said immediately.

The policeman squinted up at her. "Pardon?"

"That's Bram's pistol. I saw it in his desk drawer last Friday night. I took the ammunition, though, or all that I could find.

We were afraid that Bram might be suicidal, see. I mentioned it to Hilda too. I think she planned to take the gun as well, but she may not have bothered after the accident."

"Looks like she should have bothered," the policeman said.

■ ■ ■

"I'm surprised they didn't arrest me," Day said to Regan. "You can have my bed, and I'll sleep on the couch in the living room. There is a guest room, but it's full of cages. It's not what you're used to, of course."

"This will do fine," Regan said. The small room was furnished only with a spartan twin bed, a nightstand, a chair, and a dresser. But the walls were lined with bookshelves that boasted a motley collection of reading material as well as bits and pieces scavenged from nature—old wasps' nests, dried berries, polished stones. "The gun was so obviously planted."

Regan laid her overnight case on the bed, picked up an open scrapbook from the nightstand, and perched on the edge of the mattress. "This is nice. I've always wanted to do something like it." Pressed botanical specimens had been carefully glued to its pages, each one identified by Latin and common names.

"My sister used to have one," Day said, dropping into the chair. "But all the leaves have crumbled in it. She had little sketches that she would do with them too. I can't draw. What's going to happen, Regan?"

"I don't know. Hilda was killed so close to the time you found her that even if someone could pinpoint when you drove in, it probably wouldn't do much good. With that battle going on, nobody would notice the gunshots, of course. But it seems that with the possible exception of Paul, who was in the thick of the reenactment, nobody else has much of an alibi.

People were watching the battle rather than each other. Is that your sister?"

She indicated a studio portrait on one of the shelves: a blond teenager beaming at the camera with infectious joy.

"Yes, that's Sondra. Everybody called her Sunny, of course. Daddy used to say that both of his daughters together made for a sunny day. Daddy tended to be a bit corny. He had been a newspaper columnist, and his ideas sounded good on paper, but they were based on a flawed premise—that people are basically good and only need a little encouragement to get along with one another. Still, he could make an audience feel warm and fuzzy, and that's always helpful in politics. Especially," she added caustically, "the fuzzy part."

"Do you hear from him?" Regan asked, not sure if she was treading on sensitive ground.

"Oh yes. There's no dramatic estrangement. He's never been back here."

"Was it your sister's death that threw him?"

"Partly, I guess. That was his excuse anyway. It was," Day said, regarding her sister's face somberly, "a little like the sun had gone down for all of us. We adored her. Everybody did. She was our center, in a way. Like I said, Daddy's ideas had very little connection with reality, and Mother was his faithful shadow. I was a plain and precocious twelve-year-old who found them both embarrassing. But Sunny was all light. Not the kind of sweetness that makes your teeth ache. She could be mischievous, too, but she was never mean. Strangely enough, I was never jealous of her, but I was always afraid for her. I guess I'd bought into the idea that the good die young."

"And she did."

"Yes. The Falcos seem to blight everyone they touch. Kurt did drink some after he came back from Vietnam—until he started to date Sunny. He straightened up then, or seemed to."

Day jumped up. "Let's go out to the kitchen for a bedtime snack."

When they were seated at the table with milk and cookies, Day said, as if changing the subject, "My father should never have run for election. He was too sensitive for politics. He wanted to please everybody, and that just wasn't possible. By October his nerves were suffering. He was strung so tight, you could almost feel the thrum. He couldn't eat or sleep. He virtually lived on those quivery gelatin squares; they were the only thing he could keep down. I remember that Sunny was playing with them that last evening as she waited for Kurt to pick her up. Dad had left a plateful on the table when he went to answer the phone. She was building what she called the Grape Pyramid. She said, 'Tell Jell-O man that I'm off to inveigle the enemy again.' And she laughed as she said it. Sunny had no enemies. She really believed that Daddy could win too."

"But you didn't?"

Day shook her head. "Even at twelve, I was much more realistic than the rest of them. Frankly, I didn't want him to win. I think I knew instinctively even then that he was much too suggestible to be a politician. I was just a child, and I could get virtually anything I wanted out of him."

After nibbling at her cookie, Day continued, "Sunny and Kurt were going to a party down by the water. The weather had been warm. Bram walked to the lake on his own apparently. Sneaking into a party for grownups would have amused him. He must have known that Kurt would give him a ride home. Kurt was tolerant of his little brother's escapades.

Anyway, Bram was with them when they left. They went off the road and crashed almost immediately."

Day pushed her barely gnawed cookie aside. "The Falcos have guts. I'll grant you that. Kurt had won lots of medals in the war. He pulled Sunny out of the burning car. But then he went back for the stranger. Or he may have thought Bram was still in there. Somebody heard him say something about 'the boy.' Kurt was very fond of his brother."

Turning her untouched glass of milk absently in her hands, Day concluded quietly, "Maybe it was just a skid, the kind of thing that can happen to anybody. The road was wet, after all. It had rained a little bit. That's why the party was breaking up. Only Bram remained alive, and his concussion left him with no memory of the accident."

"They never found out who the other man in the car was?" Regan asked.

"No, just a hitchhiker, I imagine. A vet maybe. The men who came back from Vietnam were edgy, restless."

"And if Kurt was drunk? Do you hold the Falcos responsible?"

"I would hold Kurt responsible. Kurt and the war and his craving for his lost innocence. With my sister, I think he got it back for a while. She wouldn't have blamed him. How can I?"

■  ■  ■

Someone came into Bram's hospital room. At the movement of air, pain rippled over him. They had peeled off the white eschar and stapled skin from his thighs onto his face. Now the thighs burned too.

They had told him to envisage himself in another place, a peaceful place, when the pain got too bad. Focusing on the plastic covering the ceiling light, he had been pretending to be twelve again in a June pasture lying on a horse's back, head pillowed on the animal's rump as it moved desultorily from one clump of grass to the next, its tail occasionally flicking at him as it switched flies.

It had not been, he supposed, a particularly safe thing to do. Had the horse suddenly taken alarm…But it had felt safe.

"You awake?" The voice yanked him back. He turned his head carefully to look up into Tom Raines's face.

"How did you get in here?"

Raines was wearing a white jacket. With his negligent slouch, he looked like an intern. "People never stop you if you act like you know what you're doing. There was something I thought you should know. Hilda's dead. Murdered."

Bram turned his gaze back to the plastic overhead, but the June pasture was long gone. As were his father, mother, Kurt, and now Hilda. Even the light hurt. "How?"

"Shot. With your gun apparently. Newpax won't appreciate my telling you, but I thought Hilda would want you to be informed. She deserves that much consideration at least. You don't seem broke up about it."

"I know you don't like me, Raines," Bram said without moving his head. "You don't have to harp on it. Who killed her?"

"The same person who put you here, I imagine."

"I suppose Hilda found some proof. She would dig until she did. A gun seems more direct than Dame's usual style though."

"How do you know Day was responsible for that gasoline?" Tom looked impossibly tall, gazing down as from a great height. "Gavin seems more likely to me. It would have been easier, too, for him to get at the gun."

"And his motive would be?"

"Money, of course."

Bram laughed, a laugh that inflamed and raged through

his throat and chest, and gurgled into something like a sob. "Gavin doesn't inherit from me. Hilda does. Did."

"And now that she's gone? He's your only surviving family, isn't he? If you were to die now, he would get both estates, yours and Hilda's."

Bram stared into the hurting light. "Then, if he was smart, he would have killed her before he tried anything on me. Gavin doesn't have the guts. Go away, Raines."

"Day showed your roses for you, by the way. Won you the Queen."

Bram said a single, nasty word with vicious emphasis.

"I told her you wouldn't be grateful," Tom commented dryly and left.

When the nurse came in a few minutes later, Bram was alone, still looking blindly up at the fixture, the light glaring glassily off his unshed tears.

"The doctor said we could increase your morphine if you need it," she said. "Do you think that would help?"

"No," he responded dully. "Nothing will help. It's too late now."

■ ■ ■

The morning after her conversation with Day, Regan sat across the same small table from the police chief. Day had just gone out to feed Bram's horses.

"Do you know her well?" Newpax asked.

Regan shook her head. "Not really. We just spent time together at rose conferences."

"Yet she seems to like you better than most people. I need to know what's going on between her and Mr. Falco. I have the feeling they're hiding a lot."

"They're both secretive people," Regan said. "Bram not obviously so, perhaps. You must know him fairly well."

"I've known him to speak to for years. As for understanding him—" The chief shrugged. "He's not one of the pushy rich. He doesn't ask for favors. He doesn't ask for anything when it comes right down to it. I don't suppose he's ever had to."

"Or maybe he had his fill of that as a street orphan," Regan suggested.

"Now that was a surprise to me," Newpax admitted. "Nobody had ever hinted he was adopted. Once you know, it seems obvious. But Royce was dark haired. Bram could have been his son. I don't see the point of keeping it quiet." He sounded personally offended.

"Perhaps they expected some prejudice. Probably not many Hispanics lived around here at the time."

"There aren't a lot now," the chief said. "Raines's new wife, of course. What do you know about her?"

"Even less. I've seen her around with Tom here and there. It must be two or three years since he hired her. She seemed more subdued than usual at the rose show. Before she was much more take charge and intimidatingly competent. She did the nearly impossible when she talked him into computerizing his business, you know. I thought she was good for him since his occasional snappiness didn't seem to faze her."

"You don't think she's a battered wife, do you?"

Regan shot him an alarmed look. "Oh no! I think Tom's a very sensitive soul underneath. I always thought his abruptness was a form of self-protection, aggravated by incoherence. He's very lucid when he's being funny, but when something matters a lot to him, he finds it much harder to express himself in diplomatic or neutral terms."

"Does Inez matter a lot to him?"

A bouquet of roses between them was shedding onto the table. Regan rubbed one of the soft petals between thumb and forefinger. "Yes, I think so," she said finally. "Otherwise, he could be light and easy around her, and he isn't. But they don't seem happy; I grant you that."

"Would Raines think he was any match for somebody like Bram where a woman was concerned?"

Regan managed a weak smile. "Quite the psychologist, aren't you, Chief? The answer is no."

"You're sure about that?"

"Yes, pretty sure. But I think that he would just retreat. He wouldn't try to cheat by killing his opponent. Like many people with a weak self-image, Tom has a very strong sense of right and wrong. He saved Bram's life and burned himself doing it. He isn't a coward, and the person who planted that gasoline was."

"I think that gasoline was a hate crime, Ms. Culver. You can't be sure of killing anybody that way. I think this person just wanted to hurt Bram bad. Mess him up some, make him suffer."

"I don't think Day is a hater."

"She's never showed it. I agree with you there. But you have to admit she has a lot to hold against the Falcos. Kurt was driving the car that killed her sister. Some say Royce forced her father out of town. And Connie underpaid Day's mother for years. Worked the poor woman to death, some would have it. Don't you think all that must have festered? Even before Bram cost Day her job and killed those animals?"

Regan turned her face away. "Don't think all that hasn't occurred to me."

"But you like her. I do, too, but we can't let our liking get in the way of likelihood here. The woman would have to be a saint not to have a lot of anger packed away somewhere. This was one of the nastiest crimes I've seen, and we can't let her get away with it just because she's good with animals and Bram has turned out to be something of a savage under all that charisma. And there isn't any excuse for what happened to Hilda Graveston. Day was angry, wasn't she?"

"Yes, I think so." Regan came reluctantly back to his imperative gaze. "We were talking about forgiveness. Forgiveness isn't suppressing, by the way. Millie is right, that people are too quick to forgive nowadays—when the offense wasn't committed against them. True forgiveness isn't easy. But it isn't suppressing. It's walking right through the offense, suffering the pain and anger to the fullest, then getting beyond it."

"But what if she couldn't get beyond it? Did she want to forgive?"

"I don't know. I hoped so. Especially when she consented to Bram's election to the board."

"But that could have been a trick, couldn't it? Ever play chess?" He positioned his hands as over a board. "You appear to give in over here. Then you swoop in from another direction for the kill. Why do you think she took the job Bram offered, by the way? Can you explain that?"

Regan smiled. "Maybe it's just what she said—she needed the money."

■ ■ ■

Day sent the ribbons in with Gavin. When he returned, she was in the garden with a hose. It hadn't rained for a couple of weeks. She was directing the stream of water into the earthen basin at the foot of a rosebush, being careful not to splash the fungus-sensitive foliage. She pushed back her straw hat. "What did he say?"

"He said he would have to admit that the"—Gavin paused, was obviously doing some rapid rewording—"woman knew her business," he finished weakly.

"I bet."

"He also told me to give you these." Gavin dropped a ring of keys into her hand. "He said you might as well keep the house clean while you're at it. Lock it and the horses up whenever you go home. I'll be eating in town and won't be back until late most evenings, so I'd appreciate your keeping an eye on things. Keep track of the hours you work, and I'll give you a check every Friday. Is there any message you want to send him?"

"Yes. I don't like housecleaning, so I get twelve dollars an hour for it."

Gavin started to grin, then faltered when she didn't smile back. "O-kaay. I'd better get down to the factory, I guess."

He drove away then. She turned off the hose, laid it down carefully, wiped damp hands on the seat of her jeans, and walked out onto the broad lawn. She stood there, looking up at the house's serene facade, lightly bouncing the keys in one cupped hand. Gavin was, she thought, just a bit frightened of her too. It was going to make for impossibly long days—doing the work of two people besides taking care of her own animals. But she would hardly have time to think. That might be a blessing.

*   *   *

For Day, the following weeks slipped by peacefully. She rose early each morning to care for the animals in her barn. The young ones that required constant feedings during the day she took with her up to the Falco place in picnic baskets lined with heating pads.

Nestled in alongside the orphaned rabbits and possums were a couple of motherless puppies. Some people tended to ignore the wild part of wildlife rehabilitation. Day had also received her share of after-Easter, half-grown chicks, bunnies, and ducklings over the years. She passed them on to farmers when that was possible, just as she passed on unreleasable wild animals to nature centers and zoos.

She set the alarm on her watch to remind her of feeding times. After taking a closer look at the stable, she banished the horses permanently to the pasture, dragged in some big sticks for perches, and turned Ivan loose in there. That way she didn't have to muck out stalls, and the hawk would have room to practice his flying.

In the morning she worked in the gardens until it became hot. Then she retreated to the air-conditioned indoors. The housework was not onerous, Gavin not being there enough to make much mess. He usually ate in town.

She always left a note on her door and a message on her answering machine explaining where she was. The children, hunters, construction workers, and game wardens bringing wounded animals up the long curving drive often seemed overawed. Those not local enough to know what was going on would ask if she had moved.

The police chief came to see her one morning. He sat across from her at a table on the terrace where she had several animals lined up at a homemade feeding station, the puppies right in there with the squirrels.

Watching her feed a tiny bat with a tube-tipped syringe, he said, "I got to thinkin', Day. Your sister burned to death, didn't she?"

"You know she did. That was an accident though."

"An accident in a car driven by Bram's brother. Because Kurt died himself, we never tested his blood alcohol. Some people thought it was a cover-up, I suppose."

"I suppose." Day kept all her attention focused on the tiny animal in her hand. "But since Kurt was dead, what was the point? As long as you're just sitting, you might as well make

95

yourself useful." Day tucked the bat into a basket and lifted out a baby groundhog and handed it with a doll-sized bottle across the table. "What has that got to do with Bram anyway? He was only twelve at the time, like me."

The chief cradled the woodchuck gingerly. "You do know that these things are pests?"

"What people bring me, I care for. I don't make judgments on an animal's worth or lack thereof. Except for raccoons, because these days they're liable to be rabid. It's a shame, too, because coons are the most fun."

Newpax seemed to be fascinated by the animal in his arms. "I must admit, I've never seen a live one this close before. People are saying, you know, that Bram's burns are your revenge for the ones your sister suffered."

Day was inserting a feeding tube into a baby rabbit. "Just a minute. I have to concentrate, or I could get this in a lung instead of the stomach. So what are they implying, that I somehow transferred Kurt's guilt to his brother? They must really think I'm a monster. A lot of the kids who used to help me out have a different opinion. As does Millie. They all think I've sold out like my father did. That Bram killed my animals and I'm letting him buy me off."

Newpax looked up quickly. "I never said that your father sold out. Sunny's death may have been just more than he could take, and he had to get away. The election wouldn't have seemed so important then."

"Abandoning his wife and his other child in the process?" Day asked. "My father was weak, Chief. I knew that when I was twelve, and you know it. It would be unrealistic of me to blame the Falcos for that, wouldn't it? And why would I wait twenty-some years? If you're going to suspect me, at least give me a rational motive."

"I asked Bram if he killed your animals. Do you know what he said? 'It's your job to find that out now, isn't it?' I thought that was pretty brazen myself. And why are you here, Day? Let's forget for the moment what people say. You must admit it looks funny."

"Like guilt?" Dripping warm milk down the feeding tube, she said, "It's simple enough. I needed a job, and he was the only one offering. Don't feed that animal too much. It's already fat. So you visited Bram, did you? How is he? Cussing out all the nurses, I imagine."

"No, they told me he had been very quiet. It seemed to worry them a bit. You two aren't fooling me any. You plan to work your little feud out on your own, don't you, without interference from the law?" With seeming reluctance, he handed the drowsy woodchuck back. "I must admit I enjoyed that. I can see why you do this kind of thing. But maybe I see more. That it takes a certain toughness to care for these babies, then push them away from you back into the wild. I hear you feed the ones that die to your hawk."

"If they weren't poisoned. Why should the bodies go to waste? I suppose you're wondering just how cold-blooded I am. I know that a human life is far more valuable than an animal one, Chief. Than even a large number of animal ones. The Old Testament sacrifices prove that. Some people call Judaism and Christianity bloody religions. I prefer to think they're realistic. Something innocent had to die for guilty man."

"What are you saying, Day?" Newpax watched her quizzically. "Who is the innocent here?"

She shook her head wearily. "None of us. But they are." Her face softened as she looked down on the sleeping animals. "When we mess up their world, they have virtually no defense against us. I just try to compensate a little bit."

■ ■ ■

Despite her brave words, Day froze in place early one afternoon about six weeks after Bram's accident when she heard his voice in the hall. She had been mopping the kitchen floor of his house, and the shock was so great she only caught the voice, not the words.

Trying to move deliberately, she squeezed the mop dry and leaned the handle against a counter. But her hands were unsteady. The mop slid sideways and hit the floor with a loud bang that caused her to jump.

Gavin came in, saying as he came, "I'm sorry. I'm really sorry. I should have warned you, but I had no idea they would let him come home today. I don't think they wanted to, in fact, but he insisted. He said to give you this stuff."

Gavin dumped a sheaf of papers and shiny brochures on the counter only to have half of them slide to the floor. Scrambling after them, he said, "These are all about the therapy he's supposed to do, I guess. He's making me move out, wants me to take a room downtown. He says he doesn't like me staring at him. And I was very careful," he added peevishly, straightening, "not to stare. You should go too. He can't make you stay."

"Can't he?" Day absently wiped her hands on a dishtowel. "How bad is it?"

Gavin moved his shoulders uncomfortably. "Well, only one side of his face is really messed up. If you saw him in profile, you might not realize…Of course, there's his hand, too, and his chest…" He went on beating around the bush, but Day had stopped listening. She had long ago determined that Gavin wasn't going to be any help to her.

"All right," she said, heading for the door into the hall. "You can go now."

The hall was empty, but the door to Bram's study stood open. As Day walked along the silent corridor, which smelled of Mr. Clean, her knees trembled, and she could feel her pulse ticking in one eyelid. She had long ago schooled herself to the belief that revulsion was all in the mind. Because she suspected that animals could sense that shrinking away, she had trained herself not to feel it. Still, she suspected that Bram would be even more sensitive than the animals, and if she showed one flicker of shock…

She stopped to stand just outside the open door, looking in at him. He was sitting at his desk, his profile to her. From this side he did, as Gavin had predicted, look perfectly normal. Except for the hand that rested on the blotter. It was forced open by a splint and encased in an elastic glove that had the fingertips removed.

"Well?" he said, without turning his head. "Aren't you going to come and look at your handiwork?"

Setting her shoulders, she marched sturdily across the carpet to his side and aggressively imitated his remark. "Well? Let's see it."

He swiveled the chair around to look up at her. Although she felt a jolt in her chest, she carefully kept her face blank and leaned forward to examine the scars with, she hoped, the appearance of professional detachment. The puckered red skin looked, in a way, like plastic that had been left too close to a burner and had softened out of all natural shape.

"Okay." She straightened matter-of-factly. "It's pretty bad. Do you want any lunch?"

Unexpectedly, he smiled, a smile that was dragged down instead of up on the ravaged side. "You have guts, Dame. I have to admit that."

■ ■ ■

The telephone on his desk rang.

The jangle of the phone through the wood on which his hand rested irked Bram.

"Aren't you going to answer that?" he snapped at Day despite himself. She smelled of some kind of lemon detergent. Clean. The woman always smelled clean. Nothing of the disease or injury she dealt with every day seemed to cling to her. Emotionally or physically. He had wanted to be as cool and composed as she was.

"Falco residence," she said. A pause, then, "More to the point, who are *you?*" She listened without comment for a couple of minutes, abstractedly fixing her gaze on the desktop.

"I work for Mr. Falco," she said finally. Then, "There is no one else."

She raised her eyes to look at Bram. "No, he's not wearing a mask. The man is a lot bigger than I am, Doctor. How do you expect me to make him do anything?"

She appeared to be growing impatient. "It's his choice, surely. I don't think he wants to talk to you." She raised her brows, extended the receiver toward Bram. When he ignored her, she pulled it back to her own ear. "No, he doesn't. Listen, I told you, I just work here. I don't have any influence…I suggest you call me back when you've calmed down some!"

The lemon odor had intensified, emanating from the desk. It must be, Bram realized, some sort of polish. He could only hope the police had fingerprinted that surface before all evidence had been efficiently rubbed away.

Slapping the receiver back into its cradle, she said, "There's one guy who isn't used to being defied. You and he should have a lot in common. Where's this plastic face mask he was talking about?"

"I took it off."

"So I deduced. Do you really think that's wise? It won't eliminate all the scarring, of course, but it will make it less prominent."

"Would you like to wear plastic on your face full-time?"

"No. You didn't answer my earlier question. Have you had lunch yet?"

# CHAPTER 5

*Here in my scabbard, meditating that*
*Shall dye your white rose in a bloody red.*

Bram tried to eat with his right hand, but his fingers wouldn't close tightly enough over the handle, and he kept dropping the spoon. He had done better at the hospital, but he was tired. It was pretty bad when an hour's drive could make you this tired. He noticed with satisfaction that the constant clatter against the soup bowl seemed to bother Day.

She had offered to take his lunch into the dining room, but he had insisted on eating in the kitchen with her. She should have to look at what she had done.

"Why not use your left hand?" she asked finally.

"Because I'm worse with it."

He forced his stiff fingers around the too-thin handle of the spoon again. Those fingers were tired, shaking slightly as he raised the spoon to his mouth. Like an old man's arthritic appendages. *You're not yet forty, Falco, and suddenly you're an old man.* Again the sweet-acid burst of tomato, the clove-like bite of basil. When the sense of smell had come back, so had the sense of taste. For years he had eaten out of necessity rather than for pleasure. Now that the taste was back, it was almost like an assault. At least most of the hospital food had been bland.

Looking down, he realized he had dribbled some of the soup on his shirt. He glanced across at Day, expecting pity, disgust—something. But her clear-eyed gaze was unfathomable.

Surely he had been given rehabilitation. Surely he was exaggerating the difficulty for her benefit. But if so, he was a very good actor.

Day tried to think ahead. Would she be expected to cook his supper too? What would be easiest for him to manage? He wouldn't be able to cut meat.

But her thoughts refused to settle to the question. The unexpected return had unnerved her. She had known, of course, that he would come back eventually. But she had expected to have plenty of warning, time to steel herself. If only she knew what he planned to do. The known danger was never so paralyzing as the unknown one was.

"Our twentieth class reunion is tonight," she said finally to break the clattering silence. "They didn't have it earlier because too much was going on in June. I don't suppose you want to go?"

When he just looked at her, she answered her own question. "No, I didn't think so."

"Are you going?"

"No," she said. "That would make things a bit awkward for everybody. They would find it much harder to talk about me if I were there."

"I guess," he commented with that same expressionless stare, "we'll have to have our own party."

She didn't know how to respond to that, so she rose from

her seat and circled behind him to the refrigerator. The ice cream in the freezer box could be dessert. A cone might actually be easier for him to grasp than the spoon. But with no children in the house, she doubted…She began to open cupboard doors.

"What are you doing?" His tone was sharp.

She turned her head. He still had his back to her, but he seemed unnaturally tense.

He was, she realized suddenly, just as wary of her as she was of him. He believed, after all, that she had tried to kill him.

"I thought ice cream—" she began.

"The last time I checked, we didn't keep ice cream in the cupboards," he said. "Sit down, Day."

She returned to her seat like a scolded child.

"Are you willing to continue working for me?" he asked, rubbing at his scars with his left hand.

This, she thought, was where any rational person would pull out. But she was trapped. Not by the need for money but by—

She jerked her thoughts back. "Yes."

"You'll have to do the cooking, too, since I obviously can't. And I have no intention of going out. You'll eat what I eat, and I'll watch you prepare it. Who knows? You may decide that poison is an even more appropriate punishment for me than fire."

"Stop that!" she said fiercely. "Stop rubbing your face! Don't you know that grafted skin is fragile?"

"It itches."

"I'll make you some lotion for it then. It's obviously too dry." She stood and began to gather up the dishes. "Vitamin E oil and aloe vera should work. Perhaps you would prefer to watch me make that too?"

"Certainly. I think we have both of those ingredients in the bathroom. Lead on."

As she stirred the oil and gel together in a small custard dish, he leaned against the counter beside her. Outside the sun still shone as peacefully as it had in the days leading up to this one. But that peace and warmth were distant now, unattainable. In comparison, the bathroom was shadowy, antiseptic.

"All right," she said, abruptly turning toward him and raising her hand. He flinched slightly, and she stopped the hand in midair. "Unless you want to put it on yourself."

"Go ahead." He continued to grasp the edge of the counter behind him as she rubbed the oily fluid into the puckered skin.

Vitamin E was supposed to help fade scars. Small scars. These were, she suspected, beyond its capacity.

He moved suddenly and, heart thudding, she shrank back against the half-open door. "I think that's enough," he said mildly, giving her that tight, turned-down grin. "I'm going to rest for a while." He pushed past her into the hallway. "I don't want any visitors or phone calls."

To his back she said, "People may bring animals here."

"Keep them away from me."

She returned to the kitchen just as the phone rang. It was a woman this time.

"Ms. Day? My name is Nancy Slessor. I was Mr. Falco's physical therapist. Dr. Rhodes asked me to call. I'm afraid he may have been a bit abrupt with you this morning, but you can understand his frustration, I'm sure. We are trying to do what's best for Mr. Falco."

"I know."

"We gave him a Jobst mask, too, and I hope you can persuade him to wear that at least. It's made of a stretchy material that might be a little more comfortable than the plastic. It doesn't apply pressure quite as evenly, but it's better than nothing. He's already wearing a Jobst undershirt and gloves. At least, I hope he still is?"

"Yes."

"Good. Well, they will be hot in this weather, but I assume you have air conditioning?"

"Yes."

"He also needs to continue his range-of-motion exercises. I sent a pamphlet home with his cousin that explains them. We usually like our patients to come back to the clinic three times a week for outpatient therapy. Is that going to be a problem?"

"I think you can assume that won't happen."

"All right. That's his choice. But I would like you to continue those exercises with him, if at all possible. I must warn you that if he doesn't work that hand, it may become unusable. The tissue becomes too tight, which causes a contracture. That means—"

"That he won't be able to use the joints. I know. I've been reading up on burns."

"Good. We would have released Mr. Falco earlier except he never really cooperated with our psychotherapist. Physically he was far enough along in the healing process, but you should be on the lookout for some psychological symptoms. Nightmares are common. Those weeks of helplessness often lead to a loss of self-esteem as well. There may be some aggressive outbursts. You mustn't take them personally."

"I think, in my case, they would be personal."

"Pardon?"

"Never mind."

The therapist continued cautiously. "The loss of self-image is similar to a bereavement experience. Most patients have to relinquish who they were and try to build a new identity. You have me a little bit worried, Ms. Day. Were you implying that you and Mr. Falco don't get along?"

"That's putting it mildly."

"I'm afraid you're really going to be unsuitable as a caretaker then. A burn patient needs a lot of compassionate emotional support as he's recovering. Empathy, physical closeness, somebody to listen. Doesn't he have anyone like that?"

"The only person I can think of died a couple of weeks ago."

"I see. His cousin?"

"He's been sent away. Bram didn't like his staring."

"I'm afraid Mr. Falco is going to have to get used to stares, even some recoil from outsiders. That's why it's so important he have unconditional acceptance at home. Your name is beginning to sound familiar to me now, Ms. Day. Aren't you the woman who—"

"Cost him the election? I'm afraid so."

"But why...How did you get there?"

"We're neighbors. Mr. Falco asked me to look after things while he was gone."

"But this is completely wrong for him! He can't deal with this sort of stress now. Can't you—"

"Go away? I wish I could. But then he would be completely alone. You don't want that, do you?"

"Oh no. Absolutely not! But Mr. Falco certainly could afford to hire an attendant. I can recommend an agency."

"Of course he can afford to, but he won't. Since he has the mistaken idea I caused his injuries, I imagine he thinks I should have to deal with them. Mr. Falco's politics have always been very strong on justice, you know."

"He thinks you caused his burns?" The therapist was beginning to sound pitiful. "I'm sure our psychologist will agree with me that you are the last person Mr. Falco needs right now."

"Oh, *his* nerves seem to be holding up fairly well," Day commented dryly. "I can't say the same for mine. On the positive side, I am a wildlife rehabilitator. I don't suppose human rehabilitation can be all that different."

"But if you aren't responsible for what happened to him, what makes you stay when you know it could be dangerous?" And, at Day's silence, "There's something you're not telling me, isn't there?"

"Yes," Day said, "there is. Good-bye, Ms. Slessor." She replaced the receiver gently in its cradle, crossed to the sink and began to run water for the dishes. She would just have time for them before she had to feed the animals again.

■   ■   ■

Bram lay in his bed on top of the sheets. This room, too, smelled of that woman's cursed lemon polish. It beat him how she found the time for all that dusting while taking care of her animals, his horses, and his gardens. Of course, maybe the place had always smelled that way. He had no way of knowing.

Maybe she hadn't been in here at all.

The antique dresser was topped by a small mirror, but he had thrown a towel over it. In front of that mirror was a small dish that held odds and ends, change from his pockets, a penknife. On the pile lay something else that caught dim light from the curtained window. A ring. A silver hawk clasping a turquoise sphere in its talons.

He stared at it for a long time. So she *had* been in here. If she thought that thing could buy her off now…

* * *

In the small office at Relic Roses, Chief Newpax faced Inez and Tom Raines. All three sat in straight-backed chairs with no table or desk intervening. Inez suspected the chief wanted to watch their hands.

She kept her own hands folded and still in her lap. She could speak English quite well, having learned it first in her native Mexico and polished her skills when she attended college in the States. But she had learned that Americans, especially men, were inclined to like a bit of an accent. They were also inclined to underestimate anyone who had one, which had proved useful at times. So it amused her to speak charmingly stilted English, to play with tenses and throw in a not-quite-right word here and there. It had proved an almost too absorbing game in that she tended to do it automatically now.

"No," she said. "Mr. Falco enjoys women. That is not wrong. He flirts a little. What is the harm? He does not mean it. He has a pretty girlfriend, and he is not looking. He knows we like to be appreciated. Most American men do not appreciate properly." She didn't look at her husband.

Tom slouched in his chair, half turned toward her, one arm hooked over the back. His hands were still too, but stiffly so, as if he were consciously keeping them that way.

"You recognized that Mr. Falco was Hispanic?" the chief asked Inez. "It wasn't common knowledge."

"Oh yes. I do not think adoption. They say that his parents have lived in Mexico, so I think maybe his mother…" She shrugged cynically.

"Was a bit profligate? Well, I doubt that it's relevant. So

Mr. Raines here had no reason to be jealous, to want to ruin Falco's handsome face, say?" Newpax looked at Tom.

As if Tom would be jealous. She had worked for him for three years. He had strong opinions on equality and, despite occasional flashes of his mercurial temper, had punctiliously ignored her femininity. Some women might consider that respectful; Inez was inclined to find it insulting.

"No no. Mr. Falco is not handsome really."

"But he was attractive to women?"

"Yes," Inez admitted. "Very sexy," she added almost defiantly.

"Your marriage to Mr. Raines was rather sudden, wasn't it?"

Her hands tightened. It had certainly been that. "I do not take your meaning." She allowed a trace of hauteur to creep into her speech. That was only half assumed. She had come from an upper-class family and was not used to having her actions questioned.

"Only that it happened after Mr. Falco's accident. And none of your friends seems to have known about it until it was a done deal. Were you aware that we can't require wives to testify against their husbands?"

"I do not see the connection."

"Was there any coercion involved? You are, after all, also an employee of Mr. Raines. Isn't that right?"

"No, I am a partner now."

"And how long have you been a partner?"

"Since I am his wife. You cannot think that Tom could do such things. Look at him!" She turned eloquent eyes on her husband. Despite occasional bursts of his peculiar humor, he was basically a serious man, perhaps too serious. But he often succeeded in looking, as he did now, like a sulky teenager.

"Even his friends agree," the chief said mildly, "that Raines's clown act doesn't always hold up. Some of your customers describe him as curt and demanding."

"But they return," Inez replied with spirit. "Many are so stupid that Tom must tell them sharply how to care for the roses."

"What do you think of Bram Falco, Tom? You went to school with him, didn't you?"

That so-casual slouch, Inez thought, had been held too long to be comfortable. But Tom didn't move from it.

"You know I did. I was jealous of him, of course. I was the insecure nerd who overcompensated with humor. He was the senior class president who got all the girls. But that was high school. You get over that sort of thing."

"Do you?" Newpax stood. "Was it you who informed Bram about Hilda's death?"

"Yes."

"So you aren't even going to bother to deny it. And after you heard me warn Gavin not to tell him. You don't have much respect for the law, do you, Raines?"

"When it's right, I respect it; when it's wrong, I ignore it."

"A dangerous attitude. You have strong feelings about conservation, I've heard."

Tom stood too. "I wouldn't kill a man just because he was polluting a river."

"Not even if that river runs right through your backyard? Some murders are kind of like an eruption, you know. After years of bubbling resentment. Your father left town rather suddenly when you were about twelve, didn't he? He had worked for Royce Falco, and they had some kind of falling out. Was that over conservation issues too?"

"I don't remember," Tom said tightly. "I was only a kid at the time."

"Twelve-year-olds remember a lot. Do you suppose Bram Falco was telling the truth when he said he couldn't recall what had happened just before his brother's car accident twenty-five years ago?"

"I have no idea."

"Neither do I. I wish I did. I wish I understood any of you people. Thanks for your time." He went out, shutting the door behind him.

"So much for the innocently bewildered Columbo act," Tom said. "'All you edjicated people are just beyond me.' He thinks my father might have been the extra body in that car. It didn't seem to occur to anybody at the time. My mom and dad had been having problems, so everybody assumed he had just skipped out."

"Why did you not ask?" Inez demanded practically. "I know why. You wished to believe your father was in the car, that he did not return because he was dead. Then you feel sad but okay. If he does not return because he does not wish to return, you are not okay. But the police, they would ask. They would find your father. To think otherwise is not realism."

"You're the one who's not being realistic," Tom said. "These wealthy political families can always buy the discretion of the authorities. Maybe the chief is right. Maybe my father was the Damia Day of his time. They couldn't afford to have him making waves."

"Would Royce Falco sacrifice his sons to kill a book-keeper?" Inez shook her head violently. "No and no and no."

"Obviously something went wrong." Tom's tone was stiffly polite, distant. "I don't expect anybody else to see it. How do you know about the whole thing anyhow?"

"I see the clippings and the old diary in your desk."

"I suppose you read them too."

"But of course! It is a boy's fantasy you have there. You make your father a hero when he is just an unhappy man who runs away. But now you must grow up!"

"It's nice," Tom said, "to know your true opinion of me. And you might as well cut the broken English. It doesn't fool me any. I'll be outside."

Inez clenched her fists in frustration. The police car was, she realized with a glance out the window, still sitting in the drive. Even as she watched, Newpax came scurrying into view and leaned, huffing, against his patrol car, as if to imply that he had been standing there all along. He must have actually been listening at the door.

"Just enjoying your roses!" he called as Tom came into view. "Touch of mildew here. Better zap that with something before it spreads."

Inez followed her husband with her eyes. Yes...serious, moody, secretive. He had burned his hands saving Bram Falco but had been irritably impatient at any mention of the fact. He was not a handsome man either. *Why do you let such a one make you so unhappy?*

"We don't use sprays," she heard Tom reply to Newpax.

"My grandma used baking soda in water," the chief commented. "That might work. Then again," he added glumly, "it might not. Things are never that easy."

■ ■ ■

Regan sat at her office desk, looking at a print of the Apothecary Rose on her wall. Bram Falco would be getting out of the hospital soon, and Day would be there when he went home.

Regan hoped it was Day's way of choosing God, of

forgiving an enemy. But she had to admit that it could also be, as Newpax had said, misdirection. Hate could, Regan had heard, be as absorbing as love, and those feeling it didn't always show it. At least those who spouted their venom were more honest than those who, with cold patience, waited their chance.

Day called that evening. "He's back."

Regan was sitting on the terrace with Agatha. They had been watching bats and fireflies dart over the gardens. "When?" Regan said into the portable phone.

"Today."

"How is he?"

Day seemed to be considering. "Bossy," she said finally, "and jumpy. His therapist says he hasn't dealt with anything. She doesn't like my being there either."

"She may have a point. Is Gavin around?"

"Gavin has been sent away. I can't really blame Bram for that. Gavin gets irritatingly underfoot without being any real help. I bet he drives the people at the plant crazy."

"So Bram is alone in the house now?"

"Yes, as far as I know. If he's too stubborn to hire any more help, he'll have to manage."

"And can you manage—all the rest of it, I mean? The cooking and the cleaning and the garden and the horses?"

"Sure. Hey, I'm making more money than I have in years."

"Is Bram vengeful?"

"Oh yes. He's really not a patient guy either. I imagine he'll come to the point soon enough."

"The point being? What do you think he will do?"

"I have no idea. Tune in tomorrow for another exciting installment."

"Day, you don't think he will get violent?"

"He has no history of that. Not until he killed my animals anyway. But the Bram who came back here today is a complete stranger to me. If it happens, Regan, don't fuss. Millie and I dragged you into something that was never your problem."

"I might remind you that Bram isn't your problem either, Day. Get out of there."

Day laughed. The laugh seemed genuine, unforced. "Isn't he? I have to go now. I should make an attempt at sleep, at least."

"Day…"

"It's okay, Regan. Trust me. There have been too many secrets, too much bitterness. I suppose you've guessed that there's a lot I haven't told you. Somebody has to break the pattern. The other night you told me how I could do that. Pray for me, not that I'll be safe but that I'll do what's right."

"I will. May God be with you."

"He is. For the first time, I feel that he is. Good-bye, Regan."

As Regan slowly laid the phone aside, Agatha's voice came out of the darkness, more tolerant than angry. "You and your strays, Regan. They play you like a violin. I suppose you're wondering if you dare ask me to look after things here for a few days."

"Dare I? With Diane and Gina both away?"

"Why not? I'm like your little friend there. Hard work doesn't bother me. Just out of mild curiosity, will he kill her?"

"I don't know."

"Maybe you should all be keeping something else in mind. If it isn't Day herself who's responsible for all this mayhem, then somebody is out there who tried to frame her and obviously doesn't like either her or Bram very much. If I were this hypothetical somebody, I would consider the present situation to be opportunity loudly knocking. Because nobody would be all that surprised if Bram and Day both ended up dead about now. And if it looked enough like a murder-suicide, nobody would look beyond the obvious either."

Regan could no longer see the bats but could only sense their movement. They blended so well with the dark. Just like somebody might be swooping in invisibly against a murky background of old grievances.

Agatha stood. "Time for me to turn in." She touched Regan's shoulder in passing. "Just remember what happened to Hilda, and don't take anybody's innocence for granted."

"Thanks, Agatha," Regan said, "for not trying to talk me out of it."

She felt Agatha turn at the French doors. "I know by now that it wouldn't do any good. You're one of those people who was put into the world to be taken advantage of. I can't really complain about that when I have good reason to be grateful for it."

Regan turned in her chair but was unable to see her half sister's face. "You never took advantage of me, Agatha."

"Oh no? When you brought Diane, Gina, and me in as partners, we had nothing to offer, remember?"

"Yes, but it was the best decision I've ever made. One of the few, in fact, that I haven't had any cause to regret."

"Unlike your engagement perhaps? Speaking of which, what was that at the grocery store today?"

"What was what?" Regan tried to sound innocent.

"You know very well! You've barely spoken two syllables to Matt Olin for months. Suddenly you're as effusive as a prom queen. 'Oh, Matt, how are you doing? Blah, blah, blah,' and one of your hands resting prettily on his arm the whole time. Don't think he didn't notice the ring either. You're supposed to give that back when an engagement is broken, you know."

Regan smiled secretly into the darkness. "Who says it's broken? Bram Falco told me that I was giving up too easily."

"Considering the shape that Falco's in now, maybe you had better think twice about accepting any advice from him."

■ ■ ■

Day woke abruptly around four in the morning. The room flickered with a faint, fitful light, and music played in the distance.

Then something rattled against her window like hail, and her pulse jumped as she fumbled for the switch of her bedside lamp. Sliding off the bed, she ran to look out.

No, Bram's house wasn't on fire. It was just the torches that were set up throughout the gardens. He lit them sometimes at parties so his guests could enjoy the flowers. He was standing on her lawn, a dark silhouette in evening wear, gazing toward her window. When he saw her, he raised his left hand in a single, imperative, beckoning gesture, then turned and strode back toward one of the torch-lit pathways. A white-draped table was set up on the terrace with candle flame dancing over it. She thought Bram's right hand had held a bottle.

"He picks strange hours for his parties," she muttered aloud as she shucked her pajamas and reached for the white gown she had worn to his earlier dinner. When she was dressed, she wound her hair in a French twist as before and gave herself one steady, dispassionate look in the full-length mirror, her thoughts as carefully blank as her face.

"Are you sure about this?" she asked God, but there was no answer. She hadn't expected one. She draped a white shawl over her shoulders before leaving the house, carefully turning out the lights behind her.

The grass cushioning her sandaled feet was thick with dew as she headed for the torches. He had left the glass globes off, and the flames jerked and leaped wildly. Hadn't the wretched man had his fill of fire? Even its erratic illumination seemed overbright at this dead hour of the morning, the crackle like the laughter of Macbeth's witches, the hot, oily smell mixed oversweetly with the incense of roses.

She proceeded slowly along the flagged pathway. This strange promenade was like something out of a fairy tale. Beauty coming to meet the Beast, who would devour her.

He was waiting for her at the table, drinking some sort of golden liquid from a glass. He could have been part of an opulent liquor advertisement but for the marred face, the tan Jobst shirt that he wore under his dinner jacket instead of a white one, the brace protruding from the jacket's sleeve. The lighting emphasized his disfigurement while at the same time making it somehow less surprising. The music wafting from the open door of the dark house behind him was classical but with a strange, discordant, almost angry rhythm.

She thought she saw a certain reluctant admiration in the darkly hooded gaze that followed her straight-backed course up the steps. "Well, Bram," she said, "is this that private party you were talking about?"

"You do look like nobility, you know that, Dame? You took your time. I thought I might have to throw some more pebbles at your window." He took a swig from his glass. "I never knew how awful this stuff tasted before." And, at her surprised look, "Yes, I have my smell and taste back, God help me. Sit down."

When she simply looked at him, he half rose with a gallant, bowing gesture. "Sorry. Excuse my rudeness." He circled the table to pull out the chair for her. "Please have a seat, milady."

She settled into the chair then, and he took the one facing her. When she reached to push the candle between them to the side, he cringed. She understood then how much liquid courage it must have taken him to get that close to flame in the first place.

"You're drunk," she said.

He laughed. "I do like the way you say that. Not with repugnance. Just like somebody determining a fact. Yes, I'm drunk."

"Very few drunks," she said, "can manage a word like *repugnance.*"

"You're doubting me?" He held up the bottle to show her its level. "I'm quite lucid when I'm drunk. Almost, one would say, eloquent. Would you like some?"

"No."

"Don't knock it until you've tried it." He poured some of the amber liquid into her glass. She tilted the glass briefly to her lips. Even the small swallow she took seared her throat. She coughed and said, "I see what you mean about the taste. Were you like this the night you killed my animals?"

"Tut-tut," he said. "You're not supposed to discuss sensitive issues at a party. But I don't imagine you know that. Being such an industrious sort, you no doubt consider social gatherings a waste of your time."

"Not necessarily. I just don't receive many invitations." She gestured toward the silver hawk on his little finger. "I see you're wearing your ring again."

"Yes, it fits me better, don't you think? It was always a bit large for you. Where did you find it,˙ by the way?"

"In the straw near a dead robin. The robin had had its neck twisted, I think."

"Nasty. Yet you never showed the ring to the police. I wonder why. You had determined to have your own revenge, I suppose."

"*I* wonder why nobody recognized it as yours when I was wearing it, or why Gavin didn't guess when you were trying to buy it back from me that day in the woods."

"Gavin is not the brightest of lads, nor nearly so observant as your sweet self. I hadn't had the ring for long. I wonder why you would return it now? One might think that you had your revenge and saw no further use for the thing. I have something for you too, by the way."

Her gaze dropped to the covered dish by his elbow, but he pushed a vase forward instead. It held two roses, one white, one a dusky red. She looked at the white rose without touching it.

"That's the kind Hilda was holding."

"So it is. *El Niño.* Too bad I had such a good alibi. New-pax might have thought to tack Hilda's killing on me. The *mestizo* child. That's what I was. The *bastardo* who conned his way into all this." Bram waved his bottle grandiosely at the house. "And fooled everybody. Everybody but Hilda, that is. I really think she saw through me that day at the orphanage. She seemed awfully worried, but she didn't say anything."

Day watched him curiously. Did he really see himself that way? As the street kid who had succeeded in duping everybody?

"But I mustn't bore you with my sad history," Bram said.

"After all, I would do it again. I always knew it would have to end eventually, but I gave it a good ride while it lasted. Why are we sitting here anyway? This is a party. We should be dancing."

He set his bottle carefully on the table, rose, and came around the table to her.

"I haven't danced in years," she protested mildly. "I don't remember how." But she allowed him to take her hand and lift her from her seat.

It was all quite mad and somehow exhilarating at the same time. The music had risen to a savage, driving beat, and they had to move fast to keep up with it. Because she didn't remember the steps, she could only dizzily follow his lead, waltzing frantically in the shadows above the torches while the rest of the world slept. The arm at her waist was leashed and careful, the braced fingers clawlike. He was, she thought, approaching the stage where his balance, both physical and psychological, would become precarious.

"Why should it have to end?" she asked breathlessly. "You're still a very wealthy man, Bram. More so than ever now that you're Hilda's heir."

"It won't do," he said. "The beggar might become a prince, but the Beast, never. Not unless Beauty kisses and transforms him. And I don't think you're Beauty, Dame, but the bad fairy who made him a beast."

The music dropped suddenly to a slow, dragging dirge, and Day stumbled with it, smiling ruefully. "I didn't think I looked quite that bad."

"The bad fairies could be beautiful too." He regarded her upturned face dispassionately. "When they chose to be. Are you enjoying my party, Dame?"

"Strangely enough, I am."

"Good, because the dawn will be coming soon."

"And what happens with the dawn?" she asked.

"Why, the spell breaks, of course," he said, leading her back to her seat. "No, actually I'm going to fall over in a few minutes, so I'll have to hurry."

She sat with her elbows propped on the tablecloth and her hands laced together under her chin, watching him as he lifted the lid off the dish. The only item on that dish was a holstered gun. Strangely enough, she felt no alarm but simply continued to watch his hands with the same grave attention. The music rose to a final, discordant crescendo and then clicked into silence.

"I don't suppose Hilda knew I had another one," he said, as he drew the sleek revolver carefully from its holster. "It was Kurt's."

He tilted the gun so that its black eye looked up into her face, but she didn't move. The sky was paling, the torches guttering. In the garden below a bird spoke drowsily, tentatively. Now that Day was still, the cool and heavy damp sheathed her like a second skin.

"This is for Hilda," he went on. "Not for my burns. Maybe I deserved those. But your fight was with me, not her. You should have kept it that way. She never got anything but grief from my family. The least she deserves from me is a bit of justice. But I know there's very little chance you will ever be convicted. Do you have anything to say?"

"What is the other rose for? It's a Don Juan, isn't it? Does it represent you or the blood you're about to spill?"

"Neither. A dark, red rose stands for shame, for the regret you don't have."

Day unclasped her hands to reach for the white blossom.

"I knew," she said, holding the flower to her breast, "that if you wanted to kill me badly enough, there wasn't much I could do to stop you. Beauty didn't see much point in tears either. I came, as she did, to get it over with, one way or another."

"You don't believe I can. My hands aren't that bad."

"I know you can physically. I don't know if you can morally. I don't know you at all really. Except"—she looked around her—"that, as always, you do things up right. It was a lovely party."

She turned her gaze back to his. "You believe in justice, but is this justice? Are you objective enough to give me a fair trial? I think it's my father whom you really hate. I hope that what you think he took from you was more important than the rose Beauty's father stole in the fairy tale. Just remember that, like her, I came willingly."

The gun barrel remained as steady as his dark and empty eyes. The bird chirped more loudly, ending on a high note as if asking a question.

Then Bram stirred and sighed, dropping the gun with a clatter onto the plate. She started, and the rose jabbed her breast.

"You know," he said, "I really thought I could do it." He was suddenly swaying in place, as much, she thought, from exhaustion as from drunkenness. "*Despise* is the word I use for your father. Not *hate*. He isn't substantial enough to waste hate on. Like Beauty, you are stronger than your father. Maybe even stronger than I am."

"If you fall, you'll mess up all that the doctors have done," she warned sharply, jumping up and rushing around to his side.

"Then you'll have to catch me, won't you?" he said with that downward smile and crumpled against her so that she sat down hard on the flagstones, cradling his head so that he wouldn't bang his face.

"How did we ever reach this point, Dame?" he asked groggily. "Do you remember our other private party twenty years ago? Do you remember our prom? We had fun then, didn't we?"

"Yes," she said, "I remember." Hot tears were streaming down her cold face, her hands were shaking, and the fallen rose was as crumpled as her white dress. "We had fun then."

# CHAPTER 6

*No, Plantagenet,*
*Tis not for fear, but anger, that thy cheeks*
*Blush for pure shame to counterfeit our roses,*
*And yet thy tongue will not confess thy error.*

Regan spent a restless night and called Day the following morning. When the phone rang unanswered, she called Chief Newpax.

"I'm worried," she said, and told him about Bram's return.

"I know," he replied. "The town was buzzing about it all day yesterday. But there's really very little I can do, Ms. Culver, if the woman refuses to leave. Of course, we're usually talking about a rotting romantic relationship in these cases, but there was never any of that between those two before. What's going on between them now is anybody's guess. And people are guessing, believe me. I hate to say it, but if somebody is real determined to kill somebody else, there's not much we can do to stop it. If it will make you feel any better, I'll drop in up there, nose around a little."

"Please. Would it bother you very much, Chief, if I came down to Rosevale and nosed around a little too? It has occurred to me that the key to all of this might lie in the past. I won't get in your way."

"Nose all you want. I'd be glad of the help. Most murder

cases around here involve those rotting romantic relation-
ships, and they're easy, sad but easy. Drop in at my office when
you get here, and we'll compare notes."

■ ■ ■

"Something happened there last night for a fact," Newpax
told Regan in midafternoon. They had adjourned from the
police station to the diner and were drinking coffee and tea re-
spectively, eyed by a bored and curious waitress.

"I arrived around eight. Day was feeding some of those
animals of hers, and she looked pretty haggard. As if she hadn't
slept a wink. When I asked to speak to Bram, she said he was
indisposed. She finally admitted he had been drunk and was
sleeping it off. About the time I was concluding that she had
made rose food out of him, he came shambling in from the
terrace, looking like a bank robber."

"Pardon?"

"It's the truth. Really made me jump, I can tell you that.
Had this sort of stretchy thing on over his head. Said, 'It's
called a Jobst mask, Chief. Apparently she thinks I should
wear it.' Strange thing is, he was also wearing a fancy dark suit,
like he had been out somewhere."

"But he hadn't?"

"Hey, I came down here for breakfast afterward. You get
half the town in this place. If Bram had been out anywhere
around here last night, I would have heard about it. And there
was a party. One of those high-school reunions for his class.
But he wasn't there. He and Day were quite conspicuous by
their absence. He smelled damp, like he had been outside
most of the night. And somebody had been burning the
torches in his garden."

"What?"

"Lamp things. Wrought iron. Got candles in them. The wax was pretty well melted down."

"Oh yes, I do remember seeing them now. That is strange."

"Strange don't half describe that pair. 'May I speak to you outside, Mr. Falco?' I says. He comes back with, 'You can speak to me here.' And adds in a nasty, sarcastic tone, 'Ms. Day and I have no secrets from each other.'

Newpax paused. "Well, that made it awkward, of course. I tried to point out, in a diplomatic way, that some people were worried about Day's safety and did he mean her any harm? He laughs. 'Physically, no,' he says. 'I think I'm beyond that. But you might ask her the same about me.' 'I already promised his therapist I wouldn't hurt him,' she comes back, as calm as you please. 'But he could quite easily have fallen down while he was drunk and hurt himself.' I don't know if that was just a statement of fact or whether she was pointing out that she could have arranged such an accident if she had been of a mind to. Either way, from the look he gave her, I don't think he'll be doing much more drinking in the immediate future."

The chief glanced up to catch the eye of the staring waitress and winked deliberately at her. She flushed and set to polishing an already gleaming counter. "Wait until my wife hears I've been drinking with a strange woman," Newpax said. "Wouldn't do to have the boys hear me discussing the case with a civilian though. Might shake their confidence in me and all."

Regan smiled. "You might tell them you're just pretending to cooperate with me as a means of winning some confidences. Which is probably the truth anyhow. I'm afraid I'm going to disappoint you there. I scarcely knew these people."

"But you must have formed some personal opinions about them. What do you think of Paul Sedgwick, for example? Nobody's said much about him yet. He strikes me as the cautious type."

"Definitely," Regan said. "From what I've heard, he's been sweeping the amateur category of rose shows for years. Most shows will consider you an amateur if you have fewer than a hundred bushes. Paul is hardly a novice in any but that technical sense, but he doesn't want to have to compete with Bram. Because when he does, he usually loses."

"Why?"

"Why does Bram produce better roses? Some might say because he has the money to buy the best bushes—and a gardener. I think it's probably because he has a genuine passion for plants. I don't think Paul cares about the roses, but he cares about winning. It would be comparable, I suppose, to the difference between a musician skilled in technique and a maestro. The maestro contributes feeling as well as virtuosity."

"And the roses like that?"

"Apparently. Especially tea roses. They're the prima donnas of the plant world. They're beautiful, but they require a lot of attention and are inclined to sulk if they don't get it."

"Like Bram's mother."

Regan smiled. "Exactly."

"You sure he doesn't have a kind of love-hate thing going with those flowers?"

"Maybe. Do you think he hated his mother?"

"If he didn't," Newpax said, "he should have. But despite all this talk about emotion, Bram has always struck me as, deep down, a practical guy. I think he saw her simply as something he had to endure for the good life."

"But was his life all that good?"

Newpax raised his brows. "From here, it didn't look bad."

"It looks pretty claustrophobic to me, Chief. According to Hilda, though Bram did attend an Ivy League college, he went directly into his father's company afterward. This election bid was the first time he came up for air, so to speak. Hilda thought even that was more an attempt to fulfill his father's dream than his own. It was her opinion that when they rescued him from poverty, the Falcos bought his allegiance, and he felt he owed them, especially after Kurt's death left him their only remaining child. And if he did love his adoptive father, he must suffer even more from the idea that he has brought dishonor to the family name."

"I thought family honor was out of date these days."

"Not in Mexico. An eight-year-old would already have his ideals pretty well set, you know, before his adoption."

"How did we get back on Bram anyway? I thought we were talking about Paul Sedgwick."

"But Bram is so much more interesting." Regan made a rueful face. "We females do have a weakness for troubled men."

"And how do you know Sedgwick isn't troubled? How do you know he hasn't been stewing for years?"

Regan looked doubtful. "Rose competition is hardly the sort of thing you kill someone over."

"You would be surprised at the stupid little things that people kill over. Most murderers don't have grand, complicated motives like in the storybooks. Jealousy is about as common a reason as any, whether it's jealousy over a woman or over a pair of expensive tennis shoes. I think, if I was good at what I did, like you imply Sedgwick is, I might get steamed at a guy who always seems to be just a little better. With the ladies too. You know, technically speaking, this Sedgwick character is better looking than Falco. You agree?"

"Oh yes."

"But he isn't as attractive to you?"

"No. Not at all."

"See? That's what I mean. If I were Sedgwick, I think I'd find that frustrating."

"You have a point."

"Then there's Millie Childs, who thinks her fiancé died in that car with Kurt Falco."

Regan blinked. "What?"

"You didn't know that?" Newpax looked smug. "Well, I have a couple of days' head start on you," he conceded graciously. "Yeah, Millie was engaged to some guy she had never met. He was hitchhiking back east for the wedding. Never arrived. She made no bones about telling me all this, though she didn't spread it around at the time. No girl likes being left at the altar, and she couldn't prove that the guy who stood her up was dead. She is absolutely convinced, however, that her fiancé has been lying in our churchyard here, lo these many years. But like I said, she had no proof at the time and less now. She seems to have known next to nothing about him."

Newpax shook his head over such naiveté and absently stirred his cold coffee. "He got her name from a pen-pal list or something. He had been working in Arizona, but she was vague on exactly where he was from originally and who his family was. She had kind of fixated on his wanting to marry her. That, I guess," Newpax concluded dryly, "had never happened before. She was thirty-something at the time and really wanted to get married. They set a date, and he was going to hitchhike to reach her. My guess is he simply got cold feet, if he had ever planned to go through with it to begin with. But Millie moved to a house by the graveyard to be close to her dead fiancé. It's the kind of romantic gesture that would appeal to her."

The chief made a face. "Probably piles flowers on his grave on the anniversary of the wedding that never happened. I always think that kind of devotion is wasted on the dead. But, in a way, I suppose you might say she's lucky. At least the dead don't let you down. It all helps explain her hard feelings toward the Falcos though. She was just a poor girl, and a drunken playboy took away her sweetheart and never had to pay. That's how she sees it anyhow. Of course, Kurt paid with his life. He did pull Sondra out and was going back for the stranger when the car exploded. Or maybe he thought his little brother was still in there. Somebody said he was calling Bram's name."

Newpax looked into the dregs of his cup with a somberness that contained no hint of his usual staginess. "Kurt was my age, and he wasn't a drunk. He may have partied hard after he came back from the war, but a lot of us did. And Sondra straightened him up in a hurry. They say that only the good die young. But maybe it's just that you can remember them as good because they hadn't had time to rack up many black marks. Or because you want to remember them that way. Still, I think Kurt was a hero, not just in the war but to the end. He must have inherited that from someone, and it sure wasn't his mother."

Newpax gave Regan a crooked smile. "So, unlike many of my fellow townspeople here, I voted for Royce the second time around too. Maybe you're right, Ms. Culver. Maybe this case is haunted by the past. I know some of the people involved still are."

■　■　■

After the police chief left, Bram said, "I'm going to try a shower. Make me some scrambled eggs or something, won't you?"

"Don't you want to watch me?" she called after him.

"I figure Newpax is right. If your aim was to kill me, you had your chance last night."

"Such touching trust," Day muttered to herself as she stirred the eggs over the heat. The water was still running when she had finished, so she scraped the eggs into a covered dish and popped some bread in the toaster.

The toast was cooling before she heard him leave the bathroom and shuffle into his room. "Breakfast is ready!" she called.

She heard a clatter of glass and a muffled curse. Then he said something in a low voice that could either have been *Dame* or another swear word.

She approached his room cautiously. He was wearing only jeans, and he had contrived to upend the dish of aloe gel onto the carpet. His burns stood out red against an otherwise gray skin, and he was standing with hands pressed down hard on the top of the dresser, swaying slightly.

"Late night parties and hangovers are not exactly the thing when you're recuperating," she said with forced cheerfulness. "Here, put your hands on my shoulders. Then a couple of steps back, and you're on the bed. Come on now. Gentleman has to lead, you know." She nudged at his feet with her moccasins, keeping her gaze downward to avoid looking at the welter of red seams and puckers crisscrossing his chest.

"There you go," she said, as he stumbled against the bed and sat down hard. "Just lie down, and I'll bring your breakfast in here. The therapist said you had to do things yourself, but I think she might make an exception this once."

Going back into the kitchen, Day dropped the cheery expression for a moment to lean against the counter with her hand over her mouth and her eyes squeezed shut. *You are ab-*

*solutely not going to cry,* she told herself firmly and turned to assemble his meal on a tray.

Back in the bedroom, she set the tray on the bedside table before leaning to shove pillows behind his back. "Okay, breakfast in bed just like the spoiled dilettante you are. Sit up a little."

"Drop the Pollyanna patter, Dame," he said without opening his eyes. "It doesn't suit you. If I eat that stuff, I am going to be sick."

"If you don't eat something, you are going to be sicker," she retorted, perching on the edge of the bed. "Are you going to open your mouth, or do I have to force-feed you as I did Ivan the first couple of days?"

"You didn't." He finally looked at her.

"I did. That consisted of poking meat against the back of his beak with a stick. You may be a brawny brute most of the time, but I bet I'm stronger than you at the moment."

"I bet you are too. If I heave, you are going to clean it up."

"So what else is new? My family has been cleaning up after yours for decades."

He looked skeptical. "Deca—?"

She shoveled scrambled eggs in before he could finish the word. "Well, one or two anyhow. At least you pay better than your mother did."

She offered him a glass of orange juice with a straw, and he sucked at it while regarding her morosely. "How much did my mother pay?" he asked then.

"I don't know, but it wasn't enough. Did you get any of that gel on?"

"No," he said shortly, regarding his own hands with something like disgust.

When she had finished, she went into the bathroom to mix up some more of the gel and returned to apply it with deft strokes to his face, chest, and arms.

She thought he was drifting off to sleep when he said, with no trace of drowsiness, "Why are you here, Dame?"

"I need the money."

"Others would pay you as well. Housekeepers are hard to come by these days."

"Nobody wants a housekeeper who might have a vindictive streak and a stash of gasoline."

"I see." He began to laugh silently. "And nobody else is going to put up with me. So we're stuck with each other. That's kind of funny, you know."

"A real scream," she agreed, reaching for the Jobst shirt that had been thrown down over a chair back. "Time to put your leotard back on."

That annoyed him even more. "Why are you *really* here, Dame? We both know you could find another job if you wanted to badly enough."

"Regan started it. She said I had to forgive you. It's kind of a requirement."

"Christian charity, huh? Are you sure we're not talking penance?"

■　■　■

Bram proved surprisingly amenable when Day suggested later in the day that they run through his exercises. Fortunately he had a well-stocked home gym. He tired quickly, however, and seemed to find his own weakness frustrating.

Sitting on the edge of his weight bench, he looked apathetically down at the rubber ball cupped in his clawed right hand and made no effort to compress it. Day came across to sit beside him. "Maybe you need a little more incentive here." She removed the ball, slid her own hand into his. "You would like to hurt me, wouldn't you? Well, go on. Do it. Squeeze!"

Behind the mask, his expression was unreadable, but he did tighten his fingers.

"I can hardly feel that," she said. "Apply some pressure. This is your chance to make me suffer."

For an instant his hand clamped steel-tight around hers, but as soon as she flinched, he let her go.

"You know something? You look disappointed," he said, standing up and swiping irritably at the mask that held the sweat next to his skin. "You really want me to be a beast, don't you? Then you could justify your actions. Sorry to disappoint you, but I don't get my kicks out of anybody's pain. We both know what you've done. Why can't you just give me the satisfaction of admitting it? We're all alone here. I am, I can assure you, not wearing any hidden wires in this thing." He flicked at the snug Jobst shirt covering his chest. "And I've noticed, even if nobody else has, that you never come right out and deny anything. You just preserve a Christlike silence and let your friends defend you. Much more effective, I must admit, and it saves you the trouble of thinking up lies."

"*You've* never denied that you killed my animals," Day pointed out in mild tones, watching her own fingers squeeze the spongy sphere. "Catch!"

She abruptly hurled the ball, and he snagged it automatically in his right palm, looked at it as if unsure how it had got there, and tossed it back. "So Regan Culver has been getting to you, huh?" he said "I hadn't pegged you as the religious type."

"I don't think you could call it religion precisely." She threw the ball again, this time deliberately wide so he had to reach for it. "A religion is usually a set of principles, and the writer Buechner said that principles are for people who don't have God. People who think they can be good on their own. I tried that often enough when I was a child—and never succeeded. I always believed, though, that if I just exerted myself a little bit more I could make it the next time."

Sensing something of skepticism in his eyes, she said, "Didn't you ever believe you could be perfect if you tried hard enough?"

"No." He lobbed that blunt negative back at her along with the ball.

"Why not?"

She could sense a sardonic brow rising behind his mask. "I was the son of a prostitute. I learned to steal as soon as I learned to walk. Sanctity was never in the cards for me."

She stared at him dumbly, said finally, "I'm sorry." It seemed inadequate—as did her weak throw.

He caught it anyway, but her genuine sympathy seemed to surprise and confuse him. "When you finally apologize for something," he said, "that something has nothing to do with you. It figures."

■　■　■

Millie seemed quite willing to talk about her lost love. She had insisted on inviting Regan to supper. The two women sat in Millie's shaded gazebo, eating chicken salad and looking down on the adjacent cemetery. The older tombstones leaned at rakish angles under the summer sun, many of them all but obscured by tangles of rose canes. The new stones stood more primly and squarely, fronted by neat rows of geraniums and marigolds.

"They don't let us plant perennials over there anymore," Millie said, as if reading Regan's mind. "Or I would have put a rose on Francis's grave. Like in all the old songs. Francis would have liked that. He was an old-fashioned kind of guy. This was back in the seventies, remember, when people were letting it all hang loose. But Francis always wrote very formally. He looked English, in fact—very fair complexioned with fine features. He looked like an aristocrat."

"I understand," Regan said gently, "that you never actually met Francis."

"No. He picked my name from a pen-pal list in a magazine. But we didn't have to meet to know we were soul mates. Becoming engaged was our way of taking each other on faith. No one would have the courage to do that these days. Now it's all about sex."

Regan didn't know that she would call their action courage so much as rashness. But why should she measure others by her own overcaution? During centuries of arranged marriages, women routinely had gone to marry men they had never met.

"You must have a photograph then?"

"Yes. I'll show it to you when we go in. He was such a handsome boy I was surprised he could find me attractive. I mean, I wasn't a beauty like Day's sister was. But he said that kind of blatant good looks usually masked an emptiness of spirit, that he was interested in a more subtle, undiscovered kind of loveliness." Millie's pudgy face was complacent, as though she still contemplated her spiritual superiority.

Regan thought cynically that very few men were turned off by blatant good looks. And people who talked so readily about *spirit* usually hadn't the foggiest idea of what they meant by the term.

"What was his profession?"

"He was a writer. Not published yet, but he would have been. I told him we could live on what I made. I had my teaching salary and an inheritance from my mother."

Her fatuous expression was getting on Regan's nerves. Could any thirty-year-old have been that naive?

"I know what you're thinking," Millie said, "but it wasn't like that. Francis was sweet and shy and sensitive. He came all this way alone because he loved me. I had been invited to that party by the lake, you know. By someone who felt sorry for me. But I was going to have the last laugh. Because Francis was going to come that night, and we were going to the party together to announce our engagement. Only he was late. So I left a note for him on the door, telling him to join me at the party. He must have been on his way to find me when it happened." Millie's face was flushed. Almost, one might say, animated. As if she were enjoying herself.

Which, Regan realized, in a way she was. Millie had had a great romantic tragedy. It had made her, in her own eyes, important—a heroine. And nothing of greater significance had ever come along in her life to supplant it.

"Can you remember the party?"

"Like it was yesterday. It started out so wonderfully. I could barely keep from telling them all, but I wanted it to be a surprise. I must have been bubblier than usual because people kept giving me funny looks. It had been a beautiful, seventy-degree day. Then the sunset was brilliant, all flaming orange and yellow like the leaves that had fallen already. I just sat there by the fire, hugging myself, watching the path down from the parking lot, and thinking, *Any minute now…*"

Millie paused to wipe her lips with her napkin. "But after the sun went down, it grew cold. Sunny had been vivacious, but after a while Kurt dragged her off into the shadows. I think they must have been arguing because she began to look agitated."

"Was Kurt drunk?"

"I couldn't see him well enough to tell. The fire hadn't caught properly, and it wasn't providing much light or warmth. The smoke kept getting in our eyes. Nobody was having much fun. Except Bram maybe. He had walked in before his brother arrived. That boy was always sneaking all over the countryside. But people let him get away with it. The college girls thought he was cute. They were making him s'mores. He just sat there smirking until it started to drizzle and Kurt called out of the darkness, 'Let's go, Bram,' in a distinctly impatient tone. The boy knew better than to argue."

By this time Millie had forgotten all about her chicken salad. "From where we were, you could see the cars turn onto the highway above. We were all looking up just then, I think, speculating about what was wrong between Kurt and Sunny. We even thought it might be something about their fathers running against each other. The car had barely picked up speed when it just whipped around as if somebody had wrenched the wheel. For a moment—those blinding headlights—it seemed to be coming right down on top of us. But that was an illusion. It was too far away for that. It rolled down the bank and burst into flames. Then everybody started to scream and run. There was an explosion just before I got there. One of the college girls had found Bram lying a little way down the slope. She was cradling the boy's head, and his eyes were half open. I could see the reflection of the flames in them. Somebody kept saying over and over, 'He went back to the car. Kurt went back, and it got him.' Of course, we didn't know then about Francis. They must have met him in the parking lot," Millie concluded.

"Maybe Sunny and Kurt thought I'd left and offered to give him a ride back to my apartment. Of course, I didn't know that then. I was standing there, shaking, feeling sorry for Sunny, when all along…" Millie turned her head toward the lonely tombstone below.

"I went home, and he wasn't there, and he didn't call. I didn't sleep that night, but I wasn't the only one. It seemed like half the town was up. I sat there alone until morning, when I saw in the newspaper about the extra body in the car. They didn't believe me, of course. They didn't believe that somebody like me could attract somebody like Francis."

Regan didn't believe Francis had been the body in the car either, especially after Millie took her back into the house to show her a photo of the disappearing fiancé. The man in the picture looked to be in his thirties, with longish, blond hair and a face that Regan would have called more sulky than sensitive. Slouched against a weathered western building, Francis looked like something off a seventies country-music album.

He had been, Regan suspected, simply an opportunist who had decided Millie wasn't wealthy enough to merit his attention. But, in that case, who had Millie really been weeping over all these years?

■　■　■

Day was washing the supper dishes while Bram lingered at the kitchen table. "There is a dishwasher, you know," he said.

"For these few things? It would be a waste of water."

"Yes, I was forgetting. You despise waste of any kind, don't you?"

"You should too, considering what you came from."

He laughed. "Don't tell me that the story of my misspent childhood has caused you to feel sorry for me. That would be a mistake. I came out on top, didn't I?"

"Yes, and as you said last night, you would do it over again. Do what over? Your adoption?" She pulled the plug in the sink, watched the sudsy water foam away down the drain, and swabbed off the countertops.

He had remained silent, as if waiting for the gurgle in the pipes to cease, but the silence stretched. "Apparently I talk too much when I'm drunk," he said finally. "Yes, let's say it was my adoption I meant. It was worth a few bad dreams. After all, we've all had bad dreams about things catching up with us. They usually don't mean anything except that we've allowed guilt to ooze in the cracks."

He stood. "How about it, Day? You admit no culpability. But what does your subconscious say? How are your dreams?"

■　■　■

Regan drove back to the bed-and-breakfast where she had reserved a room. She had the stiff neck and bone-deep weariness that always plagued her after hours of travel. Perhaps that tiredness had caused her to view Francis with more of a jaundiced eye than he deserved. Certainly she viewed the Amish buggy she was trailing and its clip-clopping horse with more impatience than interest.

Back at the small-town Victorian house that had been turned into an inn, she perched on the edge of her antique bed and realized it was only eight o'clock. She couldn't sleep yet. She probably should have driven out to see Bram and Day. Only she suspected that neither would welcome her interference.

*Why did I come anyway? It's none of my business. What right do I have to criticize Millie's infatuation? At least when her engagement fell apart, she wasn't wimp enough to blame herself. She didn't take it quietly either.*

Staring resentfully at the phone, Regan thought, *Why not? What do I have to lose?* She dialed quickly, knowing that this rash mood wouldn't last. Then she panicked. *What are you thinking?* and started to hang up.

But a male voice had already answered, "Hayden police."

"Matt, are you busy?" She hated herself for how ingratiating she sounded.

"Not at the moment," he responded warily.

"I was hoping you could do me a favor." She hesitated briefly, waiting for some comment from him, which didn't come. Reminding herself that guys didn't respond to vagaries, she cut to the chase. "I need to know if a Francis Seton lived in a town called Ryder, Arizona, back in the early seventies. I thought you probably could find that out more easily than I could."

"No doubt. What does this Seton have to do with Bram Falco?"

At her surprised silence, he added, "I saw Agatha today. She seemed to be in an unusually chatty mood."

Just how much had Agatha told him? "It's just about an unidentified body." She plunged on quickly before he could comment. "From an accident. The one that killed Bram's brother. It was all a long time ago."

"I see," he said. "On the other hand, Hilda Graveston's death was *not* so long ago and not an accident, was it? Nor were Falco's burns. What are you trying to prove anyway, Regan? Don't you have any sense of proportion? Is murder becoming some kind of hobby to you?"

"Do you honestly think I could be that stupid," she responded tightly, "after what happened to my father?"

"I have never questioned your intelligence. I do question your common sense. You are, after all, the one who went for a solitary midnight stroll in the garden only hours after someone had tried to poison you. You should have been afraid."

That stroll had not remained solitary for long. "I had a perfectly good reason," Regan began hotly, then recalled she had gone out to collect sage leaves because it was midsummer's eve. "Anyway, I was scared enough when you sneaked up on me." According to an old saying, the sage leaves were supposed to bring her future husband quietly up behind her. That had certainly proved to be a dud.

"I didn't sneak. You just weren't paying attention. That's my point. You fret about everybody else's safety, but you never worry about your own until it's too late. Some people see that as altruistic. Gina thought you just didn't see yourself as significant enough to bother anyone. But maybe it's arrogance instead. Maybe you believe you're indestructible."

The man had the nerve to call *her* arrogant. "Don't be ridiculous. Everybody tells me I'm too cautious."

"Emotionally, yes. Physically, you go rushing in where even angels would take a detour. What do the police down there think of your interference?"

"Unlike certain insecure people," Regan said with spurious sweetness, "Chief Newpax welcomes my input. Just forget that I called, Matt. Obviously it was a bad idea."

"Oh, I'll look into it," he said. "At least now I know what this new friendliness of yours is all about. A tame cop is, after all, almost a necessity for the amateur sleuth. What's your number there?"

Regan slammed the receiver into its cradle and sat for a moment, trembling, shocked at the intensity of her rage. "Well, I must say that went well," she said aloud to the peaceful room. "You should always approach these things when you're half-dead on your feet. What you lack in rationality, you can make up for in childish retorts."

Feeling hot, she went across to raise a window. The innkeeper and his wife were chatting with other guests on the porch below. Strains of band music floated down from the town square. "Sounds like the concert is starting," the innkeeper said to his wife. "We all had better be getting along there. Suppose we should invite the dark-haired lady who just checked in? She's all alone."

"She struck me as the type who would prefer to be alone," the wife said. "Kind of distant, if you know what I mean."

"Takes all kinds," her husband said comfortably. "Well, let's go, folks." The voices moved away.

Regan sat for a while, staring at the phone. She couldn't go crying to Agatha anytime something went wrong. Besides, she wasn't particularly happy with Agatha at the minute. Well, she might as well get all her rejection over with in one evening.

She went downstairs into the sitting room to find a phone book and looked up Day's number. "It's me, Regan," she said when the other woman answered. "I'm here, in Rosevale."

"Thank goodness!" Day said. "Tell me where exactly, and I'll drive over to see you. We really need to talk."

# CHAPTER 7

■ ■ ■

*Hath not thy rose a canker, Somerset?*

"Well, I'm glad that you're glad to see me," Regan said. "I was afraid you might think I was interfering."

Regan and Day were sitting in the inn's living room. They had its rag rugs and rocking chairs all to themselves. Regan had been telling Day what she had learned from Newpax and Millie. Her account had been accompanied by the distant strains of music from the square, punctuated by a closer bumping of moths against the screens.

"I, for one, would welcome some interference," Day said, her dark-circled eyes fixed on the dried-flower bouquet filling the cold fireplace. "It's not my safety I'm worried about. I think we're beyond that now. But I'm afraid that Bram plans on becoming a recluse. He refuses to speak on the phone or to see anyone. Except Newpax, who took him by surprise. Hilda's lawyers have been calling, and he just makes me take messages."

Looking up at the blank-faced Amish dolls ranked with wooden ducks on the mantel, she added, "Isn't this place a bit much?"

"Country kitsch," agreed Regan with a smile. "But I suppose the tourists like it. I must say I find those dolls a bit spooky myself. Bram has only been home for a couple of days. He'll probably get over it."

"If he were poor, he would have to," Day said. "But, with the money he has, he can bury himself for as long as he pleases. I swear, I understand the wretched man less and less. He has something on his conscience, and I don't think it's what happened to my animals. He talks about bad dreams and things catching up with him."

Day turned to face Regan. "I said I didn't think he would hurt me, but I'm not so sure he won't hurt himself. You notice that he's not making any plans for the future? Strange as it may seem, I'm convinced that, deep down, that guy still sees himself as a guttersnipe who has succeeded in putting one over on everybody. But he's got himself convinced that his masquerade is somehow finished. I'm going to tell you what happened last night, but I don't want you to repeat it to anyone."

Leaning forward, Day proceeded to relate the events of the strange, early-morning party. When she had concluded, Regan drew a long, shuddering breath. "You're a braver woman than I am."

Day shook her head. "I would never have been that much of an idiot on my own. But I was convinced God wanted me to do it. I took it as a kind of test, I guess."

"And have you forgiven Bram?"

"I think so. I must have, to be so worried about him. I keep asking myself if he's worth it—considering that he killed my animals."

"You're positive of that?"

Day hesitated. "You've just heard what he said about the ring. What he *didn't* say would be more accurate. I think the reason I never told the police was that I started to have doubts. The whole thing didn't seem like him. I waited for an explanation, but he has never offered one. He just made his round-about attempt to buy the ring back from me that day in the woods. I should have been convinced then, I suppose, but strangely, the less he says, the less certain I am. You've only seen Bram at his worst. He wasn't always like this. Let me tell you about our senior prom."

Day wiggled back in her chair, as if to get comfortable. "Being more the studious than the social type, I had thought myself lucky to have a date. Not so lucky, as it turned out. The guy was the overly friendly type. Probably thought I should be grateful for his attentions. I disabused him of that notion very early on."

As Regan hid a smile, Day added, "You've probably guessed by now that I am not the sweet, long-suffering type. In this case, my temper got me in trouble, though, because my date told me I could find my own way home. I was too angry to stay any longer, and I started to walk the five miles. But, hobbling along the side of the road in a long dress, I shortly began to feel silly. A little nervous, too, after a couple of suggestive remarks had been yelled at me by a passerby. After that, I started to duck off the road to hide every time I saw head-lights. Of course I wasn't looking for horses." She rolled her eyes at Regan "Who would be?"

Regan laughed. "Bram?"

"Who else? He must have been in one of the cars I so assiduously avoided. Anyway, once he got home, he saddled up a couple of horses and came back. A big truck had just roared by, and I was sitting halfway down a bank with the dew soaking my skirt, my stockings ruined, and my feet throbbing in their high heels when this horse's head peers down at me from above. Then Bram says, 'Gad and forsooks, Pasquale. A Dame in distress!'"

Regan was again struggling to keep a straight face. "Well may you laugh," Day said to her. "I was feeling utterly humiliated myself. I knew who it was, of course. Nobody but Bram ever called me Dame. When we were kids, he always pretended to believe that I was a haughty grande dame, who had to be pacified constantly. I did tend to get on my high horse in response to his teasing, but there was never any real constraint between us until after the car accident. I found him attractive, of course. Almost all females do. But due to my father's inexplicable desertion and to the way my mother was treated by Connie, I stopped trusting all the Falcos." She paused as if she had lost her place in her story.

"On that prom night, however," she continued finally, "I wasn't of a mind to be choosy. When I saw that he had an extra horse with him, I just plodded up the bank, grabbed the reins out of his hand, and mounted up. Fortunately, my dress was a full one. Then I asked rather surlily what had happened to his date. He said she had given him the old heave-ho. 'This prom thing isn't what it's cracked up to be,' he went on. 'I know a place that serves much better food. Come on. We'll have our own party.' And he struck off down the road and into a field."

Day smiled reminiscently. "It was one of those crazy, spontaneous things. We have miles of riding trails around here, and I think we covered them all that night. The horses were frisky, the conversation was just antagonistic enough to be sparkling, and we were both very good riders. We went much faster than we should have, competing with each other. Considering that we only had moonlight for illumination, we're probably lucky we didn't break our foolish young necks. We finally came out at one of those all-night diners in the next town, and we must have made an unusual sight—on horseback in our formal attire. But we hitched our mounts to something and went inside."

"Didn't anyone in the diner ask about your clothes?" Regan said.

"The waitress and a couple of truck drivers gave us tolerant looks, and one of them said, 'Prom night, huh?' Well, we climbed right up on stools at the counter and had our own banquet. Then we all danced to country music on the jukebox and laughed like crazy. The waitress and the truck drivers had as much fun as we did. It was close to dawn when we finally rode home. I think," Day concluded, "that we both knew it was one of those magical times that can never be repeated. After he helped me down, he kissed my hand in the gallant, old-fashioned way and said something in Spanish."

"What did he say?" asked Regan, fascinated.

"I don't know. I never tried to find out. I had much more fun imagining what it meant. Instead of just a memory of an embarrassing incident, I had a prom that no girl would ever forget. I think that's why he did it. I found out afterward that he hadn't given me the whole story. When he told his date he was going to give me a ride home, she told him not to bother coming back. So his act of kindness cost him a homecoming queen. Maybe I wasn't so brave last night after all. Maybe I just believed a guy like that wouldn't hurt me."

Day sighed and shook herself back to the present. "That

seems like eons ago. I was surprised he remembered it. Anyway," she said more practically, "that therapist has been at me again. She wants to know if I'm touching him. People who are never touched feel isolated, she says."

Day's wry expression caused Regan to burst out laughing. "Well, I must say it's nice seeing traditional doctors incorporate some nontraditional methods into their practice. But I can imagine that one would be a shade dicey for you."

"Any unexpected touch from me would probably shoot the man's stress level up ninety percent," Day said. "But don't worry. I can handle this. I'm not shy, and I'm not sentimental. Bram keeps trying to get some reaction out of me over his looks, but a woman who's dug maggots out of wounds and recycled road kill doesn't shock easily, I can assure you. I learned practicality pretty fast too. You take steps to prevent what tragedies you can. While Bram was passed out, I cased the house and outbuildings for the more obvious weapons and poisons and locked them all up at my place. At present, no rope thicker than a parcel string is available to him and no knife larger than the one I use to pare vegetables. If he's still determined to kill himself, he'll have to work hard to do it." Her lips tightened into a firm, determined line of their own.

"But in the meantime I need somebody to find out why. You can't rehabilitate an animal or a man unless it or he chooses to live. Some of my patients just give up, you know. For Bram it has to be more than this election defeat. If we knew why, maybe we could reason with him, save him from himself."

Day slid forward in her seat and reached for her purse. "That therapist is right. Bram is isolated, and I think that happened long before his burns. If he did kill my animals, something must have changed him." She looked up again at the dolls' void faces. "We have to find out what evil spell turned him into the Beast."

■ ■ ■

"I want to speak to Mr. Falco," the squeaky voice on the phone said the next morning.

"I'm sorry," Day answered automatically, "but Mr. Falco isn't accepting calls now. May I take a message?"

"No, you may not take a message. You may go and bring Mr. Falco to the phone at once."

Unable even to determine whether the voice was male or female, Day said, "May I ask who is calling, please?"

"You can ask but you won't get an answer," the voice said. "Who am I speaking to?"

"This is Damia Day."

"What are *you* doing there?"

"Well, there seems to be a divergence of opinion about that," Day said cheerfully. "Some will have it that I am a cold-blooded killer while some hold to the kept-woman theory. The rest don't really know but abuse me simply on the basis that everybody else is doing it; there can't be smoke without fire and similar mindless clichés. May I ask which of these charming factions you adhere to?"

Since her recent notoriety, she had received several anonymous calls and had learned that unfazed matter-of-factness tended to take the wind out of the callers' sails. All of those calls had been to her own number, though, not to Bram's. And she couldn't stop answering her phone when the call might be about a wounded animal.

When this caller didn't respond, she said, "Come now, this sort of thing is really much more effective after dark, you know. I am in danger of becoming bored."

"Go ahead. Laugh," the squeak said. "Stick with Falco, and you won't be laughing long."

The receiver clicked, and the dial tone buzzed in her ear.

She hadn't noticed Bram's presence until he spoke. "What was that all about?"

Turning, she saw him standing in the doorway of his study. "Just another anonymous call. Pretty mild compared to some I've received."

"*Another* anonymous call? Have you been getting a lot of them? About what?"

"Mostly," she said dryly, "about what you and I are perceived to be doing together. When people don't understand something, they seem to delight in putting the worst interpretation on it. Usually they call at night—and to my home number."

He frowned. "I'm sorry. I hadn't realized people would put that particular interpretation on my employing you."

She stared at him. "Okay," she said finally, shrugging. "I'll buy it. You may call me a murderess yourself, but nobody else is allowed to malign my reputation."

An answering smile pulled down the corner of his mouth. "These calls don't seem to bother you."

"I have bigger things to worry about than guys who hide behind phone lines. They're the voyeurs of this world, not the doers."

"That's what I thought too," he said.

He turned back into the study before she could question his choice of tense. *Thought*? Was he implying that he had had anonymous calls too? Of course, a politician would probably be a target for all the angry extremists. But if he had received threats of any sort, why hadn't he mentioned them to the police?

* * *

Regan decided to interview Paul Sedgwick next. She found his number on a board roster, but a woman answered. Her tone was hurried, as if she were impatient to get back to something. Her husband was teaching summer classes at the college, she said. He was usually there for most of the day.

Regan stopped at the college and found Paul in his office. He had, he explained, only one class to teach that morning, and it didn't start until eleven.

He had evinced no particular surprise at seeing her, but Regan felt compelled to explain herself nonetheless. "I came down to do a little looking into things for Day. Do you mind answering a few questions?"

"Not at all." His brows rose quizzically. "I would have thought the police…" He let that trail off. "But I understand you have some experience?" His pale, unlined face would have made him appear younger than he was except that the slick, blond hair dated him.

"I've been involved in a couple of murder investigations," Regan agreed, not adding that she had been the chief suspect in one of them. "Who do you think killed Hilda?"

"That's something I'd just as soon not comment on," he said. "I don't have enough knowledge to support a premise."

"You're the only person who has anything close to an alibi."

He smiled. "And that is suspicious, I suppose. I believe that the chief has confirmed from several sources I was present throughout the battle. And the newspaper says a witness saw Hilda working at the registration table after the battle had started. I was filling in for another professor actually. I don't understand the passion for recreating history myself. You might call me progressive."

"I'm surprised you were interested in NORA then."

"Oh, a rose is a rose, as the saying goes. Though I must admit to a preference for the more modern types. The heirlooms are too floppy to suit me." He eyed with approval the elegant, straight-stemmed teas rising from a vase at the front of his desk. "Some heirlooms are, frankly, ugly. Ragged or overstuffed or blowsy."

"I can't argue with that," Regan answered. "I've seen a few I thought unattractive myself. But on the whole, I'd say they have a certain disheveled charm that the teas lack. The heirlooms look much more at home in a cottage garden setting, for example."

"I wouldn't know," Sedgwick said with polite disinterest. "I don't grow anything but tea roses. They take up a good deal of time."

"To do them right, I suppose," Regan agreed ruefully. "Mine have to tolerate some neglect, and the heirlooms survive that better."

"But the teas bloom longer."

"They're also tender and suffer more from black spot," Regan said crossly. "We really had better get back to the subject. What did you think of Hilda as a person?"

Sedgwick steepled his hands thoughtfully. "A good businesswoman and a good president. Knowledgeable and organized. A bit too sentimental perhaps."

"Sentimental? Hilda?"

"About Bram Falco, I meant. I suppose she is a typical example of a childless woman fixating on a friend's son as if he were her own. The man obviously wasn't worthy of that kind of devotion."

"You don't like Bram?"

A brief frown creased the smoothness of Sedgwick's brow. "It's not a question of liking or disliking. I was prepared to support his membership, as you'll recall. I could just view him a little more realistically than she could. Here's a boy who was taken out of his natural, poor environment at the age of eight and indulged to an unwise degree ever since. So what has he become? A man so used to having his own way that he maliciously slaughters a bunch of helpless animals when he doesn't get it—and threatens further violence. Now"—he bent a patiently reproving look on her—"I realize that Falco is attractive to members of your sex. He has a certain, shall we say, primitive vitality. But he is also arrogant, impatient, and vindictive. Can you deny any of this?"

Regan couldn't.

"I thought not." He sat back in his seat with an air of conclusion. "I certainly wouldn't condone Day's actions in regard to the lighter fluid. But she proceeded much more intelligently than Falco did. She concealed her animosity and bided her time before striking. In her defense, I must say she was not likely to have gotten any satisfaction from the law over the whole matter. Not when she was going up against such a powerful opponent. So she was compelled to take justice into her own hands, and she did so with quiet efficiency."

Sedgwick, Regan thought, admired efficiency in any form. "So you are satisfied in your own mind that Day planted that gasoline?"

"I think she is the most likely candidate, and in real life, Ms. Culver, the most likely suspect is usually the guilty one. Rather boring, I admit, but there you are."

"And would you consider Hilda's murder similarly efficient?"

Sedgwick looked pained. "Please. I regret Hilda's murder exceedingly. But I will wager her unwise devotion to Bram was behind it all. That was her weak point, so to speak. It would seem reasonable to assume that Hilda found some proof of Day's guilt, confronted her with it that morning, perhaps, and shortly paid for that most rash interference. It is really regrettable. No one had died up to that point, after all. It was apparent that Bram would survive his wounds. Day's thirst for justice would, no doubt, have been satisfied with the realization that he would regret his crime every time he looked in the mirror. Hilda's death was patently unnecessary. That is why I don't know that what you're doing is particularly wise. Stirring up such an inflammatory situation can only increase the danger to everyone involved."

*So,* Regan thought, rising, *I've been told in the most civil way possible to mind my own business.* "Where were you in October of 1972, if you don't mind my asking?"

Sedgwick had just placed his palms on his desk to push himself up. He frowned. "Don't tell me you're going to bring up the old accident Millie is always harping on. I would have been just a child at the time. I suppose I was in Florida. It's where I was raised. Now…" He glanced at his watch and got to his feet. "It's time for my class, and you will want to see my roses. Why don't you run out there now? My wife will be happy to show you around."

\* \* \*

Martha Sedgwick didn't seem particularly happy about playing tour guide. She had a little shop beside the house. As she came out from its back room, she wiped her hands on her apron, prepared with a customer-ready smile. When she found out who Regan was, the smile vanished quickly.

With a resigned glance back toward her studio, she said, "He would! Well, not your fault. Come on then."

The artsy, white linen dress she wore didn't flatter her short, stout form, and the material was smudged with damp clay. Martha led the way around the house to a series of beds in the back. Sweating under the hot sun, she twisted her hands in her apron and said, "Well, there they are then. All ninety-eight of them."

The roses stood glossily in straight, weedless, widely spaced rows. From where she stood, Regan could see no trace of black spot or insect damage. "They look well tended," she said, awed.

"They look like they're plastic," Martha said glumly. "It isn't natural. That's what I tell him. He's always out here snipping, straightening, and spraying. 'Why can't you let those poor things grow the way they want to?' I say, but he doesn't listen. You won't see any bees around here. No hummingbirds either. I bet that stuff he uses has poisoned them all. Or maybe they think the flowers are plastic too. It's too hot out here," she added, turning. "If you don't want to look at them any closer, you might as well come back inside. I suppose you really came to ask me some questions about that woman who was killed. Not that I can tell you anything."

When they were settled in the back room of the shop, Martha pumping away at her potter's wheel, the woman went on. "Maybe you're wondering how Paul got stuck with a lump like me. I used to be better looking than this, and I think the poor guy thought he could turn me into an artist. I like what I do, but I don't call it art."

"I like it too." Regan was studying a little ceramic cottage with a crooked chimney and a kerchiefed mouse sweeping off the step. "I'll bet you're a Beatrix Potter fan."

"Yes, my stuff makes people feel cozy. Nowadays, people need a little coziness. It sells fine as long as my husband isn't around to apologize for it."

Regan set the cottage gently aside. "Did your husband like Hilda Graveston?"

"Very much so." Martha eyed Regan shrewdly. "You don't think he would have shot her, do you? There's no reason. He likes being around successful people. I think that's why he joined your society to begin with. I mean, most of you are pretty well off, aren't you?"

"Some of us."

"Roses are expensive mistresses," Martha said. "And professors don't make all that much. Of course, we don't have any kids, so we can afford it, I guess. Speaking of mistresses, did you ever get a gander at Falco's? I saw her at a rose show somewhere. Now, you're a nice-looking woman, Miss Culver, but she would put you in the shade. Kind of reminded me of the roses, elegant but thorny—and expensive. She was a display piece herself. Paul took one look at her and grew even quieter than usual. 'Now see, Paul,' I thinks to myself. 'You might as well give up. There's just no comparison between you and Falco.' It's not money exactly—or looks. Falco was as hairy as Esau, and he wore his expensive togs and his expensive woman like they didn't much matter. But he had everybody in the room looking his way. Paul's always going to be in the novice class where a guy like that is concerned. Maybe it's something that you have to be born with."

"You think your husband was jealous of Bram?"

Martha laughed. "What have I just been saying? If Paul could have taken the guy's place that day, he would have done it in a heartbeat. But he would never have been able to carry it off like Falco did. Paul would have tried too hard. He's a planner. If Falco is Esau, Paul is Jacob."

"Jacob did finally triumph though," Regan pointed out.

Martha smiled secretly over her work. "Yes, but Jacob had God and his mother on his side. My husband is an agnostic. The only thing he believes is that God isn't provable. Paul will stick to what he knows. That's a mathematician for you. Remember that famous trial where the guy was acquitted despite the blood evidence? That about drove poor Paul wild. He kept saying, 'But why didn't they listen? The facts were there. So many million to one. It had to be him.' I tried to point out that people don't always go by facts, but I really don't think he can understand that. He's a great one for facts, Paul is."

■　■　■

Bram lay on the leather couch in his study where the heavy drapes were drawn against the sun and looked at the shadowy painting over the mantel. His own dark, defiant eight-year-old eyes stared back at him. They had had that portrait done shortly after his adoption, probably to make him feel part of the family.

He stood beside Connie, and Kurt rested an affectionate hand on Bram's shoulder. Connie had almost always been sitting or reclining prettily on a sofa. She had sat on a chair in the shade that day at the rectory as she looked over the group of ragtag orphans assembled for her benefit. Father Tino didn't run any official kind of orphanage. He was just a kindly old man who had taken it upon himself to teach the homeless kids to read. He let them sleep in the church, too, and managed to rustle up a meager lunch for them on occasion. Sometimes he even rustled up new parents for one or more. This had been a special occasion though. Rich American parents were not easily come by.

Connie had first singled out the lightest-skinned boy of the group. "My dear child," she had said, "*¿Qué es tu nombre?*"

"Pablo, *señora*."

"Stand up then, Pablo, and tell me why we should pick you."

Pablo stood and commenced a stiff little speech about how hardworking and obedient he would be out of gratitude to the *señora*.

Behind Connie, her husband shifted irritably and looked around at the others. Perhaps he saw a similarly impatient expression on Bram's face, because he interrupted Pablo's spiel.

"You there, what's your name?"

"Mirlo, sir," Bram said without moving. Like most of the other boys, he had picked up a good bit of English from the tourists whom he conned and cajoled.

"Blackbird, huh? Well, at least that's more original than all these Juans, Pedros, and Pablos," Royce said. "Why should we pick you?"

"You shouldn't, *senor*." Mirlo rose leisurely. "I'm not nearly as good as Pablo is. Father Tino can tell you."

"No," the little priest said regretfully. "Mirlo has charm, but he is something of a liar and a thief, I'm afraid. Of course, most of them have had to be. It's the only way they survive. He is very bright, though—and virtually fearless."

"I like his spunk," Royce decided. He turned to Hilda, who stood quietly behind his wife's chair. "What do you think?"

Hilda was then a large-boned, serious woman in her late thirties. Despite her expensive clothes, her background stance had made her seem like a maidservant.

Connie looked irritated at her husband's impatient interruption. She had been enjoying playing Lady Bountiful. She turned to her friend. "Surely we don't want a thief, Hilda. And he's so dark."

Hilda had been viewing all of the boys, one by one. Now she turned her attention to Pablo and, finally, to Mirlo. He had a hard time maintaining his relaxed pose because her sad gaze seemed to see beyond it, to realize how important this really was to him.

"Father Tino says that they must steal to live," she reminded Connie softly without shifting that thoughtful gaze from Mirlo. "As your son, he wouldn't have to. Which would you choose, Father?"

"I would never be able to choose between my boys, I'm afraid," kind Father Tino said firmly.

"I think I agree with Royce," Hilda said to Connie. "Mirlo has a certain something, wouldn't you say? An impudent charm?"

Connie cocked her head to one side and studied Mirlo critically. "Yes, I see it. This one will be much more entertaining. So!" She clapped her hands girlishly. "We will take the little blackbird, Father. We may be sorry, but we will not be bored."

They had Anglicized his name to Bram, which meant "raven." That was, they had thought, close enough to the original. He hadn't minded, nor had he minded his adoptive mother's selfishness, which, as she aged, had turned to petty insecurity and cruelty.

He had understood her enough to play up to her vanity and to show no reaction to her sniping. He had learned very young that people tended to take him at his own estimation. They admired a certain swagger and cockiness in a beggar, but they didn't like neediness. It was just human nature. Show them any weakness, and they would stomp you into the ground.

Somewhere in his playback of the scene from the rectory he fell asleep and dreamed he was staggering up a long, dusty street in the blazing sun. It was midafternoon, siesta time, and the street was empty. The houses were closed and silent against him. He looked for someone, anyone, but the light was in his eyes, and the silent town swam around him in a hot blur.

He woke suddenly, breathing hard, in a cool, shadowy room where a dark figure stared down at him. Bram jerked to a sitting position, heart thrumming.

"Jumpy, aren't you?" Tom Raines said coolly, pulling a straight chair forward with his foot and straddling it.

"Who let you in here?"

"I told Day I wanted to talk to you, and since I'd already seen the damage, you should have no objection."

"Well, I do."

"Tough. I'm going to talk anyway. Leave my wife alone."

Bram blinked. "Come again? I heard that you were married, but I hardly know the lady. I believe I met her at a show once, but that was it."

"Oh, you remember that show, all right. Another Hispanic woman rushed up to Inez, chattering away in Spanish. After I heard about your adoption the other day, things started to make sense. You understood what they were saying, didn't you?"

Bram sighed and leaned back against his cushion. "Yes, I remember it now. And, yes, I did understand what they were saying. But, frankly, Raines, I didn't care. Don't tell me—"

Bram choked on a sudden laugh. "That's why you married her. You are a quixotic idiot, aren't you?"

Raines's closed expression didn't change. "Probably. But this isn't about me. It's about those anonymous phone calls you've been making to Inez. You might as well lay off now. She has no reason to be scared of you anymore."

"She has never had a reason to be scared of me. Mr. Anonymous has been very chatty lately, but he isn't me. If I were Inez, I might have some doubts about you though. She is a very attractive woman. It wouldn't be much of a hardship to be married to her. In fact, maybe you created that necessity yourself, played the parts of both villain and self-sacrificing hero. I've always thought you were a deep one."

"And she wouldn't recognize my voice, I suppose?"

"The voice I heard was falsetto. Its own mother wouldn't have recognized it." Bram stopped immediately, cursing himself.

"So you've had some calls too," Raines said. "What did this voice talk to you about?"

"That's none of your business."

"I suppose you've mentioned these calls to the police?"

"No, I haven't. So no, I can't prove I didn't make them up on the spur of the moment. Will you go away now?"

"When things are just getting interesting?" Raines hiked his chair closer to the couch. "Unless you contend that these calls were made by Day…Do you, by the way?"

"No. I doubt it was her."

"Then how can you be so sure Day and not your anonymous prankster tried to barbecue you?"

"The calls didn't start until after that. At the hospital. And they were about something else. Okay, I know, it doesn't sound very convincing."

"You're *trying* to sound unconvincing," Raines said thoughtfully, "which leads me to conclude that you're probably telling the truth. Whatever it is, it must be something big to have you hiding away like this. I mean, you don't mind having the woman who tried to kill you in the same house, but this guy just talks and he has you running scared?"

"It's not fear," Bram said wearily, closing his eyes again. "I suppose I should thank you for saving my life. But right now I'd have to say thanks for nothing."

Raines continued to study him. "Newpax was right," he said finally. "I never liked you. I don't like big. Big companies, big money, or big guys who hog it all and leave nothing for the rest of us. And you were a hog, Falco. Class president, quarterback of the football team, valedictorian. If you had been the typical, dumb jock, I could have tolerated you a lot easier. Then I could have said, 'He's having his day now, but we nerds will come into ours later.' The really galling thing was that you took it all so easily, almost contemptuously. Back then I would have delighted in seeing you hacked down to size like this. But it didn't take much after all, did it? You were hollow all along, weren't you? Just show."

Bram opened his eyes, managed one of his downturning grins. "That's right. But I was a good show while I lasted. You should have let me burn, Raines. Blaze of glory. It's the way to go, I've been told."

Raines stood, shaking his head. "You can still do it. Make people like you who would rather not. If you're going to self-destruct, at least have the decency to let us hate you before you go. Did you kill those animals?"

Bram turned his aching head restlessly against the pillow. Looking out the door into the brighter hallway, he could see a shadow on the floor, a tense, listening shadow.

Raising his voice slightly, he said, "Will that be enough for both of you, if I tell you? Will you leave me alone?"

"I think you can count on that."

"All right. Yes, I must have done it. I was drunk that night, but I vaguely remember being there and the dead animals. Are you satisfied?"

Raines turned without a word and left the room. Bram could hear him out there somewhere, arguing with Day. After a while the outer door slammed. Then Day came into the room and stood looking down at Bram. Knuckling his itchy skin through the mask, he said, "Well? Are you going too?"

"No. How many times must I tell you to stop rubbing your face? You didn't put any of that lotion on either, did you?"

Her eyes were brimming. She left the room without waiting for an answer, came back with the dish of gel, and pulled Tom's abandoned chair up beside the couch. Peeling Bram's mask back, she rubbed the sticky fluid into the burns on his face. Tears were sliding down her cheeks now, and he kept his gaze slued away.

"Do you know how hard it is to get those animals to trust me, Bram? I don't want them tame; it would be no favor to them to make them tame. But they have to get over their natural terror enough to at least let me help them. It's kind of a pact we have that, though they have to be prisoners for a time, they're safe with me. Sometimes when I let them go, they'll stop to look back. And it's like we're both acknowledging that we were able to put our differences aside for a while, that maybe, in a better world, they wouldn't have to run away. For an instant it's almost like being back in Eden. And you destroyed that! Don't you understand? They trusted me, and you killed them! I would damn you only I take that word too seriously to wish it on anyone. Did you use any of this on your chest?"

When he shook his head, she tugged up the Jobst shirt and began to cry in earnest. Her hands were gentle, but her voice was savage. "Just give me one good reason for it, Bram! Say it was all my fault. Defend yourself. Justify. Something!"

He didn't speak. When she had finished, she went away and left him alone in the shadowy room.

# CHAPTER 8

*Hath not thy rose a thorn, Plantagenet?*

"You're in the country illegally, aren't you?" Regan said to Inez Raines.

Inez, who was sitting behind a desk in the office of Relic Roses, looked at the other woman in silence for a long moment then raised her shoulders in a philosophic shrug. "Oh well, it must come out. It is a cliché almost. The illegal alien."

"Of course," she added, "I am better educated than most. My stepfather is dirty rich. I come to attend college and never return."

"Couldn't you have applied for citizenship in the normal way?"

"My stepfather is a drug dealer. They told me I am undesirable. So I come up here where nobody can find me. How do you know all this?" She touched the phone. "Has Tom told you about the man who calls and does not give his name?"

"No, I hadn't heard. I was guessing at the reason for your sudden marriage, and that's what I came up with. It's almost a cliché itself…" Regan smiled apologetically.

"The alien marrying an American so she can stay in the

country? Yes, it is like a movie. In real life, it is not so funny." Inez didn't return the smile. "Why must you know?"

"What business is it of mine? None really. Unless it has something to do with Bram's burns or Hilda's murder. Does it?"

Fans turned lazily overhead, and the cars passing on the road sounded distant. Relic Roses was set back at the end of a long driveway.

None of the cars turned in. Few people would be planting roses until the fall.

"I would not kill to stay in America," Inez said. "That is what you are asking? There is an incident last summer at a flower show. A woman I know years ago in Mexico rushes up to me. We talk very fast. A person must know the language very well to understand us. Tom understands because he used to work for the Peace Corps. Now he finds out that Mr. Falco must also know my language. When you learn as a child, you do not forget. So Tom thinks Mr. Falco is alarming me with phone calls."

From the calmly considered way Inez was addressing the issue, Regan doubted she had been alarmed.

"Do you suspect the same thing?"

"I do not think Mr. Falco is the no-name type. There were others, you know, in college. Only they usually want to talk about sex, and I hang up on them snappily. I think they are losers. Mr. Falco is not a loser type. But Tom does not like him."

"Why is that? He has no reason to feel jealous of you and Bram, does he?"

Inez smiled. "Mr. Falco is attractive. I have said so. But I do not have flirtations, and I do not wish to marry a rich man."

Intrigued, Regan said, "Really? Why not?"

"Rich men are never full. It is never enough. They must have more money, more women. My stepfather has many mistresses. My mother does not mind. I mind, so I decide to marry a poor man who will love me furiously. Then I shall manage him. I shall not conclude like the unfortunate sister of my father who has a baby and no husband and kills herself." Inez looked Regan up and down in a challenging way. "You are Tom's old friend. Is it more than that?"

"No!" Regan hastened to reassure her. "Just friends."

"Good. So far I have not seen that he is in love with anybody. Do you agree?"

"No. I mean, yes, you're right. I don't think Tom has ever been seriously involved."

"Good. Then there is no reason he should not fall furiously in love with me."

Regan had to smile. "You are a very forthright woman, Inez. Tell me something. Why did you pick this town? Someone has pointed out that not many Hispanics come this far north. It seems a strange coincidence that both you and Bram should end up in the same place."

"That is easy. I came looking for my father."

Regan blinked. "Bram is hardly old enough—"

Inez laughed. "No, he is not my father. My real father, Javier Santos, is rich but idealistic. He becomes a Communist and goes to prison for many years. My mother, his wife, waits for him. When he emerges, he is very poor because his family does not want him. Suddenly, when his wife is pregnant, he has business in the U.S. He creeps across the border and never returns. She has only one letter. He is going to the valley of roses in Pennsylvania. Then no more. My mother gives birth. She is tired of waiting, and she does not want to be a poor communist anymore. So she marries Salvadore. But while I am here, I look for my father. Why not?"

"Did you find him?"

"There is no sign. Perhaps he never arrived or perhaps—"

Inez met Regan's speculative gaze. "Perhaps, as we are both thinking, he hitchhikes and dies in a flaming accident. Who is to say? I did not know him so I shall not fret, as Tom does for his father. *Es muy estúpido.* Tom's father is very alive."

"You know this?"

"Of course. I saw him. I ask Tom's mother impertinent questions. She does not like me, but I do not care. I poke, and I find out. On my vacation, I go to look. This man has a new family now."

"Have you told Tom?"

"I await the proper time. He may be angry. He does not like me to poke. Now…" Inez rose briskly, her speech seeming to smooth out miraculously. "If you have no more questions, the wife of a poor man must work, you know. Perhaps, as Tom's old friend, you could advise me. He wants a marriage in name only. Do you understand that?"

Regan tried to contain her smile. "Yes, I think I do. Perhaps Tom has seen too many of those movies I mentioned. He is, in his way, a very chivalrous man. He wouldn't force on you anything he thought you didn't want. I would guess that you aren't happy?"

*"Es ridículo!"* Inez said shortly. "Does he really think I married him just to stay in the country? This is not what I planned. Tom is stubborn, close-mouthed, and not manageable at all. Sometimes I do not think he even likes me. He makes me very unhappy, but I must have him! Do you understand?"

"Yes," Regan said with heartfelt empathy, "I do."

■ ■ ■

Gavin visited Day that afternoon, slipping quietly in the side door from the terrace. She was preparing supper alone; Bram apparently had given up on watching her.

"How's it going?" Gavin asked in a hushed tone, seating himself at the table.

"There's no need for the funereal voice," Day said, hoping the onions she was slicing would explain her red eyes. "I'm fine, as you can see."

"Is he…" Gavin glanced furtively toward the door into the hall.

"About the same, I would say. You two weren't close, I would take it?"

"Oh no. I hardly knew him a few months ago. I'm from South Carolina. My mother was his father's younger sister. They all grew up down there. When Royce and Connie came back from Mexico, everybody expected them to settle down in the old hometown. But they didn't. They came up here instead. They told their families where they were going but didn't want anybody else to know. Said they wanted to make a brand-new start. Everybody thought it strange at the time. After my family's business failed, my mother suggested that I look up my cousin. Fortunately, Bram needed somebody to attend to his business while he was campaigning. He said that if he promoted one of the guys already there, a lot of jealousy and backbiting would result. But if he brought in an outsider, they would all have to band together—against that outsider. I thought he was joking."

Day had to smile. "But he wasn't?"

"I don't think so. Well, they seemed to tolerate me okay before. But now they keep asking when my cousin is coming back, like they had just expected me to be temporary."

"Were any of them close to him?" Day asked. "I really think Bram could use a friend about now."

Gavin looked uncomfortable. "Well, you know how it is. He was the boss. They haven't seen much of him this past year. Then there was all that fuss about your animals getting killed. People don't know what to believe, and Bram…well, he's not an easy person to understand."

Day was sautéing sliced onions and peppers in a pan, preparatory to cooking a steak. "How about his old girl-friend then? She called today, wanting to know if she could come to see him. I said okay. I thought maybe he would talk to her."

"Paula?" Gavin looked worried. "I don't think that's a good idea. She's kind of finicky. She won't like how he looks now, and she'll show it. I never understood what he saw in her myself. I mean, yes, I suppose I do know what he *saw*—she's very beautiful—but Bram's a smart guy. You would think he could see through her…" Having gotten entangled in the sight metaphors, Gavin stopped and started over. "Of course, he is kind of cynical about women. He was telling me the other day that a guy couldn't show them any weakness because they would use it against him. Anyway, maybe you had better warn him that she's coming. He might not like it."

"I know he won't," Day said cheerfully. "But she might be the best thing for him at the moment. He can't hide out here forever. Well, he probably can, but I'm not going to help him do it. He will have to get used to people's reactions eventually. I always think it's best to face the worst at once and get it over with. If her reaction is that extreme, it will probably be the worst he can expect. Everything after that should be relatively easy. It's called tossing him in at the deep end."

Gavin stared at her with something like horror.

■  ■  ■

Gavin had gone before Bram came into the kitchen. "Well, what did my cousin want?" he asked Day, not meeting her eyes. "I suppose the guys down at the plant are getting a bit tired of him?"

"It looks that way. Medium rare okay?"

He nodded, sat down with his back to her. That could mean he had decided to trust her—or simply that he didn't care anymore. On the other hand, perhaps he was avoiding look-ing at her because her earlier emotional outbreak had made him uneasy.

She flipped his steak onto a plate, piled onion and pepper rings on top of it, and cut the whole thing into bite-sized pieces. "Are you just going to make your poor cousin deal with things indefinitely?"

"It will be good for him."

She slid the plate in front of her employer and took a seat on the other side of the table. "He's not happy, but he feels ob-ligated."

"That's a pretty good description of half the human race. If they have to deal with it, so can he." Bram began to eat without looking at her. He could, she noticed wryly, use that hand fairly rapidly when he had to.

"You mean it's a good description of you. After Kurt died, you were an only child. Someone had to carry on the family business. Someone had to erase the blot on the family es-cutcheon. Do you really like politics, Bram? Did you really want to win that election?"

He gave her a knowing look. "Or does Ms. Day really want to clear her conscience over ruining my chances? Of course I wanted to win. And of course it wasn't the river you cared about but that your father lost last time."

"He didn't lose. He forfeited. Why did he do that, Bram? It wasn't just my sister's death, was it?"

Bram resumed eating. "Trust me, you really don't want me to tell you."

"But you do know. You've as much as admitted that."

"It's no use, Dame. I promised my father I wouldn't blab, and I won't, no matter how emotional you get about it."

"So my little outburst did offend your machismo?" Day eyed him sardonically. "No doubt you considered it part of the great female plot to discover your weakness that Gavin was telling me about. I cried because I was angry, buster, and don't you forget it."

"Gavin got it wrong as usual," Bram replied coolly. "I think that what I actually said was that women looked soft, but they had some almighty big thorns—like the roses. And, yes, I was talking about you at the time."

He set down his fork beside his plate. "I do owe somebody an apology. I realize that. What happened to those animals was vile. I offered no excuse because I have none. I could say I was drunk, but I was the one who chose to drink. I could say you started it, but that wasn't the animals' fault either. You may call Newpax, if you want, and tell him that I will confess to the crime. I doubt I would get more than a fine out of it—perhaps probation—but the public humiliation should be enough to satisfy even you. I will replace the cages that were ruined. I will even buy you some good incubators, if you want. But I will not apologize to you for the animals' deaths because, as you have said yourself, they don't really belong to you." Bram paused momentarily.

When Day said nothing, he continued. "I do apologize for saying that you may have done it yourself. That was an irrational striking back. I wanted desperately to believe you had framed me somehow. Human nature will go to almost any lengths to still be able to think well of itself."

"Personally," he gestured at his mask, "I think the punishment has been more than sufficient already. So what's it to be? Are you going to make that call, or shall I finish my steak?"

"Go ahead," Day looked steadily into his challenging eyes. "Christ just said to forgive. Of course, you don't deserve it, but that made no difference to God, as long as you're sorry."

A flicker of something like surprise or indecision showed on Bram's face. "You're not going to call?"

"No, your humiliation wouldn't give me any satisfaction. A fine wouldn't bother you. And you are right about the animals; they weren't mine. So I expect you will make your apologies to him instead."

"Him?"

"The owner."

"Oh, *him*. Are you implying, perhaps, that the punishment came from him? Fire from heaven, so to speak?"

"No. He comes back at you with something that hurts far worse than flame."

"And that would be?"

"Love."

■ ■ ■

Day sounded subdued when she called Regan that night. "Well, Bram has confessed—to killing my animals, I mean. Even offered to go to Newpax with it."

Regan's heart sank. "I was so hoping that wasn't true. How are you handling it?"

"I did something I've been doing too much of lately. I

cried. I was just so disappointed in him and so angry. I guess I had hoped something larger lay behind it than spite."

"I hoped for some supreme reason for my father's death too," Regan said. "But there wasn't. Loving your enemies isn't so easy in practice, is it?"

"How did you manage to forgive?"

"I just did what I would do if I had forgiven. It felt hypocritical at first, but eventually I discovered the hate had withered and died on its own—from lack of nourishment, I suppose. I go to visit the killer in prison. It's someone I was close to once. But I see no repentance on that person's part. That makes it harder. Still, the forgiveness releases me too. It proves I still have free choice, that my reactions are determined by what I am and not by what is done to me. Is Bram sorry?"

"Yes. But it's hard to say if he hurts for the animals or because his opinion of himself has been tarnished. He was willing to take his punishment though and was surprised, almost disappointed I think, when I declined."

"Strangely enough, most people would rather pay the strict price of justice than accept forgiveness free. It's easier on their pride. They can feel that they have, in a sense, compensated. By the way, I have some new speculation on the identity of the burned body, from Inez Raines of all people. She came from Mexico too and is only here because she was looking for her father, a Javier Santos. It seems he started for Rosevale in 1972 and never made it back to Mexico. She also strangely introduced into the conversation that her aunt had an illegitimate child and committed suicide. Now if that was her father's sister, don't Mexicans have a thing about avenging family honor?"

"Kurt!" Day said.

"Yes, he would have been about eighteen when the family left Mexico—an age when one is prone to raging hormones and a carelessness about consequences."

"And that's why he was killed? But this Javier's vendetta must have really gone to extremes if he was willing to wipe out Sunny, Bram, and himself in the process."

"Well, considering how long the government thought it prudent to keep him in jail, he must have been something of a hothead. Jail does give people plenty of time to brood. Perhaps he and Kurt struggled and no one intended the accident to happen. Maybe that's what Kurt meant when he was talking about the child. He wanted to know about his child, and he wouldn't if Javier died."

"You think Inez was hinting at that?"

"I would say she considers it a possibility that she didn't want to state in so many words out of loyalty to her family. But if she, knowing more about her father, thinks it could have happened that way…"

"And it does seem," Day contributed slowly, "that the Falcos were running from something when they left Mexico. They asked their relatives not to tell where they had gone."

"I wonder what happened to the child. Too bad it couldn't be Bram, but he's too old. He was only about ten years younger than Kurt. I don't see where your father could come into the whole thing, though—unless he spent some time in Mexico."

"Not that I know of."

"Maybe it *was* your sister's death that sent him into a tailspin. You said he was more of a nervous type. Maybe he had a breakdown of some sort."

"Again, not that I know of. And why abandon the ones who would be most able to help him through it?" Day asked. "That was just stupid."

*And it hurt,* Regan thought. Even a precocious twelve-year-old wouldn't have been able to understand so complete a rejection.

"You are sure that your father's alive? I mean, there's no chance he was the body in that car?"

Day laughed shakily. "Nope. That's out, I'm afraid. I did go to see him once when I was eighteen. One of those finding-yourself, put-the-past-behind-you sort of things."

"How did it go?"

"It didn't. I would have liked to have hated him, but Bram is right. My father isn't substantial enough for that. He was cordial but evasive. I asked for an explanation, but looking back on it, I realize he talked a lot and didn't say anything. There was just no connection anymore."

There was, Regan thought, too much fatherlessness in this case. Too bad people didn't realize the havoc that could play with young minds. Matt had never known his father either.

"Would you mind if I talked to him, Day?"

"Be my guest. I can give you his number. I hear from him once in a while."

After Regan had jotted down the phone number, she said, "I feel as if I'm poking around the edges of this thing instead of addressing it directly. But it's around the edges that you tend to find something you can get ahold of. I've had a call from Agatha about some papers that I need to sign. So I think I'm going to run back home tomorrow and stop to see your father on the way. I'll return as soon as I can. Are you and Bram going to be okay for now?"

"Oh yes," Day said. "If the bird won't fly, it's usually because it's too comfortable where it is. After all, why should it go back to a hardscrabble life when it's being taken care of?"

"Uh, Day…" Regan began uneasily.

The other woman gave a more genuine laugh. "Don't worry. As I told you, I've had a lot of experience at this. In the long run, it's more important that the animals get back to normal than that they like me."

■　■　■

Paula arrived the next morning. Day was in the garden at the time, foliar feeding the rosebushes with a fish-kelp emulsion. The emulsion was in a bottle, attached to the hose, which metered out the proper amount with each spray. It had to be replenished frequently from a gallon jug. Since Day was also adding some Superthrive to the mix, her sticky fingers smelled of decaying sea life and vitamins. The morning sun shone directly in her face. Wiping her sweaty forehead with the back of one hand, she bent to fill her bottle again.

"Hello," said a cool voice behind her.

Day jumped and splashed emulsion on her moccasins. "Darn! Must you sneak up on me?"

"What is that?" The tall and elegant brunette had backed off a hasty few steps. She was staring, with a wrinkled nose, at the sludge on Day's shoes. "I rang and rang the doorbell, but nobody answered."

"Ground-up fish leavings," Day said helpfully. "You must be Paula."

"I am. You would be the housekeeper I talked to yesterday?"

"That I would. Also groom and gardener and general dogsbody."

"Where is Bram?"

"I think I saw him wandering down toward the barn a minute ago. You might try there."

Paula, who was wearing high heels, didn't look enthusiastic. "Do you suppose you could go and get him, Ms. uh—"

"Call me Day. No, I couldn't, because he wouldn't come. Remember, I told you he wasn't seeing anybody and you would have to take him by surprise."

Paula eyed her suspiciously. "I don't think Bram likes surprises. You're kind of young for a housekeeper, aren't you?"

"We come in all makes and models. Maybe I could just yell for him."

"That's all right," Paula said hastily. She apparently didn't want this reunion witnessed. "I'll just go down there, as you said."

"Good." Day, watching Paula pick her way down the gravel walk, said as an afterthought, "Look out for the hawk."

"What?"

"Never mind." Day had just remembered she had never told Bram that his stable was now an aviary. He was not, she thought, going to be very happy about that. Among other things.

With a sigh, she sat down on the terrace steps to hose off her moccasins. Leaving them on the warm stone to dry, she padded gingerly up the steps in her bare feet to feed her animals.

■ ■ ■

Day was sitting in one of the terrace chairs, a foot tucked up under her and the other dangling free, giving the groundhog its bottle, when Paula stalked back. Her heels rang on the steps. "You!" she said, taking in Day's barefooted insouciance. "Don't think I don't know what you're up to! Well, as far as I'm concerned, you can have him, you—" Her gaze froze on the furry bundle that had turned its head calmly to regard her. Then that gaze rose to Day's hair. "—rodent!" she finished and bolted.

"It's very insensitive of her," Day said consolingly to the woodchuck, "to use your family name as an insult. But the cat clan does have its prejudices, you know."

From a distance, Bram was bawling her name.

"I'm here," Day said in a tone that could not have carried past the edge of the terrace. Turning over the woodchuck, she rubbed his stomach.

Bram found her soon enough. He was carrying his mask in one hand, and his burns stood out even redder than usual. But then his whole face was redder than usual. He stomped up the steps and just stood there, breathing hard and glaring at her.

"There's no point in roaring at me like a browbeating baron," she said. "I am not your personal slave. And, now that I've brought up the subject, I would just like to add that I've had enough of doing the work of three people while you sulk. I thought the pretty lady might be a help, one way or another."

Bram's expression changed as she spoke to one of bemusement. "Can you tell me," he asked quietly, "why you smell like a dead fish on a hot beach and why a possum is in your hair?"

"Oh," she said. "I forgot about that." She reached up to disentangle the pointy-nosed rodent. "That's the way they like to sleep, hanging on to their mother's fur."

"Not to mention," he said, "why my horses have been replaced by your hawk?"

"Did he fly away?" she exclaimed eagerly. "His wing is completely healed now. He should be able to leave, but he won't. I chase him back and forth until we're both wheezing, but he won't go out the door."

"Well, he still hasn't," Bram said, seating himself at the top of the steps with his back against the terrace wall. "He just flew to a higher perch and sneered at me."

"The horses are fine. They can stay out in the pasture for the rest of the summer. But Ivan has to have a place where he can stretch his wings."

Bram began to laugh. "So one very expensive stable is emptied for the convenience of one very ungrateful hawk. Only you, Dame! Pray, tell me, how was hauling in my ex supposed to help?"

Day leaned to set the groundhog on the terrace tiles and pushed it forward with her foot. "Here, put him down on the grass. He needs to learn to eat something besides milk. Well, I figured," she said, reaching into her basket for a hairless mouse, "that either she would help or she wouldn't. And if she didn't, that might be the best help of all since it would give you a taste of how people were likely to react. Which would be hard, but then you wouldn't have to be afraid of it anymore."

She dipped a rag in formula and held it for the mouse to suck on.

"You have a ruthless practicality, Dame, that is priceless." Bram seemed more relaxed than she had seen him in some time, leaning back with his hands laced around one drawn-up knee. "And that," he added, dark gaze sweeping from her tousled head to her bare feet, "is not your only allure, believe me."

"It must be the eau de fish," she said.

"My face is not what is bothering me, Dame. Granted, it's not much fun to look at, but it wasn't all that pretty before. Just out of curiosity, how many of those do you have in there?"

Day had just withdrawn a couple more mice from the basket. "A whole litter," she admitted with a sigh. "I don't usually bother with mice, but it was a little girl who found them. Her cat had caught the mother, and the girl was so upset…Go on. I'm listening. You said your face wasn't what was bothering you."

Bram had turned his head to watch the groundhog's progress. "If that animal eats my roses, I'll wring his—" He stopped abruptly, and there was a sense of constraint between them again. "Sorry, I wasn't thinking."

"It's all right," she said, but he had already stood up. He walked across to the door leading into the house where he stopped and turned to look back at her. "I thought I could manage a pitchfork, but the stalls don't need cleaning. I'll do the roses instead. I know now that you didn't try to kill me, by the way. I always had a hard time believing that, but it was preferable to something else."

"So you know who did do it?"

"I have a pretty good idea. And I have to admit that I deserved it. But…" His face tightened. "Hilda didn't. Hilda definitely didn't deserve what happened to her. They should have listened to Father Tino that day at the orphanage. They should have left me there."

Day felt for an instant she was holding something else thin-skinned and vulnerable between her fingers. "Why, Bram? What did you do?"

He shook his head. "The priest said it best. 'The boy has charm, but he's a thief.' You have a soft heart, Day, and you're a natural healer. But you're also practical. You know that some things even you can't fix. You're doing this out of some misplaced Christian charity, but you're only endangering yourself. Walk away while you can."

"Does that mean I'm fired?"

He shook his head. "If I were a gentleman, I would make

you go. But I'm just a gutter rat, who will take whatever is offered. Don't say I didn't warn you."

When he was gone, Day sat looking down at the blind mice, who tugged urgently at the milky rag. *That's one of your problems, kid,* she thought. *You've always had a weakness for rodents.*

# CHAPTER 9

*Ay, sharp and piercing, to maintain his truth;*
*Whiles thy consuming canker eats his falsehood.*

The next morning when Day arrived for work, the house was silent. Usually Bram was up by then, showering and preparing for breakfast. She stepped cautiously out into the hall to listen. A moan from the direction of the study. Day ran for the open door, only to pull up short once she reached it.

Bram lay on the couch, apparently asleep and dreaming. The heavy drapes were drawn, and she couldn't see him clearly. The cushions, which usually made up the back of the couch, were dark heaps on the floor. He was tossing agitatedly. Suddenly he cried out, "No! Look out!" This must be one of the bad dreams she had been warned about.

His hands were clutching at nothing, and Day felt a distinct impression of someone falling, grabbing for any hold. Then he gasped, as if at impact. She rushed forward, stumbling over the cushions to kneel by the couch and tug at his shoulder. "Bram, wake up! You're having a nightmare."

His eyes opened but appeared glazed, unseeing. "The flames," he whispered. "The burning flesh."

"Bram!" She shook him harder. "It's just a dream!"

When he sat up, he was still shaking. She perched beside him, stroking his arm and speaking to him in the low, soothing tone she used on frightened animals. "It's over, Bram. It's all over. That was a month ago. The burns are healing. You're getting better every day."

"Not a month ago," he whispered. "Twenty-six years ago."

She stiffened momentarily, realizing he was talking about the car accident. She forced herself to relax. "Well, that's over too, a long time ago." She wondered briefly if the loss of his sense of smell could have been partly psychological, a blocking out of odors that were too awful. Perhaps that was why another fire had brought it back again. "Do you want to talk about it?"

"No," he muttered, and she felt a stab of disappointment. Perhaps in his dreams his subconscious did remember. But considering the state he was in now, she didn't have the heart to force him to grab for those memories before they slipped back where they had come from.

"It should have been me," he added, "instead of Kurt."

"I used to feel the same way about Sunny," she said. "But there's nothing anybody can do about it now. We thought they were better than we, that they should have been the ones to live. But it wasn't our choice to make. We've just had to go on. We might not be good, you and me, Bram, but we're survivors."

"And that's close enough?" he asked, a touch of humor returning to his husky tones.

"I think so. Going forward with hope. That's what they did. We idealize them now because they died young, but they weren't perfect. They did go forward, though, no matter what. Even Kurt, after the horrors he had seen, had the courage to be happy, to see life as a gift."

"I think your sister taught him that."

"Yes, but he had it in him already. 'An earlier music that men are born remembering.' We all have it if we can find it. Something is haunting you, Bram. You're tight all the time. It was there before Hilda's murder and your burns. It was what made people think you might kill yourself. I can't help you because I don't know what it is, but God does. He already knows, so there's no point in making pretenses with him. That relieves a lot of the tension, having somebody who really knows."

Bram stood and pulled her to her feet. "Don't you remember what I said? Sanctity isn't in the cards for me. God is the enemy."

"Are you sure?" She smiled at him. "That's your fatalistic Mexican upbringing talking. The idea that things happen to you instead of the other way around. It isn't the cards, but what you do with them that counts."

That afternoon a package arrived for Bram from Hilda's lawyers. After palpating the bundle and deciding it contained books of some kind, Day ripped off the wrappings. It was always possible, of course, that a killer had been clever in his choice of a return address. But, if so, he should also be clever enough to know that men like Bram didn't always open their own mail.

The package contained a series of brown, leather-covered notebooks and a letter explaining Hilda had requested her journals be mailed to Bram after her death.

He was taking a nap and had looked like he needed it. Maybe he didn't sleep much because of the dreams—or because he still knew himself to be in danger.

Bram had told her that she was to look over his mail and sort out what was important. This, Day told herself firmly, certainly qualified.

She sat down at the kitchen table and leafed rapidly to the

last page of the most recent journal. She was disappointed to discover that Hilda's last entry had been made several days before her death, the day after Bram was burned, in fact. It was maddeningly cryptic.

> Something someone said this morning has me worried. I suspect—but, no, that seems impossible. It must have been a coincidence. And if it isn't, I don't quite see what it can mean. But I'll have to find out. More later.

The trouble was there wasn't any more. Day glared at the empty pages and turned back to the prior entry. This apparently had been written in the hospital. *It's too like that other night,* Hilda had scrawled, the words spilling in a forward slide of haste and agitation.

> When he was twelve. He was the only one who escaped the flames that time, but now they've caught up with him. In a way, I think it's something he's always expected. Ever since then he's had that careless air that some women find sexy but which always seemed to me to be born of resignation. I knew he wasn't telling something that time. But I thought maybe he and Royce were protecting Kurt, so I didn't push. Whatever it was, Bram has felt guilty about it ever since. Why wouldn't you tell me, Royce? You trusted me the other time. But now you've left your son to bear your secret alone—and to take the punishment for it.
>
> I know this isn't just about that cursed woman's

animals. Her father was taken away from her when she was twelve, and you can't tell me that twelve-year-olds don't hate.

I might even feel sympathy for her—if she had taken her revenge on anybody else. But Bram has always had so little! Ever since that day in Mexico, when he was slouching there, pretending not to mind whether he was chosen or not, we had a connection. I could feel his desperation when no one else seemed able to.

He always seemed a bit afraid of me, as if to be understood was to be weakened somehow. But I don't think he ever lied to me. That's why I never asked him about the accident. I didn't want to know.

Perhaps we connected because we both felt extraneous. We both attached ourselves to the Falcos to feel part of a family, but even that didn't seem to work.

Day dropped the journal she was holding and shuffled quickly through the others. Each covered a period of several years. Hilda had not made her entries consistently. But Day seemed to remember the other woman had come down to join the Falcos in their time of grief. Finding the notebook that included 1972, Day riffled through the pages to the end of October. There was no entry for the date of the accident. There was one, however, for the following day.

November 1
     Kurt dead. I still can't realize it. So much laughing gallantry gone up in smoke. I always thought

Kurt inherited the best of both of his parents—his mother's acuity without the cruelty, his father's courage without the stringency. He carried his sweetheart out of the flames then went back for a stranger. That's how the Kurts of this world die.

But it's Bram I can't stop thinking about. Bram who came so close to dying too. Tossing in delirium on the white hospital sheets and muttering over and over, "It was my fault. It was my fault."

I pray God that it isn't so. Bram is Royce all over again in many ways. He will never forgive himself if he caused his brother's death.

I had doubts that the adoption was a good idea that day in Mexico. But those doubts were dispelled forever when I saw Royce sitting for hours beside Bram's bed. The boy is all he has left now.

Connie has acted typically, going into a dramatic collapse, demanding attention for herself. I have to remind myself that Kurt accepted and loved her as she was. He would want me to be tolerant. Above all, he wouldn't want his little brother to suffer.

November 2

I hope Bram's fears have been allayed. After he regained consciousness today, Royce talked to him quietly for a long time. I couldn't hear what was said, but Bram did seem to calm down some then. Still, several times he looked at his father as if he wanted to speak, then turned away again. And there is a deep isolation in the boy's eyes.

November 3

The girl has died, and her father has forfeited the election and gone away. I don't understand any of this, but I think that Royce does. This is one secret he apparently is unwilling to share with me. People will believe the worst, of course. They always do. He says that Bram remembers nothing of the accident.

Connie has been strange too. This afternoon, while I was napping, she apparently had a visitor. When I woke, the house was empty, and her car was gone. When she returned, she simply said she had to run someone to the bus station and refused to explain further. But after Royce returned from the hospital, she picked away at him all evening. There was what I could only call a triumphant malevolence about it, as if she had finally found him out, so to speak.

It was pretty horrible to realize that, at a time when they should be comforting each other, she was trying to undermine him. I wonder how many marriages are like this. Perhaps I haven't missed so much after all.


Interrupted by the sound of Bram's footsteps in the hall, Day froze for an indecisive moment. Then she grabbed up the journals and stuffed them under the animal boxes in one of her picnic baskets. When Bram came in, she was still bending over that basket.

"Mail?" he said, catching sight of the pile of envelopes she had yet to open. He scanned desultorily through the stack, scaling the junk at the wastebasket and using a paring knife to slit open the top of one envelope and extract a sheet of paper.

"What did you mean when you said it was your fault?" Day asked him.

He glanced up from the letter to look at her unseeingly. "What?"

"Somebody said, after that car accident, you kept muttering about it being your fault. Why was it your fault?"

Despite her urgent tone, her hands pressed flat on the table as if to hold back, like Hilda, a truth she really didn't want to hear. Day didn't seem to be getting through to him. His gaze was distant, preoccupied, as if he were trying to figure some equation in his head.

"You lied, didn't you," she persisted, "when you said that you didn't remember?"

"Apparently."

It was an illogical, inadequate answer, and Day slammed one palm down on the table hard enough to bring stinging tears to her eyes. "Royce protected you, didn't he? You were the only son he had left. He told you what to say."

"No, my father never in his life told me to lie. He was a just man." He turned his back and began to walk out of the room, still carrying his letter, as if the subject were closed.

She surged on bitterly. "A normal little boy, when the brother he adored had died, would speak the truth. I never questioned that you had. Did you really love Kurt, or was that a lie too? It was very convenient that you were thrown out of that car, wasn't it? So that you, the adopted son, became the only child, the only heir. Maybe you're not Esau after all, but Jacob, the one who stole the birthright."

"That's close," Bram said. "That's very close."

■  ■  ■

Henry Day lived in a poor town in upper New York State. Regan had called ahead to make sure he would be home when she arrived. He worked as a clerk at a hotel, he had informed her, and lived on the premises. So he was almost always there. She should look for him in the office.

It turned out to be one of those cheap, one-story motels that squat at the edges of towns just off major highways. This one was near a red light. The office sported fake wood paneling, vending machines, and an old living-room suite with bad springs.

Regan perched on the edge of one of the chairs, and Henry sat on the couch. The constant stop and start of traffic made a restless background to their conversation.

She would have a hard time remembering what he looked like afterward. He must have been at least in his sixties, but he had flattish blond hair similar to Sedgwick's, glasses he could hide behind like Raines, and a constant patient smile.

"I want to talk to you about the accident back in the seventies," she said. "The one in which your daughter was killed."

He continued to smile—and to wait.

"Sunny would have been in her early twenties at the time."

"Yes, she was a beautiful girl." He sounded proud but strangely untouched.

"So I've heard. You were running against Royce Falco for the Senate, but your daughter was dating his son. Didn't that cause some awkwardness?"

"No, not at all. Royce and I waged a friendly campaign. Neither of us believed in mudslinging. We were both for peace in our own ways."

"You were a writer?"

"A reporter. I had also written some little columns that happened to catch the public attention. I still do write occasionally. I don't get published too much anymore, though, except letters to the editor. People think I'm outdated, I guess—and they've always called me idealistic." Despite a self-deprecating little shrug, he seemed unbothered by this lack of success too.

"Do you remember the day of the accident?"

"Certainly." Henry cocked his head to one side. "It was one of those warm, lazy days that seem to be left over from summer. One of the first I'd had off from campaigning in a long time. The election was getting very close by then, of course. I was trying to write an acceptance speech—just in case. We lived in a big, old house in town at the time. The windows were open. Day was in school. Maureen had a headache and was lying down. The spinster lady next door was humming to herself as she planted bulbs. I was leaning back with my eyes closed, thinking that it had a lavender-y color, that song. Anyway, the afternoon got away from me. Day came in from school, and Sunny came home from work, and I still hadn't gotten anything done. And I knew I wouldn't have any time free over the next few days. Maureen had fallen asleep, so I told the girls to get themselves something to eat. Sunny said she was going to a party on the beach and would eat there. By the time I came out of my study later, she was gone. She had been eating some of my Jell-O. It wasn't a lavender day after that but a horribly dark purple night."

"How did you find out about the accident?"

"Royce Falco told me himself. He was driving home from some election dinner and came upon the scene shortly after it had happened. So he came to inform me. I thought it was very kind of him. He couldn't stay because they had taken his surviving son to the hospital, but he had some of his people make arrangements for me to go away."

"But why?" Regan asked, leaning forward and trying to connect with the eyes behind the glasses. "Why did you have to go away? Why would you abandon your wife and daughter at such a time?"

"My wife agreed that I should go," Henry said, as if he were the one being reasonable. "Everybody agreed that it was the best thing. I couldn't continue with the campaign then, of course. But they all knew it was an accident, that it wasn't my fault. So I've always thought there is no point in rehashing it."

"Yes," Regan said softly, straightening, but feeling as if her heart were actually sinking down into that sprung couch. "So you feel no guilt?"

"No," Henry said simply. "It's like the psychiatrists say. Things happen. We all do our best, but things happen. Guilt is not constructive. So I've just put it all behind me. Only the present is important."

Regan couldn't have described afterward any of the scenery she passed through on her way back to Massachusetts. She kept an automatic eye out for the cars around her and the route numbers, but that was all she saw. She felt a blank kind of horror, and she didn't know what she was going to tell Day.

After she had pulled into her garage, she just sat for several minutes. Perhaps Agatha, not knowing the characters, could offer some dispassionate solution to the dilemma. But, even as Regan approached the house, she remembered Agatha had a meeting in Boston and was staying there overnight.

Regan snapped on lights in the living room, went out onto the terrace, and looked down over the gardens. A lot needed doing down there, but it was already growing dark.

The stone walls and flower borders had that air of remoteness that familiar things sometimes assumed when one had been much more immediately involved elsewhere. Agatha, too, perhaps, would have been too remote from it all.

The doorbell chimed just as Regan moved restlessly back inside.

He was half turned away from the door when she opened it, looking away down the porch with an abstracted gaze. "Evenin'," he said, turning toward her. "I was wondering…" He stopped.

"Good evening, Matt." She smiled faintly. "You didn't know I was home, did you? Actually, it's just for tonight. I'm going back tomorrow."

"I was intending to give Agatha a message for you. Since," his tone was dry, "you neglected to leave me your number the other night."

"So I did, didn't I? Well, now you can give me the message personally. We might as well have a seat." She led the way to the porch swing.

Matt, casting his cruiser in the drive an uncertain—perhaps yearning—glance, followed her reluctantly.

Feeling his weight settle down beside her, she kept her own gaze on the streetlights below, beyond the wrought-iron fence. A jasminelike perfume rose up to them from the nicotiania fronting the porch. "I suppose it's about Francis Seton?" she said.

"Yes. Fortunately that town you mentioned isn't a very big place, and the chief has been there for ages. He vaguely remembered the guy himself. Did a few months of odd jobs for ranchers in the area and then moved on. The chief thought he might have gone east. He used to receive letters from some female in Pennsylvania. This the guy you want?"

"I think so. How did the chief describe him?"

"Blond, blue-eyed. Hispanic."

"What?" She turned to look him full in the face.

"You didn't know that?"

"I knew the guy I had in mind was Hispanic. I just assumed he had sent Millie a fake photograph."

He grinned at her tolerantly. "Not all Hispanics are dark, you know. That's probably what you would call a stereotype. His real name was Javier Santos."

"Not much of a jump from that to Francis Seton."

"Scarcely a hop. So, if that's all you needed to know…"

He shifted his weight, preparatory to rising. "Matt, wait. I need to talk to you about something." At his wary expression, she added crossly, "Not about us, about this murder case."

He settled back gingerly. "I'm not sure which of those subjects should scare me more. Go ahead."

"I'm going to have to fill you in first." She did so, holding back very little, except the conversations that had pertained to him.

When she had finished, he expelled breath in an exasperated sigh. "The things you get yourself mixed up in! Well, frankly, I think your present dilemma serves you right."

"You do see it then?"

"Oh, I see it all right. Those gelatin squares should have given it away from the start."

"Yes, but not all of us are as well-read on illicit drugs as you cops are. It was LSD that they took that way, wasn't it?"

"Yep. You have a lot of the other signs there too: low appetite, insomnia, hearing color, losing track of time. This Henry was criminally careless, and he should have gone to jail. If I were this Royce Falco and my son had just been killed, I would have insisted on it."

"So you think it could have happened that way? Sunny ate LSD by mistake in some of that gelatin. Everybody said she was agitated that night, but they misinterpreted it. Somebody who wasn't used to the drug could have a very bad trip, couldn't she? Become difficult to handle?"

"She sure could. The stuff can make you confused, paranoid, or downright delusional. Back in its heyday, people were known to walk out high windows because they thought they could fly."

"So she might have grabbed the wheel or something?"

"Or something. Maybe she thought the car could fly." Matt eyed his ex-fiancée sardonically. "So what did I tell you about getting mixed up in messes that didn't concern you? It isn't much fun, is it, deciding whether you should tell your friend that her father caused her sister's death?"

"He didn't really cause it. He didn't mean it to happen. Like he said, it was an accident."

"Carelessness that kills somebody is still a crime. Why do you suppose Falco let him go?"

"Maybe Royce thought Henry already had been punished enough through the loss of Sunny. And Kurt wouldn't have wanted Sunny's family to suffer the added blow of Henry's imprisonment. But Royce had to make sure Henry didn't stay around to endanger his other daughter—or to possibly win the election. So Royce forced his opponent out, with the best possible motives, and smeared his own reputation in the process."

"The only question is how this Royce found out if, as you say, Kurt was dead and Sunny never regained consciousness."

"My guess would be that Henry blurted it out himself." Regan leaned wearily into her own corner of the swing. "When Royce came to deliver the shocking news. Henry must have been at least a little uneasy when he found out his daughter had been playing with that gelatin. What am I going to do, Matt?"

The look he gave her now was more sympathetic. "I don't give you these warnings to spoil your fun, *cara mia,*" he said.

"Having to play Solomon can lead to a lot of sleepless nights. I know that from experience, and I'm considerably less sensitive than you are."

The endearment from their courting days apparently had slipped in unconsciously, and she decided to ignore it. "Yes, you do know, don't you?" she said, briefly turning her cheek against his arm that lay along the back of the swing. "I'm sorry I hung up on you, Matt. I was in a really bad mood that night. It was good of you to find out about Seton for me anyway."

"Hey, that's what I'm here for, remember," he said tweaking her hair. "Protect and serve. Only I can't protect you when you're way down in Pennsylvania."

He had been moving the swing to and fro with his foot, and the gentle rocking was making her drowsy. "I won't be staying much longer. I can't impose on poor Agatha forever, and if I find out much more stuff like this, those people down there are going to be happy to see the last of me. Besides, I'm awfully tired."

"You look it." The hand resting on the back of the swing dropped to her shoulder, pulled her over against him, stroked her hair. She was too exhausted to think much about it except that it felt good.

Eyes shut, she smiled. "Are you implying that I'm haggard?"

"No fishing for compliments, lady," he growled. "You know you always look good to me. One of these days, though, you're going to have to slow down."

"I know. I miss you, Matt."

He didn't respond to that, but the hand stroking her hair snuggled against her throat.

She lost all sense of time then, swaying in the gentle darkness with his warmth beside her. A buzzing brought her groggily half awake, and she realized it must be the cellular phone he carried. "I'm sorry, Matt," she mumbled, sitting up straight to allow the damp night air to come between them. "What time is it?"

"Just about midnight." He walked a few paces away to address the phone and then returned to her. "I have to go. Come on. You had better get inside to bed if you're going to drive tomorrow."

"It's you who has to play Solomon now, I suppose," she said seriously, as he helped her across to the door. "I don't envy you."

"Nor I you." He pushed her gently inside the door, clicked on the light, and, squeezing her shoulder, said close to her ear, "Just be careful, *cara mia*. Okay?"

When Regan woke the following morning, she had a hard time believing the scene with Matt had happened. She had been so tired that she had dropped, fully clothed, onto the couch instead of going upstairs. Sitting up, feeling stiff and disheveled, she listened to the silence of the big house and wished she didn't have to go back to Pennsylvania.

Nothing compelled her to return. Day would understand that she had other duties, other responsibilities.

After showering and changing her clothes, Regan ate a lonely breakfast on the terrace. The flower beds were weedy; many of the plants were overgrown, past their prime. The summer was slipping away from her, and she had had no time to enjoy it.

*Maybe that would be the best thing—just to stay here. Especially now when there's the possibility of a new start with Matt. Then I wouldn't have to make this difficult choice that has no right answer.*

She remembered an old man named Amos Hargrove saying to her, "Everybody has a right to know the truth." Perhaps because, when you didn't know the truth, you were apt to imagine worse things. It would be hard to get worse than this though. Regan locked up the house and stopped at Thyme Will Tell for a few minutes to chat with her staff, check the mail, and sign papers. Then she started the long drive back to Rosevale. At least she would have plenty of time to think.

When she arrived at the bed-and-breakfast again, she had come to no decision. She would have to tell Day something about the conversation with Henry, but which parts? *Maybe if I just give her a factual account, she'll figure it out for herself. No, she won't. She was too close to see it. Really, I have no proof. It wouldn't be right to give her guesses about which there's no proof. But who could verify it? Henry's too wily to come right out and admit it. Wait a minute! Didn't Day tell me Bram knew why her father left?*

Regan punched out Bram's number. She didn't have any hope he would answer so, when a masculine voice said, "Hello," she waited for a message to follow.

At his impatient second "Hello," she jumped to life.

"Bram? This is Regan Culver."

"Oh hi, Regan. How's the campaign to recapture the boyfriend going?" He sounded casual enough.

"Much better," she said, "thanks to you. Listen, Bram, I need to ask you something—or tell you something, I guess I should say. I've found out what caused the car accident that killed your brother."

Silence.

"I mean, I know about Henry and the LSD?" She let her voice go up interrogatively at the end.

"You are good at this, aren't you?" His voice was guarded now.

"This is no surprise to you, is it?"

"My father told me. He made me promise not to tell, but

I don't suppose there's much point in denying it. Are you going to inform Day?"

"Should I?"

"Since my father sacrificed his career to keep that knowledge from her, I would have to say no. On the other hand, she's a very tenacious woman who's probably not going to give up until she is told something. It's dangerous for her to be here. I didn't realize how dangerous until I received an anonymous letter today."

"What did it say?"

"Something to the effect that I was going to get mine. There hadn't really been any physical threats before."

"You've had other anonymous letters? Why didn't you tell the police?"

"And phone calls. The calls didn't start until after my burns. I thought it was just your run-of-the-mill prankster until a certain name was mentioned. And, no, I am not going to tell you that name. You had better go back home to your cop. If something happens to you, he would kill me, and I wouldn't blame him. Of course, he would have to get in line. It looks like that car accident may have been my fault after all. In that case, there's no reason Day has to know that her father was a junkie. Don't worry. I started this thing, and I'll end it too."

"Bram!"

He laughed. "No, I didn't mean suicide. Though, if I fail, I may end up dead at that. Just in case, I'll give you a clue. My eyes are brown. Good-bye, Regan."

# CHAPTER 10

*Well, I'll find friends to wear my bleeding roses,*
*That shall maintain what I have said is true,*
*Where false Plantagenet dare not be seen.*

That evening, perusing Hilda's latest diary further, Day could find nothing more relevant to the case at hand. *Hilda was right, though, when she said that the two of us were very much alike. Two independent, single women who prefer to do the hardest stuff ourselves,* Day thought.

She wondered if her volunteers had been discouraged as much by that spirit as by the scandal itself. Maybe, after all, they had simply been looking for an excuse to leave.

It also had meant that Hilda herself was too busy around the time of the primary election to realize how hard her heir had taken his defeat. Only when she had come to visit, arriving a couple of days before the board meeting, had she seen the depth of Bram's depression. She had been furious.

Gavin should have informed me. But the man is palpably spineless, one of those who believe that things will somehow work themselves out. I wonder sometimes how he can be Connie's nephew.

It's not like Bram to be a bad sport, but he may

be right that the game was rigged. Henry Day's family has always caused trouble. People around here felt sorry for Maureen because she appeared to be so poorly paid. The truth is, of course, that she was paid plenty but insisted on sending a good percentage of it to the husband who had deserted her.

Day looked up from the notebook to stare into the darkness beyond the circle of lamplight. *That can't be true.* But a heaviness in her stomach acknowledged it was the sort of thing her mother might very well do. Maureen Day had been slavishly devoted to her husband, more so than to either of her children.

*Maybe it would be better not to read any further,* Day thought, *not to have my own perception of the facts undermined as if it were a house built on sand with a dark tide curling around its foundations. I shouldn't have demanded the truth. People can't stand too much truth, somebody said.*

Day had not cried the afternoon before, though she had felt like it. Why must she keep feeling such disappointment in Bram?

He had admitted to her, after all, that he had been a thief and a liar since childhood. Had he been a disappointment to his adoptive parents too? Day had hardly known Royce.

She remembered his coming on the night of the accident though. A dark, handsome man, deathly pale and smelling of smoke...

At a sudden, peremptory knock at the back door, Day started and thrust the diary behind a sofa cushion, staring at that door, horrified, as if it would again be Royce Falco on the other side.

Only bad news came knocking late in the evening.

"Who is it?"

"It's me, Millie. Let me in. I want to talk to you."

When Day opened the door, she thought that her usually kind neighbor looked different somehow—harder, tenser. "You have to stop, Day," Millie said at once. "There are rumors about you all over town. I don't know what kind of bleeding-heart drivel Regan has been feeding you, but you're becoming a pariah."

"I thought you were a friend of Regan's," Day said mildly, the lump of dread in her chest dissolving all at once in her relief. She waved Millie to a seat at the kitchen table, reached for some glasses from the cupboard. "Would you like a lemonade?"

"Yes, thanks. Of course, I'm a friend of Regan's. I was of her mother anyway. But both of them tend to carry things to extremes."

"Including their religion?" Day asked, pouring lemonade over ice cubes. "I thought you were a Christian too." The crackling fizzle of the cubes seemed loud in the silence that followed.

"I am," Millie said finally, stiffly. "But I do try to retain some common sense. What you're doing is not sensible. It's scarcely rational."

"Apparently, you skipped the part about loving your enemies." Day sat down across from her neighbor, pushing the extra glass over to her.

"Don't you preach at me, Damia Day!" Millie was suddenly shouting. "I was a Christian before you were born. And suddenly you know more about it? The Falcos of this world don't deserve any love!"

"Maybe not," Day responded in the same quiet tone. "And I'm *not* claiming to know more than you. But I do know that Christ never said anything about loving people only if they deserve it. I don't question the worth of an animal that needs me after all. Why should I do any differently for a man?"

"Because animals can't help what they are, but people can."

"And what do you think Bram is?"

"A taker." Millie leaned forward over the table, face flushed. "The Falcos have always been takers. They took your father away from you, for goodness sake! They worked your mother into her grave!"

"No," Day said sadly. "I suspect my mother worked herself into the grave, for the sake of my father who definitely didn't deserve that kind of devotion."

"More fool her then! And more fool you, because you're doing exactly the same thing."

"Not exactly," Day said. "I never thought that Bram merited my help. But if we're going to be judged on our merits, all of us are sunk. Christian love, as I see it, is not affection. It's something you have to do despite your feelings. Maybe even against them. And it certainly isn't logical as this world sees logic. But where has all our worldly logic gotten us? Into a trap where hatred and violence must be met by an equal hatred and violence. I think it's time that some of us broke that vicious circle. There is no perfect justice, after all."

"There is no justice at all! Francis was all I had, and the Falcos took him away from me. It should have been he, not Bram, who survived."

Day stared at her, appalled. Then Day reached to lay a hand over the other woman's. "Millie, listen to yourself! You're saying that you hate Bram because he lived and Francis didn't?"

Millie shook off the touch. "And wasn't I right? Look what Bram has proved to be. Latinos are cruel; everybody knows that." She lurched to her feet. "Those people are right. You're unnatural. You're not the person I thought you were at all."

"Neither are you, Millie," Day said sadly after the other woman had banged out. "Neither are you."

After she drank her lemonade, Day called Regan at the bed-and-breakfast. "I'm glad you came back. I wouldn't have blamed you if you didn't though. Millie was just here. She hates Bram, you know. I never realized that until tonight. I think she has some twisted idea that if he had died her fiancé would have lived."

Regan sounded shocked. "She would wish death on a twelve-year-old?"

"And I thought I knew the woman," Day said. "I thought all that emotion proved a good heart."

"Somebody said that sentimental people are more concerned with their own emotions than they actually are with other people."

"There's a broad streak of racism in Millie too," Day said. "I was tempted to tell her our suspicion that her dear Francis was Hispanic. But I thought she would really have gone ballistic then. Besides, I would have had to add that Francis was only using her, and I didn't have the heart to do that. She implied, by the way, that you were leading me astray with some very strange ideas."

Regan laughed. "Well, I never said they weren't strange. They feel strange, if it comes to that. They go against the grain."

"Do they ever! I think Bram knows more about that accident than he's told. He as much as admitted it. Do you have any guesses?"

Regan let the silence stretch too long.

"Maybe," Day said finally in a controlled tone, "I should ask how much you know."

"I would really rather not do this over the phone."

"All right. I can drive up there."

"No! Really, Day, it's late. We had better leave it until tomorrow. Maybe we should leave it altogether."

"That bad, huh? Sorry, Regan. I'll wait until tomorrow if you think that's necessary, but no longer. I've waited twenty-six years already, and I think that's enough."

"Okay." Regan capitulated. "I'll come over there. It will be more private."

After hanging up, Day was overwhelmed with languor. She went into the living room to stretch out on the couch, reminding herself firmly that she must not fall asleep. Not when she was finally going to hear the truth about her father. An uncomfortable truth, apparently, but at least it was something. Some knowing, some firmness.

When she finally succumbed, she dreamed of a beach where she waded through shifting, slipping, dragging sand toward a flat rock that never seemed to get any closer. And, at the back of her mind, was still the urgency. Must wake. Must wake. But the sand only deepened until it finally dragged her down into its grainy darkness.

■　■　■

After knocking on Day's back door and getting no answer, Regan tried the knob. It turned, and she was looking into the lighted little kitchen where two glasses, one empty and one full, sat on the table.

"Day!" Regan called softly. "It's me! Are you here?"

No sound answered her except a stealthy brush of wings as a moth sailed past her and headed for the ceiling fixture. A firefly flitted about the room, pulsing a fluorescent green. Outside the cicadas chirred their unending chorus.

"Day!" Regan said more shrilly and urgently, yanking the door shut behind her.

Still no answer came except for the moth's banging at the bulb.

Skin crawling with sudden dread, Regan tiptoed across

the kitchen floor to look into the living room. A lamp still shone on a table beside the empty couch. The bedroom and bathroom were dark and, as Regan discovered when she flipped on the lights, also empty.

A loud knocking at the front door brought her up short, heart thudding. "Who is it?"

"It is I, Inez."

The door opened reluctantly, as if it were not often used.

The Hispanic woman, stepping into the room, frowned around her and then at Regan. "Where is she—the little blond?"

"She doesn't seem to be here. I just arrived."

Inez tapped her fingers impatiently against the doorframe. "I do not trust little blonds when they ask my husband for help. That one is not the type to need help. It is very suspicious."

"What is? When did Day ask for help?"

"A message was on the machine that had not yet been erased. Tom must have listened to it because he was not there when I arrived home from mass. It was this Day woman's voice. She asked him to come and see her after dark. She said that she was in danger. It did not sound right to me."

"It doesn't sound right to me either," Regan said shortly. "I was just talking to Day on the phone fifteen minutes ago. She knew I was coming over. If she had to go out, she would have left a note."

"Perhaps she prefers her male visitor," Inez suggested, eyes blazing.

Regan shook her head. "Not tonight, she wouldn't. I had some important information for her. Really, Inez, Day has never showed any romantic interest in Tom. Besides, his car isn't here."

"Yes, it is. It is down the road, hidden in a little lane. Tom, he would think it fun to creep about like in a spy story. Tom, he has much imagination, but he does not see what is right there in front of his face. He likes his stories better."

"You haven't told him about his father yet, have you? Listen, Inez, do you think it possible that he believed his own stories enough to want to hurt Bram? To want to punish the Falcos for his father's death?"

Eyes narrowing, Inez said. "You will not pin that on Tom. He is fair. He does not blame Bram for the accident. Bram was only a boy. It is not rational."

"Yes, but Millie blames Bram for living when the man she thinks was her fiancé died."

"I know this Millie. She is a fool. Tom is not."

"Maybe you're right. I hope you're right." Regan looked around again distractedly. "We shouldn't just be standing here. We should be looking for Day. Was her station wagon out there? Did you notice? I wasn't paying any attention when I came."

"Yes, the car is there. And a Rover, which I suppose is yours. We must search thoroughly. This Day is small." Inez produced a pencil flash from her bag and began a businesslike scouring of the house. She even got down on her graceful knees to peer under the bed.

Finished, she dusted herself off and said practically, as they returned to the kitchen. "Okay. Perhaps she is at the big house." Inez looked up at the moth. "Perhaps the little blond returns once too often to the flame. We will go there."

But before they could go anywhere, Tom Raines opened the back door and walked into the kitchen. "What are you doing here?" he asked his wife.

Inez turned to Regan and said with elaborate sarcasm. "Do you hear that? *He* asks what *I* am doing here?"

Regan, who was losing patience, said to Tom, "More to the point, what are you?"

"Looking for Day. She left a message asking me to come and see her, but the house was empty when I arrived. So I've been looking around outside."

Just then another pair of headlights swept into the drive. Regan hurried hopefully across the kitchen to stand in the doorway that Tom had left open. The headlights clicked off, and a car door slammed. "Am I late for the party?" Paul Sedgwick asked. Emerging into the light, he added, "Not that I understood it to be a party. I had a message from Day—"

"So did I!" Millie's strident voice called out of the darkness as she hurried across her lawn. "Which doesn't make any sense. I didn't find it until just now, but I've been to see Day since she left the message, and she never mentioned it at all."

"It did sound kind of stilted," Tom commented. "Unnatural wording. Something like 'This is Day. Come after dark. I am in danger.' Thing is, she sounded cheerful enough, saying it."

"Why would she send the same message to all of us?" Sedgwick asked, sounding a bit disgruntled. "And why after dark?"

"Maybe so Falco couldn't see," Tom suggested. They were all standing outside now and, as one, turned to look at the big house next door. A single light burned on the ground floor in what would be Bram's study.

"Has anybody checked over there?" Sedgwick asked.

"We were just going to," Regan said.

A certain reluctance seemed to hold them back, as if the big house were some kind of haunted castle to be approached only as a last resort.

"Why are you all frightened?" Inez asked impatiently. "Mr. Falco is just a man with a burned face. He is not an ogre.

I will go ask him myself." She cut across the lawn, and the others followed sheepishly in her wake.

Once on the gravel drive, Inez stomped straight up the steps to the front door and stabbed at the bell. "Myself," she said, "I think this blond likes to make herself interesting. If she really is in danger, why does she not call the *policía?*"

"Who is it?" Bram's voice called irritably from within.

"*Señor* Falco, it is I, Inez and Tom and Paul and Regan. We wish to speak with you, please."

"Come in then. It isn't locked."

They all trooped down the hallway to the open doorway. Bram was lying on the couch with a book, which he turned facedown on his chest when they came in. The mask did make him look like a bank robber.

"We're looking for Day," Regan explained quickly. "She's disappeared."

It was hard to read any expression through that mask. "Disappeared?"

"After leaving strange messages about being in danger on our answering machines," Paul said. "I have to agree with Tom that she sounded unusually cheerful for someone in fear for her life. And, as Mrs. Raines here has so astutely asked, why didn't she call the cops instead?"

"What did she say?" Bram asked but made no comment on being told.

"Are you sure it was Day?" Regan asked. "She certainly didn't sound frightened when I was talking to her. And that was only a half-hour ago."

Tom Raines nodded reluctantly. "It was her all right."

"No doubt about that," Paul agreed.

Millie was glowering down at Bram. "I warned her. Not

more than an hour ago, I warned her to stay away from you. But would she listen?"

"*Aquí es ridículo,*" Inez said. "*Señor* Falco, might we search your house?"

"*Mi casa es su casa,*" Bram said sardonically. "But I wouldn't be surprised if Day has disappeared for good. She hasn't been too happy with me. Also, she seems to have made off with some journals Hilda's lawyers sent. I found the wrappings in the trash and called to find out what had been in them. All Damé has to do is lay low, and every living soul around is going to say I must have done away with her. She always was a clever girl. If that's her game, though, I think she'll find that I do still have a few friends in high places."

They didn't find her. The big house was neat but empty of other life. And though Inez probed in closets and under beds, she found nothing unusual. "This woman is a good housekeeper," she admitted, rising finally to her feet. "No dust rabbits."

At some point, Tom had gone quietly downstairs to call the police. When Newpax arrived, he said he couldn't do anything. An adult couldn't legally be considered missing until a certain time period had elapsed. But as long as Mr. Falco was being so obliging… The chief searched the house quickly as well. Then, after thanking Bram, who had not stirred from his couch, Newpax asked Millie to retrieve the message from her machine so he could listen to it.

"I'm getting a strong odor of fish from the whole situation," Newpax told Regan in an aside. "People who are in danger don't take the time to call everybody they know; they dial 911. Maybe Falco is right. Maybe something was in those journals that implicated Day, and she decided her best move was to disappear. She didn't mention them to you, did she?"

"No," Regan had to admit. "She knew I was coming over though. Maybe she was going to wait and show me."

But when they returned to Day's house, Newpax found the latest of Hilda's journals almost at once, behind a cushion on the sofa. And it took only the most cursory of searches to discover the others piled on a bookshelf in the bedroom.

"All right," Newpax said with a sigh, dropping onto the sofa beside the lamp. "I'm stumped." He had sent the other members of the rose society home, and his men were still out searching the woods and fields in the vicinity.

■ ■ ■

When Day opened her eyes, she was in the wrong room, a room she had never seen before. She could see sunlight, white painted furniture, and sheer white curtains blowing in on a fresh breeze.

Her head was throbbing, and a bedside clock read nine o'clock. She had a strong sense of *déjà vu,* but at least she wasn't cold this time. Nights in late July were seldom chilly, and a light cotton blanket was tucked around her.

Just then Bram Falco padded, barefoot, into the room, wearing only a pair of jeans and rubbing at his wet hair with a towel. "Good, you're awake," he said, tossing the towel over the back of a chair.

Day continued to look around blearily, trying to recall how she had gotten to this place, but it was all blank. She sat up abruptly, and the room swam.

"Don't panic," Bram advised, perching on the edge of the bed and easing her back onto the pillow. "You didn't do some-thing you're going to regret for the rest of your life. I spent the night on the couch. I have gotten quite used to sleeping on couches lately. Somebody drugged you again. And I say *again* advisedly. Granted, I may have killed your animals while I was drunk, but I think the drugging part would have required more forethought than I was capable of at the time."

"That hadn't occurred to me," Day admitted, rubbing her head. "I suppose it was the lemonade last night. But then, Millie should have…no, come to think of it, she never drank hers. But I have been keeping my doors locked lately," she added crossly.

"Did it never occur to you that our friendly drugger might have made a copy of your key the first time?"

"Oh." Day continued to massage her temples. "How did I get here anyway? Wasn't Regan coming over? I remember trying to stay awake because she was going to tell me something important."

"By the time she arrived, you were gone. It seemed you had left messages first on everybody's answering machines asking for help. It was quite a search party; they combed my house."

"Oh," Day said again. "I don't remember calling anybody but Regan. And they didn't find me?"

"Nope. It's a good thing you're a small woman. You recall the leather couch in my study? I just put you under the back cushions. It did make them a little higher than usual, but fortunately nobody seemed to notice. Of course, I had to lie on the front ones the whole time, since your intrusion pushed them out pretty far, and I was afraid that, if I got up, they would all slide off. After all, you do see that their finding you in my house would be pretty incriminating for me."

Day began to laugh. It made her head hurt, but she enjoyed it. "You would!" she gasped. "How did you get stuck with me anyway?"

He regarded her frowningly. "You're not suspicious of me?"

"It's my turn to say, 'If you wanted to kill me, you had your chance last night.'"

"Right. Well, I heard somebody sneaking in the terrace door. I've been thinking that the murderer would show up sooner or later, so I've been leaving the doors unlocked at night to make it more convenient for him. Though, since he got in to find my gun that time, I suspect he might have a key to my place too. Anyway, I've been sleeping on the couch in the study just in case—and not doing much sleeping at that."

"And to think I was so impressed by the way you had been making your own bed every morning!"

He grinned. "So I picked up my golf club and tippie-toed out there, but by the time I arrived, he had gone again, leaving you shoved under the dining room table." Bram's facetious air drained away. His face and voice tightened. "With a plastic bag over your head. Fortunately, it hadn't been on long enough to have the intended effect. I could see across to your place and all the cars arriving. I knew everyone would be on the way over to see me shortly. There wouldn't be much point in somebody planting you unless he also had made arrangements to have you discovered. Besides being unconscious, you seemed to be doing okay. If I'd thought you were in real danger, I would have called the EMTs. But otherwise I didn't intend to go to jail for you, thank you very much."

Day laughed again. "You are such a gallant, Bram. I suppose I'm just lucky that your cushions didn't smother me."

"I made sure you had air. Though you did stir a bit once. That gave me a couple of bad minutes."

"I imagine." Day pushed herself to a sitting position against the pillows. "Where are we now, and what are we going to do? If I turn up, people are going to want to know where I've been. And I'm pretty sure I didn't make those phone calls you're talking about."

"I'm pretty sure of that too." Bram stood to retrieve his dish of aloe vera gel from the dresser. "I suspect your voice was recorded and the words rearranged, probably from some of those anonymous phone calls you've been getting. Maybe even the one I heard you taking. It seems to me you gave your name that time and said something about after dark as well. That would explain why it all sounded slightly stilted, and the tone was wrong. He had to use what he had."

Bram returned to hand her the dish and to half lie across her feet so she could apply the gel to his face and chest. "We're about an hour from home. This is a cottage that belonged to Hilda. On Hearn Lake. Very few people know about it because she used it for a hideaway when she wanted a few days alone to recharge. I drove us up here last night after everybody left. It's obvious that this killer is trying to implicate me through you. I'm going to have to go back to have any chance of nabbing the guy, but I think you should stay disappeared for a while."

Day shook her head vigorously. "I can't do that. I have my animals to look after. Besides, I thought you knew who he was."

"I thought I did, too, but the guy I'm thinking about is not a member of our little circle. Of course, he wouldn't necessarily have to be to have committed any of these crimes. Still, whoever is doing this seems to know an awful lot about us. He may have deliberately misled me into thinking he was this person from my past."

"You're sure it is a he?"

"Not really. The person from the past is male, but all I've heard from Anonymous is a squeaky, obviously disguised voice over the phone and a threatening letter. It could be a woman, I suppose. Like I said, you're not very big. Any female who was fairly strong probably could manage to carry you."

"I suppose you're still not going to tell me who this person from your past is—or why he would have cause to hate you so much. But, really, I can't stay here." Having finished with the gel, Day set it on the bedside table. "Anybody walking in right now would put the wrong construction on this scene, for one thing. We look much too cozy."

"Cozy?" Bram made no move to get up. "That's not quite how I would have expressed it, but this is rather *comfortable,* isn't it?"

That dark gaze of his held hers, and she could feel heat creeping up her cheeks. "For you maybe," she said tartly. "But I'm losing all feeling in my feet."

"Well, we can't have that." He sat up. "I think you had better stay in bed awhile. I remember somebody saying that this drug really wiped you out last time. Regan was going to stay over at your place to look after the animals."

"Regan does not know the first thing about looking after the animals," Day objected, starting to pull her feet out from under the blanket.

Bram grabbed one of those feet through the cotton and pulled her down so that her head rested on the pillows again. "She'll figure it out if she has Millie to help her. You are not indispensable. I'll go try to find you some breakfast. But with my doing the cooking, you'll probably have to settle for cold cereal. I'll also call Regan and tell her the truth. Maybe she can figure out something to tell Newpax."

"You know," Day said crossly, "I quite fail to see any of this charm that everybody else claims you have. All I get from you is insults and manhandling." It did feel good, however, to sink back into the bed, to let the flaccid tiredness surge in again.

He turned his head to wink at her. With his distorted face, the gesture should have been grotesque but wasn't. "Hey, I've never tried to snow you, Dame. I didn't think it would be possible."

■ ■ ■

Regan, who hadn't slept, was vastly relieved—and angry. "Bram, you are the most infuriating man! Why couldn't you have told me this last night?"

"I didn't know how far your inclination to trust me could be stretched."

"It's getting close to the breaking point," she warned. "I agree with you that maybe Day should stay gone, but I don't think it's fair to keep the people who care about her in a state of worry. I would advise you to tell Newpax. Then he can refrain from reporting her disappearance to the papers and can assure everybody that he knows where she is and that she is hiding out for a while for her own protection. I imagine he's going to want to hear her voice, though, to make sure. Frankly, I don't think being with you is the safest place for her since this killer seems to have you as a target, but since most of her other friends are suspects…You're sure she's all right?"

"Positive. I virtually had to hobble her to the bed. Are you and Millie managing with the animals?"

"Well, you might say it's that teenager named Joan who is managing. We're just taking orders from her. I had better hurry up and tell Joan that Day is okay. I think she's been working herself up to bearding you in your den."

"If she's anything like her mentor, I would have been suitably cowed, believe me."

"I bet," Regan said. "Listen, Bram. Don't you think it's time you told us what is behind all this?"

"I would if I were sure myself. Be careful, Regan. This person apparently has no qualms about harming the innocent."

"I've already heard the warnings from Matt."

"Incidentally, have you told your boyfriend where you are? If he called your hotel last night and you weren't there…"

"Oh no! I never thought of that."

"You females," Bram said. "No consideration for our tender feelings whatsoever. Would you happen to know, by the way, what happened to those journals another heartless female stole from me?"

"Newpax has the most recent one. He's allowing me to read the others. Do you want them back now?"

"I don't think so. I only know of one secret Hilda ever kept from me."

She hoped her silence was encouraging.

"You're not going to ask? That my adoptive father is supposed to be my natural father too."

After Bram had hung up, Regan scrambled through the journals for those that had been written in Mexico and found the entry that talked about the trip to the orphanage. The three had stopped to eat first at a café in the town.

When Connie went to use the rest room, Royce dropped his bombshell on me. He said, "Hilda, I don't have much time to explain this to you, but I need your help. I've heard that a certain boy is at this orphanage, a boy whom I believe is my son. Do you remember Calida?"

Of course I remembered Calida. Knowing what Connie was like, I was not surprised that Royce had had an affair. But to have chosen somebody like that! Although from a high-class Mexican family, Calida was similar to Connie in frail appearance, and, like Connie, she loved to play the martyr.

Actually, having an illegitimate child gave her the perfect opportunity. When she was kicked out by her uncle, she could have moved in with friends. But she preferred wrapping her disgrace about her, so to speak. She moved to another town, but because she never took a job of any kind, we all deduced that somebody must be sending her money. In letters, she kept up a constant, wistful commentary on her betrayal. She actually called it that, as if, as they say, it doesn't take two to tango! She never came right out and said who the father was, though she threw out lots of hints.

She was famous for her suicide attempts. She was always careful not to take too many sleeping pills and to be discovered in time. But one day she must have miscalculated because she actually died. By the time her friends found out about it, the boy, named Mirlo, had disappeared.

This was two or three years ago. You can't believe how disappointed I was in Royce. I mean, Connie herself is preferable to that frail creature! And now he wanted to adopt the boy while pretending to his wife that the child was just another orphan!

In the end, I went along, of course. I could see that Royce had long since regretted that affair and was probably punishing himself for it much more than anyone else could have managed. No doubt he blamed himself for the suicide. Anyway, the child was a charmer, dark and daring and doing his best to hide that he desperately wanted to be the one chosen.

Knowing that he is Calida's child, I have some qualms. Nothing good has come out of that family. Calida's brother is a Communist rebel who goes in for self-aggrandizement and who, I have heard, has sworn to avenge his sister's disgrace. He may make trouble if he ever gets out of jail.

But since we are returning to the States shortly, we will leave all of that behind us. I only hope the child can adapt to a different culture.

Bram appeared to have adapted quite well. So Royce was the one on whom Javier would have been seeking revenge, not Kurt. But Javier may well have thought the best revenge was to kill Royce's own son. Still, why subject himself and his sister's child to the fiery punishment too?

Regan went back to the beginning of the journals and settled herself to read. But, though she learned much more about Hilda herself, little of it was to the point. Hilda had had a wonderfully dry sense of humor about her own plainness. She had once been in love with a Mexican who could be called dark and daring, but had sensibly turned him down due to the suspicion that he was really interested in her father's money. Perhaps that partly explained her soft spot for Bram. He was indeed the son she never had.

Hilda had not languished, however. Although somewhat shy and backward up until her father's death, she had stepped in afterward to take over his business enterprises and had made a surprising success of them. As her confidence grew, she also had become a leader in various clubs and charities, including one involving heirloom roses...

Was it that involvement that had cost her her life? Or was it her weakness for dark and daring males? Had her fate been decided the day she found a ragged orphan to have a certain impudent charm?

# CHAPTER 11

### ■ ■ ■

*Now, by this maiden blossom in my hand,*
*I scorn thee and thy fashion, peevish boy.*

After eating some cereal and speaking drowsily to Newpax over the phone, Day lapsed into half sleep again. She was conscious enough to be aware of the cool sheets, the lapping of water outside, and the curtains that blew lacy sunlight over her face, but her thoughts floated pleasantly. Surprisingly pleasantly, considering the circumstances.

The morning drifted away. Bram brought her some soup from a can for lunch. It, too, was surprisingly good, and she announced herself ready to get up.

"All right," he said. "Hang on to my arm, and we'll take a stroll outside." He plopped a straw hat on her head before leading her down the front path and past a tangled garden surrounded by a picket fence, to where sand had been trucked in to make a small, private beach.

The day was clear, the temperature in the seventies, the breeze blowing in off the lake almost cool. Trees circled the cleared space around the cottage and reached farther to encompass the peaceful water. A single canoeist fished far down the lake.

"Nice, huh?" Bram said. "Hilda bought up most of the land on this end to keep it secluded."

"Nice," Day echoed, "if you can afford it." The "cottage," which she suspected was only used a few days a year, was larger and better furnished than her house.

"There are also hiking paths in the woods," Bram said. "But for now, I think you had better continue to take it easy. Why don't you sit in the sand for a while?" He brought out blankets, a beach umbrella, and some books.

For once, though, Day felt no interest in the printed word. The sand was warm and the breeze cool. She felt satisfied to simply laze in the sun and watch the waves. It had been, she realized, a long time since she had done nothing at all.

Bram lay on another blanket nearby, reading. He wasn't wearing his mask—she and the doctor were, she feared, going to lose the battle on that—and his burns were clearly delineated in the bright light. Rough and red and ugly.

Looking up to catch her eye, he smiled and set the book aside. "Comfortable?"

"Very. What are you reading?"

"*The Great Divorce*. Lewis. Heaven and hell. Hardly a topic for the beach."

She watched the lone fisherman rock gently on the reflected sky. "You say sanctity was never in the cards for you, but I've noticed you have a lot of books on the subject."

"We all want what we can't have."

"Who says you can't? One of the strange things about God is his apparent willingness to take all comers."

"It's hard to repent when you still possess the benefits of your sin."

"Bram, speaking of sin, what was it my father did? What was Regan afraid to tell me?"

He turned his head away, but Day pursued. "She's going to tell me anyway. I'd rather hear it from you since you were there."

Still looking out over the water, he said, "Your father was a junkie. The gelatin your sister played with that night was laced with LSD."

What was surprising now was her lack of surprise. She hadn't suspected the truth, but she was not taken aback by it.

"Sunny caused the accident then, not Kurt?"

"That's what I believed for a long time. Or tried to believe anyhow. Now I think it may have been something—somebody—else. That would make it my fault, not hers. So don't harp on it."

"I hadn't intended to. It wasn't her fault even if she did cause the accident. It was my father's. Jell-O man. That was a joke of hers, but it hits close to the truth. There was no solidity in him. All words and no substance."

He smiled faintly, turning back to her. "That's how I wonder where you came from. Considering that your mother was hardly there either. Maybe two negatives can make a positive. Are you okay?"

"Yes. I was disillusioned with my father long ago. Why did your father let him get away with it?"

"You. An awkward little thing with braids and braces. Royce couldn't bring himself to destroy what was left of your life. Of course, I knew you better. I could have told him you were on the acerbic side and would probably prefer to know the truth. But I didn't get the chance. Then, too, my father's sense of sin weakened him. He had violated his own strict ethics with the result that his mistress killed herself. It was very difficult for him to condemn anybody else after that. I think maybe he gave himself too much credit. I don't think she intended to die."

"Was she Javier Santos's sister?"

"Yes. How did you find that out? Regan, I suppose. I swear, the woman must do it by osmosis or something. Calida was the name."

Day felt a surge of excitement. "She was your mother, wasn't she? Royce was your real father."

"So they say."

"And Javier was the unidentified body in the accident?"

Bram stared at her. "That's the first I've heard of it. Where did you get that idea?"

"Regan got it from Inez. She's Javier's daughter, which makes her, I suppose, a cousin of yours."

"And nobody ever thought to mention all of this to me?"

"I guess not. Well, first we got the idea that Kurt might have been Calida's lover, but you would have been too old to be his son. Do you suppose Inez could be responsible for all this mayhem? Because of what happened to her father? No, I don't suppose that's likely. She never knew him."

"But she might know some other stuff," Bram said, frowning. "I accused Raines of making those anonymous calls to her himself. It never occurred to me that she might have made up the anonymous calls."

"My head is beginning to spin," Day said crossly. "Why would she do that?"

"As misdirection. So that nobody would suspect her of being an anonymous caller. Could she have been the voice you heard?"

Day considered. "I don't know. There was no accent or unusual word choices, but I kind of suspect she puts that on anyway. For her own amusement. In that case, why would she marry Tom?"

"Because she was in the country illegally. The possibility that there were no anonymous calls wouldn't disprove that.

Hey, you look beat. Let's drop the whole thing and talk about something else for a change."

"Like how you're going to go off tonight and leave me here?"

"You'll be much safer here, believe me."

"I know. But you're not going to be safe there. Your little game of trying to trap a murderer could backfire. You could end up quite dead."

"No kidding. I'm rather surprised to still be here actually. But, remember, I never planned to survive our little party that night. Everything else has been borrowed time for me."

Day gaped at him, appalled. "That's why your face doesn't bother you. You don't expect to be around long enough to use it."

His lips twitched. "I wouldn't have put it exactly that way, but, yes. Still, I plan to put up a good fight. He may get me, but I'm determined to put the mark of Cain on him somehow for Hilda's sake."

When tears welled up in her eyes, his grin vanished, and he said harshly. "Don't cry for me, Dame. I'm the guy who was going to kill you, remember?"

"You never did get beyond suicide, did you? This is just another form of it."

She lurched up to her knees to glare at him. "When I think of all the advantages you've had…" She flung a hand in an eloquent gesture that encompassed the cottage and the serene lake. "All that stuff that Tom mentioned. Intelligence, strength, sex appeal, more money than you know what to do with—and it's not enough for you! You are a hog—an ungrateful swine, who will just flick God in the face and say, 'Thanks, but no thanks,' in that careless way of yours. While people like me have had to get along on plainness and poverty and just hoping we could hold things together for one more day! It takes a lot more guts to live than it does to die, and you simply don't have what it takes, do you? I'm not crying for you. You disgust me!"

He had turned pale under the lash of her voice so that the burns stood out even redder. She recognized that as a sign of anger, but her words tumbled on, as if compelled. "Even Hilda!" Day snatched off the straw hat. "I suppose this belonged to her. She died for you. She could still be here today, enjoying her cottage and her lake, but she was trying to save your life. A life that you don't even have the decency to want! All because you failed once. Because the voters decided you weren't the best man after all, you're going to throw it all over."

"Shut up, Day!" he snapped. "You don't know what you're talking about."

"Don't I? You've always despised us all, haven't you? You couldn't be bothered to listen to me about those ducks, but I wasn't the only one. Maybe you had a reason to despise your father for his weakness. He deserted you and your real mother after all. But was that any reason to transfer your hatred to the rest of the world? You even chose women you could despise for your mistresses. I saw that the other day. You didn't care how Paula felt; you enjoyed repulsing her. How much is it going to take? Tell me that! How much? Hilda died for you. *God* died for you! But that isn't enough. Nothing is ever enough for you, is it?"

He caught her by the shoulder, thrust her down again on the sand, leaned over her. "You're one to talk about selfishness. All I was asking of you was one peaceful day. Sun and sand and good company before I die. Was that too much?"

She stared defiantly back up at him. "Yes, it was. Because I'm not letting you die easy, Bram. Not after all you've put me through."

His narrowed gaze searched her face, as if he were not quite sure of her meaning. He grinned suddenly, recklessly. "You don't know how sorely I'm tempted to live, Dame!" She thought that he was going to kiss her. When he released her shoulder and rolled away from her, she was blindly, irrationally disappointed.

*You little idiot! You wouldn't have put up any fight either, would you? All these years you've been subconsciously comparing every man you meet to this one—and finding them wanting. No wonder you cried when you found out what he really was. But even then you didn't learn.*

"But I think I owe this guy a try at me at least," Bram was saying. "A life for a life. That's in the Bible."

"You killed someone?" *Would even that,* she asked herself wildly, *rid you of this infatuation?*

"No," he said. "I didn't despise Royce, by the way; I admired him. And I hated you at times, but I never despised you. The only person I despise now," he concluded quietly, looking up at the puffy white clouds, "is myself."

She hurt for him. The worst punishment he could have inflicted on her, she realized now, was to die himself. How he would have laughed at the irony if he had known.

She sat up. "You said a life for a life. He's had one. He's had Hilda's. She took the punishment for you. That's in the Bible too."

■　■　■

That afternoon Tom Raines brought Regan and Joan a duck he had pulled from the river. "It didn't put up much of a fight."

The bird felt too light for its bulk, and its eyes were glazed and indifferent. "It must be poison again," Joan said, after running exploratory hands over the duck's body. "We can try activated charcoal, but it usually doesn't work. Why won't anybody do something?"

Tom shrugged. "They investigated Falco's factory after the election, but they didn't find anything. I was hoping he had cleaned up his act. In more ways than one." To Regan, he said, "Any news on Day?"

"You must not have been home. I left a message with Inez. Day is all right. Bram found her and took her away somewhere for her own safety."

Tom regarded Regan disbelievingly. "I hope you're not taking his word on that."

"No. Newpax talked to her over the phone. He knows where they are. Bram says that she was drugged, with a plastic bag over her head, when he found her."

"And exactly when was that?" When Regan didn't answer, he added, "It seems to me you're risking a lot on Falco's unsupported word."

"Bram isn't the killer, Tom. He was in the hospital when Hilda died, remember?"

"So? Money like his can buy any number of hired assassins. He's the only one who benefited from her death. He got a big inheritance and the pleasure of seeing a woman he hated framed for the crime."

"You think he was calling hit men from the ICU? He was fond of Hilda."

"He could have made the arrangements before he got burned. And I don't think that guy cares about anybody but himself."

Tom turned away. Watching him go, Regan remembered Hilda's own words about how people reacted to Bram. Extremely.

Joan had quietly been mixing activated charcoal with milk and oil. Coming back to the present, Regan found the girl using a baster to squirt the liquid down the duck's throat. "I'm sorry, Joan. I should have been helping."

"That's all right," the teenager said. "We'll have to repeat this every fifteen minutes, but I don't think it's going to help." She stroked the duck's drooping neck. "Do you think Day's going to be all right?"

"I don't know," Regan said. "I really don't know."

"I asked her why she was helping Mr. Falco," Joan said. "She said it was like what we did with the animals. 'Reversing the damage,' she called it. Somebody had to step in and turn things back the other way. I asked her what if they wouldn't turn."

"And?"

"She said in that case she was likely to get run over. But she had to make the effort. I think people can be like the animals sometimes and not realize that you're trying to help them rather than hurt them. Because some people are more used to getting hurt."

"And?" Regan encouraged softly.

"She would say that's the risk you have to take. She does that, you know. She will even take injured coons sometimes, though she's not supposed to, if she's pretty sure they're not rabid. She keeps them separate and never lets us volunteers handle them. She says she doesn't want us to suffer for her errors in judgment. It wasn't really fair of her not to let us take the risk too. That's why, when I found the gun, I threw it out of the car."

Regan gaped at the teenager, speechless.

"Right after Day found Ms. Graveston's body," Joan explained patiently, "she signaled me to look after the animals. So I stopped to get the ones that were in the station wagon before heading back to her place. The gun was in one of the baskets, under a heating pad. I knew if I told where I'd found it, things would look bad for Day. So I dropped the thing on the ground. I knew nobody would believe she was stupid enough to leave it out in the open like that. I'm probably guilty of tampering with evidence or something. But I don't mind. I wanted to take that risk for her. You understand?"

"Yes," Regan said.

■　■　■

"So the little blond is all right after all," Inez said to Tom. "I thought so. And now she has the falcon man to look after her. I would be very careful if I were that one. He will become a tame hawk if he does not watch out."

Tom looked at her blank faced. "Jealous?"

"No, I am not jealous! But now everybody forgets that this blond is an icy-blooded killer. Just because she makes peculiar phone calls and vanishes, we must all worry about her? I think maybe it is the falcon man who is in danger, not her."

"You would!" he said. "Every female around is under the guy's spell, it seems. Moths to the flame, all of you."

"I am not a moth! I do not stick and cling. It is you who do that. Always you are saying 'It is the way I have always done.' Does that make it right? It is you who flutters round and round without going anywhere. I do not understand you at all. You were very nice to me when I came here. You were very nice until you married me. Then you became," she flung up her hands, "a different person entirely!"

"We all do, lady," Newpax said from the doorway. "You know, I'm thinking that maybe Regan Culver was right about this red rose–white rose thing. It's turning into the war between the sexes all over again. I heard from a guy I took to be Regan's boyfriend today. He's a cop from up New England way. Seems he's been calling the hotel where she was supposed to be staying and not getting her. The man was not happy, wanted me to forbid her interference in the case. As if I could do that. My way of thinking is that all citizens should take a little bit of the risk for a civilized society, not just us cops. And I don't mind a little help now and then such as you, Mrs. Raines, can give. Regan tells me you know that your husband's father is alive. Know, even, where the guy is. That true?"

Inez felt Tom stiffen in shock, avoided looking at him. "Yes, it is true," she said sullenly. "I know. It was not hard to find him."

"So Tom would have had no reason to hold a grudge against the Falcos? Unless, that is, he didn't know."

"All right, Chief," Tom said in a soft tone that was yet razor sharp. "I didn't know. That was a piece of information my wife apparently didn't think important enough to share with me."

"Now, now," Newpax responded. "You can see why she didn't. You're not taking it at all well. One would think you would be relieved."

"Relieved that my wife lies to me? I think not."

"I did not lie to you!" Inez cried. "It was your mother who lied! She has known where your father was all along, but she never told you. She wants you to think that she has been treated badly."

"And wasn't she?"

"If I were your father," Inez snapped, "I would have left her myself!"

■ ■ ■

Back on the shore of Hearn Lake, Day and Bram talked away the afternoon. By common consent, they ignored the subject of murder. But once, when Day went into the cottage to use the bathroom, she stopped in the bedroom on her way out. Pushing up a screen, she looked sharply at Bram's truck, which was parked on that side of the cottage, taking special note of the tarp that covered several sacks of oats in the truck bed.

She left the screen open when she returned to the shore.

The conversation didn't languish. They talked like two people who had a single day to know each other but wanted that knowledge badly.

The weather changed gradually around them. The blue sky dulled to a hazy gray, and the clear air became thick with a humidity that couldn't be shrugged off. As the time drew closer that Bram would be leaving, Day felt a rising panic.

The water looked almost oily in its torpidity now. The fisherman had gone home.

"It's going to storm," Bram said. "We had better have some supper. I need to be getting back."

Day opened a can of clam chowder. The potatoes tasted chalky, the clams gritty, and the humidity clung to her skin like sweat. She rejected all of Bram's conversational sallies now and ate in silence. He was having trouble with his spoon again, and it clattered irritatingly against his bowl. For her fledgling plan to have a chance of working, she must whip up an argument with him now and that wouldn't be difficult.

"Listen, Day," he said finally, laying down the utensil. "I don't want to leave you here, but you must see it's the best thing. You'll be safe."

She stood to gather up the plates. "If safety was my priority, I would have scrammed before you ever left the hospital. You said you weren't a gentleman. It's a little late to start now, isn't it?" She turned her back to dump the plates into the sink.

"Could be, but I would like to go out on a high note. And I'm not taking a chance on somebody else having to die for my sins." He stood and came up behind her. "Let's not part angry, okay? Tell me you'll be all right."

She turned to glare up at him. He took her hand and started to raise it to his lips, but she jerked it free. "So you can make another romantic exit? I'll do no such thing! Like I said before, exits are easy. It's the sticking around that's hard. Go then, but don't expect me to be waving a tear-stained hanky after you!"

She brushed past him, stalked across the tiny living room and into the bedroom, slammed the door, and locked it behind her. She heard him come up on the other side.

"Dame, please…"

"I said go!" She was already up on the chair beside the window, sliding a leg over the sill. She paused, straddling that sill with head ducked under the sash long enough to yank the shade down behind her. Then she swung both legs to the outside, dropped, flexing her knees, to the ground, and ran for the truck.

She heard the front door open and close as she scrambled up onto the rear bumper, ducked her head under the loose end of the tarp, and wriggled over the tailgate. Bram shouldn't be able to see her until he came around the corner of the house. It was a tight fit, the edge of the tarp scraping painfully down over her shoulders and back, catching briefly on her hips. She writhed frantically and was through, dropping onto the unyielding hardness of tight-packed grain sacks.

She heard Bram's footsteps moving up beside the truck, and she cringed, expecting the tarp to be yanked back. It had been a stupid idea after all, one she had not expected to get away with. But she heard him open the driver's door and pause. Was he looking at her window, noticing the absence of the screen? If a breeze blew the shade into the little room, he would be able to see no one was in there.

As she huddled close to one of the sacks with the tarp only inches above her, a film of grain dust raised by her impact floated around her face. She pressed a finger hard under her nose, fighting the itching at the back of her throat that threatened to erupt into a sneeze.

Then the truck door slammed, and the engine started. She compressed herself even tighter against the sack. He would be looking in his rearview mirror now, and it would only take one ripple of the canvas...

The truck reversed out into the lane then lunged forward. Bram was either angry or upset, because he was taking the bumpy lane at quite a clip, causing the sacks to bounce on the hard truck bed and Day to bounce with them, *oof*ing as silently as possible every time she slammed down on the unforgiving grain.

Between oat dust and road dust, she was sneezing, also as silently as possible, between the oofs. Fortunately, the truck was rattling enough to cover her expulsions of breath. When the vehicle finally turned onto a surfaced road, she wiped streaming eyes with a gritty sleeve and crept forward on aching ribs toward the front of the bed where the ride might be smoother.

As she did so, the vehicle swerved off the road, and she froze, thinking he had finally suspected something. But then she heard the ding of a bell and footsteps approaching over cement.

"Help you, sir?"

"Fill it up," Bram said shortly.

She heard the nozzle thrust into the tank, the flow of the gasoline, the clicking of the numbers. There was, she thought, a certain awkwardness in the silence, the attendant's reaction, no doubt, to the sight of Bram's face. If she sneezed now...She buried her face in her palms.

Bram flicked on the radio. An oldies station apparently. The song had been popular when they were kids. "Don't Let the Sun Go Down on Me." He switched it off quickly.

"That will be $17.65." A whisper of bills, a clink of coins, and the attendant said, "Thank you, sir. Have a good evening."

Day almost giggled into her cupped hands. The truck pulled back onto the road. A breeze was tugging at the tarp now. Day pillowed her head on her arms. *You are pitiful,* she told herself. *The real reason you crawled all the way up here was just to be as close to the guy as you could be. Admit it. A guy, moreover, who made no bones about wanting to leave you behind.*

# CHAPTER 12

■ ■ ■

*Turn not thy scorns this way, Plantagenet...*
*I'll turn my part thereof into thy throat.*

*Yes,* Day thought, huddled miserably in the back of the truck like cargo. *Even if he dies, Bram will have the last laugh. I can scorn his easy affluence, but deep down, my real complaint is that one of the chattels he acquired so easily was me. And I thought I was so much smarter than the others.*

Her initial, adrenaline-spurred burst of energy had faded. The lassitude that was one of the aftereffects of the drug began to creep over her again. The thrum of the wheels was lulling, and even the stiffness of her bed couldn't keep her eyes open.

A sudden crash awakened her. Like a confused animal, she kept very still while she tried to remember where she was. Facedown in darkness under a claustrophobically close roof.

Thunder grumbled away in the distance, so perhaps it had been the initial clap that she had heard. Then she felt the hardness of the grain under her breast, and a beam that was not lightning played over her from behind. The crash must have been the tailgate going down. Bram was going to be really annoyed with her.

But the voice that spoke was not Bram's. It was the same

squeakily anonymous one she had heard over the phone one day. "So this is where you hid her body," it said. "I wondered about that. Though how you managed the voice on the phone to Newpax…You should have been smart enough to get rid of her by now."

Horrified, Day realized the speaker thought she was dead. Thus, it could only be the person who had put the plastic bag over her head the night before. She continued to lie as flaccidly as possible though some kind of small bug was creeping up one of her legs. Her arms, still folded under her head, felt numb. A gust of wind flattened her shirt against her back.

There had been no response to the voice's comments. But she heard muffled grunts and groans, as if the person was now trying to lift some heavy weight. Dear God, Bram! A final heave, and something heavy rolled into the truck bed. The tailgate slammed to again, and the darkness was back.

Then the truck started and began to back up. Again Day waited for it to creep forward before she moved. She started up to her hands and knees, but the tarp pressed down tautly over her head and shoulders. Dropping to her stomach again, she writhed her way around so that she faced in the opposite direction. Then she elbowed on half-numb arms toward the back of the truck. She was half panting, half sobbing when she came up against the body crumpled there and patted at it frantically.

It was a big man with hair on his arms and…her hand groped upward…burn scars on his face. She fumbled agitatedly for the base of his throat. For an instant all she could feel was the tingle of life returning to her fingers, but then a heavier throb that was outside them.

"Thank you!" she gasped, slumping against his chest. "Oh, thank you!"

The truck stopped, started, stopped. The driver seemed to be trying to angle it into some kind of half-turn. *I must be ready.* Day crawled over Bram's limp body until she was right up against the tailgate. Then she lay down with her head and shoulders across his legs, her hips right up against the gate, and her legs curled back against her chest. Pure rage coursed through her with the heightened pumping of blood through her veins.

The truck wasn't moving now, though it was still running. She could feel the vibrations in her back. Footsteps clicked on blacktop, coming closer…The tailgate crashed down again, simultaneous with a roar of thunder, and Day's feet lashed out, catching the dark shape looming over her in the chest.

That shape stumbled backward and half fell. All smaller noises were lost in the thunder.

Day sat on the gate now, waiting, her feet still poised and ready, straining her eyes for any trace of movement. As the roar died down to a mutter, she heard the patter of running feet going away from her.

Only then did she scramble down off the gate, slam it shut again, and hurtle to the cab of the truck. Once inside, the first thing she did was to stab at the automatic lock, its click a jolt of relief. The headlights were pointed out over a deep darkness. Beyond and below it was a gleam of water. She realized where she was—at the same point above the lake from which Kurt's car had plunged back in the seventies. *Someone,* she thought savagely, *has a very sick sense of humor.*

She eased the truck into reverse. She must be very careful not to back too far—or she could end up in the ditch behind her. But, if she didn't back far enough, she could complete the intended accident. At the same time, she must hurry. Otherwise, the killer might scramble into the truck bed.

*Don't think about it. Just do it.* She thrust down on the gas, and the wheels spun. She yanked the four-wheel-drive lever, and the vehicle lurched backward. The front tires bumped up over the edge of the blacktop and, an instant later, the back tires dropped down off the blacktop on the other side. Day slammed on the brakes, twisted the wheel, and stomped on the gas.

The truck shrieked forward, burning rubber. For a heart-stopping instant, one of the front tires again dipped off the asphalt. But then the vehicle slued back like a horse on a tight rein to catch the road solidly underfoot, and she was off. She threw a quick glance at the rearview mirror as lightning blossomed like a flashbulb and died as quickly. She thought she saw a ghostly figure standing in the roadway, staring after her. But she couldn't be sure.

At the hospital, a couple of interns were watching the storm through the all-glass doors of the emergency bay when she squealed the truck in from the street—horn blaring. They grabbed a gurney, ducked their heads, and dove out into the downpour.

"He's in the back!" she yelled at them, jumping down from the driver's seat to dart around to the tailgate.

The interns exchanged a disbelieving glance but followed. Catching a glimpse of Bram's scarred face, one of them made a stifled exclamation.

"Isn't this—" the other began sharply, looking at Day.

"Bram Falco," she finished.

"What happened to him this time?"

"I don't know. I think somebody must have hit him with something."

■ ■ ■

Regan was with Chief Newpax when he took the call. "Come on!" he said to her, slamming down the receiver and heading at a trot for the door of the police station. "Somebody's made another try at Bram. Day's rushed him to the hospital. But if we make it out to his place in time, we might find out who."

"I didn't even know they were back," Regan wailed, following the chief out into the rain and diving into the front seat of a cruiser beside him.

"Neither did I," Newpax snapped, squinting against a veil of water as the wipers whapped frantically and the car crept out onto the road. "Seems Bram had intended to leave Day at the cottage, but somehow she stowed away in the back of his truck. Claims she fell asleep and only came around when somebody was heaving his unconscious body in with her. So she can't say where he was waylaid. This joker apparently had the cute idea of sending them down the same slope that killed Kurt and Sunny. Assuming that Day's telling us the truth, of course. It's quite a story. Concludes with her kicking the killer into retreat and stealing the truck back. Says she got mad."

"I wouldn't want Day mad at me," Regan commented.

"Neither would I. That's been my point all along."

Having almost missed his turnoff, Newpax jammed on the brakes, and the cruiser spun in a violent arc on the wet pavement, ending up facing the way they had come. Regan had made no sound during the slide, simply reaching out convulsively to place a steadying hand on the dash.

Casting her a sardonic glance, Newpax said, "Wouldn't want to go up against you either, if it comes to that. I don't think we're going to make it in time." He eased the car around again and proceeded more slowly. "So there's no point in killing ourselves trying. Presuming our murderer ambushed Bram at his place, an extra car should be parked around there somewhere. But it isn't that far to the lake from the Falco house, especially cutting cross-country. And this guy or gal would have a pretty big incentive to hoof it fast. Of course, in this mess…"

"Couldn't Day tell who it was?"

"Nope. It was dark, and she was concentrating on survival. She would say a guy if she had to guess—not much give in the chest—but she wouldn't want to swear to it. Uh-oh, what's this?"

"Somebody coming," Regan answered automatically, leaning close to the windshield to squint at the watery lights advancing toward them.

"Yup. And nobody's going to be out in this unless they have urgent business, if you catch my drift."

Then it was as if those lights, like eyes, had spotted the oncoming car. The gleaming orbs slowed, stopped, began to angle away as the driver began a U-turn.

"He's going to run," Newpax said, pumping his brakes. "Listen, Regan, we're right in front of Day's place. I want you to go call everybody. Find where all your rosy friends are right now. Okay? Go!"

She jumped out into the downpour, slammed the door, and watched the cruiser shoot away after the receding red flick of taillights. Her hair was hanging in soaking strings by the time she turned the key in the door at Day's cottage. The rain had dropped the temperature in minutes, and she was trembling as she switched on the light. She hoped the car Newpax was chasing was really the killer and not someone whose inspection sticker had run out or something.

The little house seemed quiet except for the drumming of rain on its roof. Regan hurried across to the wall-mounted phone, wiped her wet face with a wet sleeve, and consulted a list of numbers that was tacked up beside the phone. She dialed Millie's first.

After four rings, the answering machine came on. "Sorry, I'm out. Leave a message…"

"This is Regan. I'm at Day's. Call me as soon as you come in, please."

Regan cut the connection, tried Tom Raines's number. Again, unanswered rings, a click, Tom's recorded voice, "Either we're not here, or we don't feel like answering the phone at the moment. Better luck next time."

"Tom!" she said urgently. "Inez! It's Regan. Please pick up if you're there. This is important!" Nothing. She left her message again.

There wasn't even a recording at Gavin's apartment. Listening to the phone shrill unanswered, Regan began to feel very alone. Finally she gave up and dialed the last number—Paul's.

A board creaked somewhere in the house, and she turned quickly to put her back to the wall, crossing her free arm tightly over her chest.

"Hello?"

"Martha, this is Regan Culver. Is your husband there?"

"Nope. He stayed on to work at the college this evening. Said he might attend some play the community theater was putting on there tonight. He will probably be home soon. Want him to call you?"

"Yes, please. I'm at Day's place. He probably has the number."

"Oh, so she's back?"

"Not exactly. She's at the hospital. I mean, she took Bram to the hospital."

"Uh-oh. Somebody had another whack at him?"

"Yes, but he's going to be all right. Just have Paul call. Thanks." Springs squeaked in the living room. "Martha, don't hang up! I think somebody is here."

"Okay. Don't panic. Yell out a name as soon as you see who it is, and if this person has any brains, he won't try anything after that. This is a portable, and I have another phone line in the shop. I'll just trot out there in case I need to call the cops."

Regan's gaze fixed on the doorway to the living room. "Who's there?" she demanded, raising her voice in an attempt to cover any faltering. Somewhere water was dripping at an even pace like a metronome that couldn't keep up with the rapid beating of her heart.

Someone, she was quite sure, had been sitting in the dark, waiting for Day to come home. Because that someone couldn't afford to leave a witness alive?

Then a young face materialized out of the darkness. Joan. "It's just me, Ms. Culver. I thought maybe I should wait until you came back. In case anybody called about animals needing help. I was taking a nap on the couch. It was still light out when I went to sleep." She glanced at the clock. "Oh, man! My mom is going to be nuts."

"It's all right," Regan said to Martha. "It's just one of Day's teenage volunteers. I'm sorry for making such a fuss."

"No problem," Martha said. "Injected a little drama into my dull evening anyhow. Under the circumstances, I think you had better be a bit jumpy. See you."

"Right. Hold on, Joan!" Regan called as she hung up. "You can't ride your bike home in this weather. I'll take you in the Rover."

The teenager was standing in the open doorway, viewing the drenched and still-dripping night with surprise. "Wow!" she said. "There must have been quite a storm, and I slept right through it."

"Yes," Regan agreed. And thinking about what Day had almost slept through, "I don't think any of us had better be here alone after dark anymore. Somebody's out to get Day, and it isn't safe. I'd better go back to the bed-and-breakfast myself."

Only after she was partway to Joan's did Regan remember she had told people to call her back. Well, with any luck, Day's answering machine would record the time they called. Or with better luck, Newpax had already caught the fugitive.

That wasn't to be, however. Regan phoned the station after reaching the bed-and-breakfast, only to find the chief was back—damp and disgusted. Somewhere along the curvy road, he had been given the slip. Newpax figured the suspect had pulled into one of several gas-well lanes, quickly doused his or her headlights, and waited until the police cruiser had passed before heading back the other way. "Did any cars go by Day's place while you were phoning?" he asked.

"I'm sorry. I wasn't paying any attention. Nobody answered my calls, by the way, except Paul's wife."

"Figures. I tried after I got back with the same results. Martha Sedgwick said you had a little scare."

Regan flushed. "I wasn't going to mention that."

"I shouldn't have left you there by yourself. The killer might have made a stop on his return trip. If I were this person, I would be a little nervous about whether or not Day had recognized me. I've made arrangements for her to stay with my sister, who lives not far from the hospital. And I've put a guard on Bram's room. If you have any bright ideas about who this joker is, don't hold out on me."

"I'm not, believe me! I think I'm going to sit up and try to piece things together. I won't be able to sleep tonight anyway."

"You might as well come down here to do it then. I'll send a car for you. We'll go over the whole thing from the beginning. Maybe it will get your boyfriend off my back. You can hardly be safer than in a police station. Can't you at least give him a call to reassure him?"

"No," Regan responded tartly. "He would demand to know everything that has happened, and then he would insist I abandon the whole mess and go home. The last I knew, he wasn't my boyfriend anyway. So I don't see that he has any say in the matter."

After changing her damp clothes, she went downstairs to find the inn's host locking up for the night. "Oh, I'm sorry," she told him. "I have to go out again. There's a police officer coming to pick me up."

At his alarmed glance, she added quickly, "It's nothing really. I'm just helping them with their investigations." She remembered too late that an old euphemism used to indicate a suspect was the cryptic comment that he or she was "helping the police with their investigations." The host didn't appear reassured, but he reluctantly produced a key for her.

At the station she found that a couple of officers, who had been sent to check on the suspects, had returned. Nobody, as it turned out, had much of an alibi. Millie had gone shopping and to a movie—alone. Tom supposedly had been working late at the office of Relic Roses while his wife had retired to bed with a book and declined to answer the phone. The officers opined that the couple had been arguing before going their separate ways. Paul had also worked late at his college office and attended a play afterward. He had sat in the back, however, and had spoken to no one, so he doubted his presence there could be verified. None of them had an alibi, not even Day, who might very well have hit Bram herself and made up the rest of the story about the incident.

"Of course, in that case it isn't likely she would have rushed him to the hospital," Newpax conceded grudgingly. "Though I can see her braining him. At times I would have liked to hit the guy with something myself."

They were all seated around a table—the chief, Regan, and the two officers who had offered to stay after their shift to help with the brainstorming. Regan had made notes after many of her interviews and was going over them while the chief reviewed reports from his men.

"There are a few small things," Regan said. "One of these people knew Bram's age at the time he was adopted. I found that peculiar, since, as Hilda pointed out, very few people even knew he was adopted at all. This is also the person whom I consider to have had the best chance to do the shooting."

The policemen exchanged glances.

"I think we all know who you're talking about," Newpax said. "But why the so obviously planted gun? That wasn't a bright move on the killer's part. If it had been left by the body, I probably would have arrested Day right off. But she isn't stupid enough to just toss the thing beside her car."

"It wasn't meant to be so obvious a plant." Regan flushed. "That's one thing I haven't told you. I didn't want to get Joan in trouble."

When she had finished her explanation, Newpax turned

his thoughtful gaze on one of his officers. "I had my men search you people's cars soon after the body was discovered. So this gun was lying on the ground beside the station wagon the whole time?"

"It was lying in a clump of grass," Regan put in quickly. "Hard to see until the sun caught it just right."

"I suppose I'm lucky the officer didn't trip over it and hurt himself," the chief said ironically. "Okay, let's say we're agreed on a suspect for the moment. So far as proof goes, we have *nada*."

"We need to find some," Regan said.

At eleven o'clock the next morning, Regan was still at the police station. She and the men had spent most of the night discussing the whys and wherefores. It was like, the chief had pointed out disgustedly, trying to put together a jigsaw puzzle for which half the pieces were missing. Even when they were finished, the picture wasn't complete.

"That's what happens when a story is spread out over decades," Regan had concluded wearily. "Bits of it get lost along the way."

There had been enough, though, to point them in a certain direction. They had made a list of subjects requiring further investigation. Newpax had then called in all his officers, on-duty and off, so enough personnel would be on hand to take routine calls while others pursued the leads. One excited young officer had even been sent to catch a flight to Mexico, though the chief had grumbled about the expense.

Regan sat quietly apart in an interrogation room, reading the rest of Hilda's journals while phones rang and men came and went.

Once Newpax burst in on her. "That idiot has come around and is checking himself out of the hospital!"

"Is Day with him?"

"Where else?" The chief paced moodily around the room. "It would take a whole squad of men to guard that place of his, and I don't have them to spare right now."

"Maybe," Regan suggested quietly, laying her book aside, "you shouldn't have an obvious guard."

"I doubt the killer is stupid enough to be lured in that way. On the other hand, if I were this creep, I would be getting edgy about now. I guess I'll have to go myself. I'm the only one who's free at the moment. You stay, hear?"

# CHAPTER 13

*How I am braved and must perforce endure it!*

"Cops will be hanging around here somewhere," Bram told Day. "The killer knows that, and he knows he would have been arrested by now if you had been able to identify him. I'm betting he will lay off for a while. Still, I don't want you out of my sight."

"That's new," Day said. "Yesterday you wanted me as far away as possible."

"Well, if you won't stay away, you had better stay close. Not that I have anything to protect you with, seeing as *some-body* removed everything that could possibly be construed as a weapon from this house days ago. What did you do with Kurt's gun?"

"It was at my place," Day said. "Oh no!"

"Oh yes. The killer was in your place a short time ago, if you'll recall. He probably jumped on it with cries of glee. On the other hand, a revolver isn't a distance gun. To use it, he will have to get pretty close. That's an advantage for us."

That afternoon Bram decided to teach the filly to lead. With Day perched on the rails of the riding ring and eyeing the surrounding hills nervously, he coaxed the young horse into the enclosure with a bucket of oats. Once he had clipped a line to her halter, however, she turned recalcitrant. And his fingers didn't close as securely over the rope as they should.

For the third time, she lunged past him, ripping the lead out of his hands, and dashed to the far end of the ring, where, Bram saw, Tom Raines was now standing outside the rails on which Day sat. Day leaned to grab the rope dangling from the horse's halter. But the movement was purely mechanical. She looked dazed.

"What's the matter?" Bram asked sharply, rubbing his stinging palms against his jeans and berating himself for not keeping a better eye on things.

"Tom has something to tell you." Day's tone was also blank, and Bram started cautiously toward the two, keeping an eye on Raines's hands.

"I thought she would be happy," Tom said, sagging against the fence. He looked the worse for wear. An angry-looking red scrape marred one side of his face, and his glasses were out of whack. "I've found the source of that pollution in the river, and it looks like we owe you an apology."

"Looks like the source smacked you around a little bit," Bram commented suspiciously, wondering if the other man could have tangled with one of the police guards.

"You could say that. I was out hiking this afternoon, and I thought I saw a pet rabbit, a white one, on the loose. I lunged after it up a brushy slope and literally tumbled into a hole. Fell smack into the stream in a cavern below. Any comments about Alice in Wonderland will not be appreciated. I didn't break anything, and no rabbits were down there, white or otherwise. But I did see a slew of rusty barrels lying in the water. They had been there for some time. They were also leaking. Of course, I can't be positive until somebody has verified what's in them, but the stuff didn't look very healthy. And that stream flows into the river. Seems to me, the guy who used to own that land also owned a factory in the next town. It must have made a very convenient landfill for him. He's dead now, though, and some tourists from Pittsburgh own the place. I doubt they even know the cave is there. So…" Tom looked speculatively from Bram to Day and back again. "This cave is downstream from your factory though. It is something of a puzzle how the sample Day took was polluted."

"Isn't it?" Bram agreed.

Day unclipped the rope from the filly's halter and hung it over the fence. Then she climbed down and turned away, all of her movements still stiff and slow. When she reached the stable door, she slipped inside, as if seeking relief from their stares.

"Is she going to be all right?" Tom asked.

"She will be fine," Bram said. "Why don't you go call the EPA? No, on second thought, I'd better do it myself. I may have to pull some strings. If worse comes to worst, I'll pay to have the mess cleaned up. The sooner we get this behind us the better."

"Good," Tom said, eyeing him almost belligerently. "Well, I found out that Inez was right too. My father is alive. We were over at my mother's for lunch today. Inez went upstairs, purportedly to use the rest room, but she poked around and found a bunch of unopened letters addressed to me back in the seventies. From my father, of course. I don't know why my mother kept them except that she keeps everything. Inez made quite a scene. She and my mother were screaming at each other."

Bram grinned. "I imagine your wife can hold her own."

"Especially since half of what she was screaming was in Spanish. Mother couldn't understand it, but she knew it was bad. Finally I just had to hustle Inez out of there. After I got her home, I went for a long walk. And that's how I happened to stumble on the cave. I suppose somebody meant me to find it. But I would think he could manage that without literally pulling the ground out from under my feet."

"Sometimes that's what it takes." Bram climbed the rails and jumped down on the other side. "So we Falcos didn't pollute your river, and we didn't kill your father. You're going to have to find yourself another scapegoat, Raines."

"I'm really going to miss hating you," Tom said, pushing away from the fence and hobbling toward his car.

"And I think somebody ought to tell you that your wife isn't happy."

Raines froze in place without looking around. "She wants an annulment?"

"No. Rather the opposite. She wants a real marriage. Maybe it's time to stop looking at what you don't have and start paying more attention to what you do."

■　■　■

Leaving her Rover idling in the drive, Regan hurried up the walk to Relic Roses. She had only one question to ask Inez, but it was an important one. And nobody had answered the phone at the Raines's house or office. That was peculiar on a weekday, so Regan had driven out to see if anything was wrong.

Inez sat at a desk, writing furiously in longhand. Her eyes were red rimmed, but whatever she was writing seemed to be giving her a certain morose satisfaction.

"Good afternoon," she greeted Regan. "I am quitting."

"Quitting what?" Regan asked, startled. "Your job?"

"Everything," Inez replied shortly. "I proved to Tom that I was right. I found letters his father had sent years ago, hidden by his mother. But was he happy?"

"I would guess no."

"You are right. He allowed his mother to scream at me, and he dragged me out by the arm as if I were a bad child. Then he left me here and drove away. He said he was going hiking. Maybe I would like to go hiking too, but does he ask me? No! I get to stay here and watch the office. Do you want something?"

The phone rang.

"Don't you need to answer that?" Regan said.

"What have I just told you? I don't work here anymore."

"Well, it would have been a little more convenient if you had answered my call earlier," Regan said impatiently. "You never knew your aunt, I realize, but I was wondering if you just might be able to tell me what color her eyes were."

"Blue," Inez responded promptly. "High-class Mexican women are always proud of a baby with blonde hair and blue eyes. It is too bad that I was not light-haired," she added spitefully. "Perhaps Tom would like me better then."

"I like you fine the way you are," a voice from the doorway said. With his glasses askew and his face bruised, Tom looked more than ever like an awkward teenager.

Inez's eyes narrowed. She jumped to her feet. "You have a fine way of showing it! Where have you been?"

"Wonderland," Tom said.

Something in the way he was watching his wife made Regan smile to herself and begin edging toward the door. "Thanks, Inez. I hope you change your mind about resigning."

"Resigning?" Tom said sharply.

"Yes," Inez declaimed grandiloquently. "I quit!" She snatched up the scrawled pages, waved them at him by way of illustration, then threw them down so hard that they scattered over the desktop and onto the floor. "The job, the marriage, everything! For three years, you have growled at me and stomped on my affections. And now you give me a wedding that isn't a wedding after all."

"I didn't know you had any affections for me," Tom said.

"Oh no?" Inez said with exquisite sarcasm, leaning forward across the desk, hands pinning down the mussed sheets on the desktop. "Do you think I enjoy pain? Do you think I am a ma—, ma—" She snapped her fingers at Regan.

"Masochist," Regan supplied hurriedly.

"Thank you." Inez turned her hauteur back on Tom. "Do you think I am what she said? That I would put up with all of this otherwise? I am a beautiful girl from a high-class family. I can do much better than a dreamer who does not see me. Yes?" She appealed to Regan again.

"Absolutely," Regan agreed, having reached the door.

"And what," Inez exclaimed, finally seeing his scratches, "were you doing in Wonderland? Wrestling with the smiling cat?"

She circled the desk to rush across to him, wringing her hands. "Your glasses are broken. Your face…"

She stopped abruptly, perhaps finally noticing what Regan had recognized in his eyes. "Tommy…"

"I've always seen you, Inez," he said, reaching to cup her face in his abraded hands. "Much too well, in fact. Even in my dreams. But I've seen the way other men look at you too. Richer men, younger men, nicer men. Men who can give you much more than I can."

Tears welled in her eyes. "But I don't want a rich man or a young man or a nice man. I want you to love me furiously."

"Now that," he said, "I can do." And he kissed her so hard that his glasses went even more awry, but neither of them seemed to notice.

Slipping away down the walk, Regan doubted that either of them would notice her exit either.

■ ■ ■

After Tom had gone, Bram went into the stable, looking for Day. She was sitting on a bale.

"You were right," she said dully, as he stood looking down at her. "I planted the arsenic. I'm sorry."

"Of course you did," he responded impatiently. "That's what I've been telling everybody all along, remember? Move over."

Dropping onto the bale beside her, he added, "Though none of them believed me. Why did you do it?"

She shook her head helplessly. "I was just so tired," she whispered. "The ducks kept dying, and nobody would listen, least of all you. And all those years I'd had to scrape and scrounge and make do. I thought, like Millie said, that your family had taken everything from me. It just wasn't fair. I convinced myself that all I was doing was providing evidence of what was really true, that the end justified the means. Then, after I'd done it, I was horrified at myself. I knew your killing the animals was partly my fault. They died because of my sin. I was terrified where it would end. Everybody thought you might commit suicide. I'd never meant things to go that far. I never even thought that you would lose the election over it. Everything just got so out of hand."

She was weeping silently. "Then, when Regan started talking about Christian charity, it seemed like a good excuse. I couldn't tell people why I was really helping you. You were right about that too. It was penance. The only scrap of justification I had to cling to was my confidence that your factory was doing the polluting. And now it turns out I was even wrong about that. I'm a horrible person!"

He put his arm around her. "Well, that's what Regan has been trying to point out to us all along, isn't it? We are all horrible people."

Day's sobs intensified. "Wait until she finds out how I've deceived her!"

"I wouldn't be surprised if she knows."

Day stopped crying to peer up at him. "I thought you were going to be furious."

"Been there. Done that. Besides, compared to me, you are only a minorly horrible person. And, like most women, once you get going, you tend to take personal responsibility for every bad thing that has happened back to the day of your birth. If I killed those animals, it was my choice and I have to take the blame for it. Even if I had killed myself, that would have been my choice too, not something that was forced on me. You're the one who told me there was always a choice, remember?"

"'For love or against it,' Regan said." Day mopped at her tears with the back of her hand. "'For God or against him.'"

"See? You heard her, but you didn't hear her. The poor woman must get very frustrated. Are we done now so I can go back to breaking my horse?"

"Yes." Day stood resolutely. "I'm going to call the newspapers."

"Hey!" He grabbed her arm and pulled her back down again. "Your sin was against me, and I have forgiven you. Once people hear about this cave, I'll be exonerated anyhow.

You didn't require my public humiliation, and I'm not going to require yours. Besides, people might stop bringing you animals, and why should the animals have to pay again?"

When she continued to stare at him with that utterly desolate expression, he shook her gently. "I know it's much harder to forgive yourself, but that's necessary too." He picked up one of her clenched hands and pried open the fingers. "There, you're letting it go. Now," he raised the hand, "you're waving bye-bye. See, it's history."

She managed a watery giggle. "All right. I'll help you train the filly. I have an idea you could try."

"Okay," he agreed, rising to lead the way out of the stable. Anything to distract her. "What is it?"

"Something I read. You get a long line, stand in the middle of the ring, and toss the line at the horse to keep her loping around you. You keep turning so that you are always facing her full on. Eventually, she's supposed to incline her head toward you, then make a chewing motion. When she lowers her head, you stop and turn your shoulder toward her, averting your eyes."

Increasingly skeptical, Bram said, "And where does that get you?"

She smiled mysteriously as they came up to the riding ring. "Wait and see." Light from the low sun shone full in her face, revealing the tracks of her tears. Droplets still glittered in her lashes.

"Whatever." He took the rope down from the fence, and opened the gate, closing it quietly after himself. The filly snorted and stayed where she was, at the far side of the ring.

As he started toward her, she paced nervously along the fence. Stopping in the center of the ring, he flung the end of the line. She picked up her pace at once, and he turned to follow her with his eyes and the rope. It seemed almost to be the stare as much as the rope that kept her moving. She tossed her head worriedly.

In a way, he thought, this animal acted much as he had done for years. Trapped in his own deception. Constantly pacing the limits of that trap with his fascinated eyes fixed on the goader at the center, the conscience that never let him rest in that deception. *God is the enemy,* he had told Day. And she had said, *Are you sure?*

The still air smelled of warm wood, dust, and the sweating horse. Scents were no longer overpowering. The powder stirred up by the horse's movement drifted down through the long rays of the sun like gold dust. Day watched quietly from outside the fence.

He was, he realized, hopeful for the first time in years. He didn't know how long the filly had been bobbing her head before he really noticed it. Then she dropped her head lower and began to chew.

Remembering Day's instructions, he let the rope lie still and turned so that his shoulder was toward the horse. From the corner of his eye, he saw her raise her head and look across at him with pathetic eagerness.

Feeling rather foolish, he waited. He was facing Day now, but a bar of the fence shadowed her expression.

He could hear the filly blowing softly. Dust gritted under her hooves as she took a tentative step toward him. Although nothing bound her, nothing pulled, he could feel a palpable something stretched tight as a rope between them. Her next step was more confident. Then her pace quickened. As she came up behind him she was almost prancing, lighthearted.

Her breath mixed for an instant with the warmth of the sun on his nape. Then, as he still did not turn, she nudged his shoulder in a friendly way with her nose.

Tears sprang to Bram's eyes. He felt as if something in him had cracked and melted. No, God hadn't goaded to torment but to tame. A man, like a horse, was no good to anybody until he was broken.

Bram pivoted slowly, reached up to rub the horse's neck, to clip the line onto her halter. This time when he stepped out, she followed easily, happily.

A patter of applause came from Day. She was standing halfway up the rails, beaming. "It worked!"

Bram shook his head dazedly. "What was that?"

"Well, the guy who wrote the book said a wild horse receives those signals after she has been chased out of the herd for some infraction and is being permitted to return. The lead mare holds the offending one off with the stare for a while, but when she turns away, that means all is forgiven. I think it might have something to do with trust, myself. You show her that you trust her by turning your back, so she trusts you."

Perching on the top rail, Day reached down to rub the filly's forehead. "And I've heard it said that the natural animal is a tame animal. That they were all tame at one time. Maybe they feel some need to get back to that. Just as," she added ruefully, meeting his gaze, "the natural man was a tame one. Ever since he revolted, he has known he was missing something."

Bram unclipped the rope and tossed it over the fence again. Then he climbed the rails beside her and dropped down the other side. "Come on," he said roughly. "I have something to tell you."

She didn't ask questions but followed him back to the stable and seated herself on the bale again.

He thought it would be easier if he didn't have to look at her face, so he dropped down on the floor with his back against the straw.

"To start it off short and sweet," he said, "I was not Royce Falco's natural son. He thought I was, but I wasn't."

She didn't make a sound, but far up in the rafters, the hawk stirred uneasily.

"I was what I told you, the son of a prostitute. My name was Pablo. I was expected to shift for myself, and I did. By the time I was six or so, I was the leader of a little band of street kids. We would steal food from the stalls in the marketplace or beg from the tourists or even run errands for change. Mirlo Santos didn't have our street smarts. He was lucky that we found him and let him join up. Most of the guys didn't like him much because he always was bragging about his mother's rich family. Mirlo was terrified of his convict uncle though. Afraid that, when Javier was released from prison, he would come looking for his nephew and force that nephew to join his band of rebels. And Mirlo was a smart kid. He had a pretty good idea what would probably happen to those rebels, and he wanted none of it."

Bram stared at the floor as he talked. "Still, he was something of a weakling. If Javier had shown up, Mirlo would have gone along meekly. He harped on the subject so much that I finally said, jokingly, that I could change names with him. Then the uncle would get me instead. I wouldn't have minded being a rebel myself. And Javier had never seen the kid. I was surprised when Mirlo took me seriously and pestered me about it until I finally agreed. I had never particularly cared for the name Pablo, anyhow, and Mirlo fit me better than it did him. The other guys thought it was a good joke and went along. Nobody else knew us well enough to call us anything but 'You, boy' or worse."

Bram stopped for a moment to gaze blindly at the sunny world outside the open door. "Eventually Father Tino took us in. He never knew me as anything but Mirlo. A friend named Diego and I happened to be hanging around a certain café on the day Royce Falco came to town. We liked to attach ourselves to Americans because they tended to have money and soft hearts. We overheard the conversation between Royce and Hilda when he told her about Mirlo Santos being his natural son. Diego and I looked at each other. He was laughing, and I think we both knew at that moment what I was going to do. The only thing Diego said as we started back for the rectory was, 'He's the one who insisted you take his name.'"

Bram rubbed the back of his neck and continued, "I think you've already heard most of the rest of it. The real Mirlo was the lighter-skinned boy Connie was interested in. That was the irony. Poor Diego could hardly contain himself. It was really the sort of thing I'd been doing all my life—pushing my luck. I'd done it so often, in fact, that I had very little fear left. The only thing that could really scare me was the thought of having to live my whole life as a beggar."

He stopped again and, after a moment, Day said softly, "That isn't all, is it?"

"No. I wish it were. I can't say I felt any compunction at the time. Kids are pretty selfish creatures, you know. So I came to the States as Bram Falco. I found, though, that my secret created an invisible barrier between my family and me. I never had the courage to tell Royce the truth. I was afraid of how he might react. Royce was very big on fairness and justice and doing the right thing. He tried to bring me up that way, and I did my best, considering I'd always been a rebel at heart. And Kurt was great. He accepted me from the start. He was a smart kid, and I think he had some idea I might be his real half brother. I did feel a little guilty about that. Connie had no suspicion I was anything but a street kid. And, strangely enough, she was the one who was right. If I got out of hand, she would remind me of my humble beginnings and of what I owed them."

Hearing Day suck in her breath with disapproval, he added quickly, "Hey, that didn't bother me. She was right, after all. Besides, as a young thief, I had been used to having much worse hurled at my fleeing back. I knew my parents' marriage wasn't all that good, but I also knew the kind of guy Royce was, and I thought he would stick to it. I had expected to despise Royce for a fool. It's quite common for rich men in Mexico to have mistresses, but most don't feel guilty about it. As it happened, though, I came to admire him for his discipline and high standards. I don't think he ever had another liaison. He was a deeply unhappy man, though, and I did my best not to add to that unhappiness. I was in clover myself. I never had to worry about where my food or clothes would come from, and I had more than any kid could need of toys and horses. Kurt's having to go to war did put a bit of a damper on things, but he came back safely. He was a bit different there for a few months, quiet and depressed, but then he met Sunny, and things started to look up. I felt good at the party that night. Kurt was himself again, and I was positive Royce was going to win the election and maybe that would make him happy."

He paused in silent acknowledgment of how wrong he had been, and Day put a hand on his shoulder. "I didn't really lie when I said I couldn't remember the accident," he went on. "I did remember following Kurt and Sunny up the steep path toward the parking lot. She was distraught by that time, mumbling incomprehensibly and trying to tear away from him. He was a strong guy, but she almost pulled him over the edge at one point. That was when he snapped at me to take her other arm. I asked what was wrong with her, and he said, 'Some kind of drug. LSD, I expect.' I suppose he had seen it in the army."

Bram studied his hands unseeingly as he continued, "I didn't ask any more questions. I knew it wasn't in character for her, but it seemed that nobody was quite in character that night. And I felt this sort of uneasy crawling on my skin like somebody was watching us. Next thing I knew, I was waking up in a hospital. And after one look at my father's face, I knew something terrible had happened. After he told me, I remember thinking, 'He's never going to be happy now.' He asked me what I remembered, and only one thing came to me. It was more like a fleeting flash than an actual memory. Mirlo jumping into the middle of the road, staring accusingly into the headlights. I wasn't even sure it was a memory. It could have been just a bad dream or a hallucination that happened when I was unconscious. Besides, I would have had to tell about being an impostor to explain who Mirlo was. And I couldn't do that to my father. I couldn't tell him the only son he had left was a fake. But I realized that, if the vision was what had truly happened, the accident was my fault. A result of my deception. Not of the drug your sister took."

He waited for Day to speak, but she said nothing.

"My father convinced me it was the LSD. Henry already had confessed. And I had seen myself how out of control Sunny was. Also, it seemed impossible that Mirlo could be in Pennsylvania, that another twelve-year-old could have found me. So I agreed to keep Sunny's condition that night a secret.

I think it was for you that my father did it. He described once your opening the door to him that night, unaware of the awful news he was bringing. He couldn't let you find out that the accident was your father's fault. Maybe you'll say it was worse to have your father abandon you for no apparent reason. But Royce thought he was doing the right thing at the time."

Still no sound from her.

"As you know, I lost my sense of smell in the accident, but I gained something else, something I didn't want. Guilt. Not for the accident itself, since I'd convinced myself that what I saw was a hallucination. But guilt over how I'd deceived Kurt, who, as a result, had never known his real brother. And guilt over how I was still deceiving Royce. I was just egotistical enough to convince myself I'd made him a better son than the real Mirlo ever would have, but I also realized that wasn't the point. Maybe I hadn't convinced myself as well as I thought about that hallucination because I've spent most of the rest of my life waiting for Mirlo to come and denounce me. I realized that Diego would have told him what had happened after I was gone. Diego wouldn't have been able to resist telling him."

Still Day said nothing.

"I began to receive the anonymous letters when I was running for election. 'Wouldn't the voters like to know who you really are?' That sort of thing. They weren't specific enough that I could tell for sure…But then, the day after I lost the election, the mysterious writer told me, unambiguously, who he was and that he was coming to demand what rightfully belonged to him."

"But he couldn't do that, could he?" Day asked. "Your father made no stipulation when he adopted you that you had to be his own blood. And once adopted, you were his legal son. Mirlo couldn't demand your inheritance."

"He could make an almighty big stink. I had been afraid he was going to do that during the election."

"But he still hasn't come forward, has he? Might that not prove it isn't really Mirlo at all but someone else trying to extort money from you?"

"Possibly. That's what I meant when I said I couldn't be positive that Anonymous is male. But whoever it is hasn't asked for any specific amount, and I wouldn't have given it if he had. I would rather go down in one big smash than to be bled white over years."

"So that's why you took it so hard," Day said. "It wasn't just the election."

"No. Though that was bad enough. After my father's death, I had pledged myself to carry on his dream of a successful political career. To, in that way, be a real son. To make things up to him. And I failed, only bringing another scandal on his name. Oh, I was angry enough at you, but I also expended on you the rage I felt for the enemy I couldn't see. And I did think it was you who tried to kill me. Mirlo could only lose by my death. If I were dead, my estate would go to my heirs, and he would have a much tougher job of proving his claim. His best bet was to play on my guilt, and I think he realized that."

"If it is him. I still think it's suspicious he hasn't shown himself." And sharply, "Bram, when you said that the name Mirlo or 'blackbird' fit you better, were you implying that he was lighter haired?"

He turned to look up at her. "Yes, Mirlo was blond. Why?"

"Are you sure Gavin is really your cousin? He said he came here looking for you. Had you known him well before that?"

"Hadn't seen him in years. He does have some of the family features though."

"But he would," she insisted. "Don't you see that? If Royce was his father. He claims to be only in his twenties, but he may look younger than he actually is. Would you recognize Mirlo now?"

"It's not likely. Thirty years can make a big difference in appearance. But Gavin knew a lot of our family background."

"It wouldn't be so difficult to find out that stuff, would it? You said yourself that Mirlo was something of a coward. Maybe he thought the safest way to proceed was to make himself your heir."

Bram stared into the shadows, trying to visualize Mirlo's face next to Gavin's. But it had been too long. The face of Mirlo was only an accusing blur. It had a certain perverse logic, though, that the enemy could be invisible by being so close. "I don't know. I really don't know. I wouldn't think that Mirlo would have the gall to do that. Of course, carrying your unconscious body across my garden would take a certain amount of brass."

"But it was in the darkness," Day said. "And he didn't kill me outright but left me to smother to death. He does seem to be more the indirect type. Unlike you. So that's what you meant by being a thief. As usual, you had to do it on a mammoth scale. You didn't steal any one thing from the guy; you stole his whole life. Why didn't you tell this to the police?"

"Like I said, I didn't believe it had anything to do with the attempt to murder me or with Hilda's death. And I didn't want to see it in the papers. I had no wish to give up my fortune. But in the last anonymous letter I received, he made it plain the gasoline was his idea. Couldn't help gloating, I guess. Maybe his hate is stronger than his avarice. But why Hilda?"

"Might she have recognized him?"

"It's unlikely. He was just one kid in a bunch of orphans

that day in Mexico. Maybe Tom was right. If Gavin is the culprit, maybe he just wanted to eliminate my heir. If I had known what I was going to bring on Hilda, Royce, and Kurt, I would have stayed in Mexico."

The shadows had been growing longer on the grass outside. Bram had been staring unseeingly at one that lay just across the doorway. Now that shadow moved, and a man was silhouetted against the rectangle of green. "No, you wouldn't have, Bram," Paul Sedgwick said, stepping inside, looking as sleek and neat as the gun in his hand. "You were born a thief, and you'll die a thief."

# CHAPTER 14

■ ■ ■

*O, pity, pity, gentle heaven, pity!*
*The red rose and the white are on his face,*
*The fatal colors of our striving houses...*

Day stiffened but felt Bram lay a reassuring hand on her ankle. "So it was you, Paul," she said. "You're much more the right age and as blond as Gavin is. I always thought you two looked something alike. I suppose it's the family likeness of the Falcos. So Gavin really is Bram's cousin after all?"

"*My* cousin," Paul corrected her gently. "I'm the real Falco, remember?" Taking in their position, Bram sitting at her feet, he added, "I have to hand it to you, Ms. Day. I never thought Bram would admit all that to anybody. You must really be a tamer after all. But now that he has, he has cost you your life too. Because, of course, you can't be permitted to tell anyone about it. If the police investigate our pasts in depth, they will discover I didn't arrive in Florida until I was twelve."

"So you were on that road the night of my brother's accident," Bram said bleakly, as one who hears a long-dreaded supposition confirmed.

"Oh yes. I was with Javier Santos. He came looking for you once he was released from prison. I didn't tell him I was the real Mirlo because I didn't want to be claimed by a disinherited rebel. I was still with Father Tino then, although the rest of your little gang had moved on. They dumped me soon after you left. I did tell Javier that I was a friend of yours though. He took me along to identify you and Royce Falco, since he had never seen either of you. He wanted to make sure he killed the right man. Of course," Paul added almost as an afterthought, "I had other reasons for going along with his plan. In reality, I was the one using him."

"He didn't have a child with him in Arizona," Day said.

Paul's voice was as mildly reasonable as ever. It was hard to take the gun in his hand seriously. "Oh no. He waited until he was quite sure where Royce was before smuggling me across the border. Quite by luck, he had found a female pen pal in the same town, from whom he picked up some further details. He wasn't planning on staying long enough to get acquainted with poor Millie though. In fact, he dyed his hair so she wouldn't recognize him. He already had a wife back in Mexico. He was just going to kill Royce, kidnap Bram, and hightail it for the border. He was not a very nice man, I'm afraid."

"And he probably would have dumped you as soon as your purpose was served," Bram said.

"I wouldn't be surprised if he meant to kill me," Paul replied. "Like I said, he was not a nice man. He did have a certain quickness of mind, however. After we had stumbled on your beach party, which we did quite by accident, he hit on the idea of passing himself off to Kurt as an old friend of Royce's from Mexico. I decided it might be prudent for me to stay behind, and he didn't have time to argue with me then. I had to do some fast thinking myself. I certainly didn't want him to kill Royce. My plan was, of course, to reveal myself to my father as his true son. Even if my likeness to my mother didn't convince him, I had a couple of her possessions that I was sure would do the trick. So I couldn't let Javier kill the man. Also, I had the foresight to realize Royce might have become fond enough of Bram to forgive him for the deception and allow him to stay on. People do seem to like Bram, though I've never understood why. I would not have been able to tolerate that. But then, I realized, with a shock of inspiration, that a single serious car wreck would remove all obstacles."

Bram's hand tightened on Day's ankle. "My brother and Sunny were simply expendable, I suppose?"

"My brother," Paul corrected him. "Not yours. But he was older and, as such, would be the natural heir. I had not come all that way to be satisfied with being a poor, younger son. Besides, with both of you dead, Royce would be more willing, even eager, to believe my story."

"You're inhuman," Day breathed, feeling a first cold breath of horror on the back of her neck. "Did you really believe he could so easily swap his dead sons for another?"

"As it happened," Paul said, "Bram's cursed luck still held. Someone directed me to the Falco house, but Royce was always at the hospital. So I never had a chance to talk to him." A first hint of peevishness had crept into his tone. "So when I got cold and hungry enough to be desperate, I made the mistake of approaching his wife instead."

Bram laughed. "You idiot! You incredible idiot! Did you really think she would fall on your neck?"

Paul stiffened resentfully. "Nobody told me she didn't know you were supposed to be her husband's son. In Mexico, the wives of rich men take that sort of thing casually. She seemed a quiet and delicate little thing. She listened to my story calmly."

Bram was laughing silently. Day could feel it through his hand. "Dear, dear Connie," he muttered, as if he knew what was coming.

Paul stared at him coldly. "When I was done, she told me to my face I was a liar. But I knew she believed every word I told her."

"Of course she did," Bram agreed. "She was not a stupid woman."

"She said that, even if the story were true, it meant I was a…an illegitimate child, that I had no claim on her husband at all. Then she wanted to know how I had reached Pennsylvania from Mexico."

"I can see you might have trouble answering that one."

"I said I had hitchhiked, which was true enough. Then she leaned forward and looked me in the face and said, 'I think you're somehow connected to the man whose body was in that car, the man who, I am sure, cost my son Kurt his life. Because you are still just a child, I will give you the benefit of the doubt. I will put you on a bus to Florida. Like other aliens, you can get yourself hired as a crop picker. If you ever come back here or try to contact my husband again, I will have you arrested.'"

"You should have expected that," Bram reproved him. "Royce was running for the Senate on the conservative ticket, and she was quite determined he would win. She would not allow a scandal of any kind."

"It wasn't fair," Paul Sedgwick complained. "I was just lucky an older woman was on the bus who felt sorry for me and took me in." He turned to Day. "Don't you agree with me? I was telling the truth. The way Connie Falco treated me was not fair."

"You killed her son," Day said.

"I was just a child. I couldn't stand against someone like that. She intimidated me. She hustled me out of there before I could think of any way to fight back. She kept the proofs that I had brought with me. It wasn't fair."

"You killed her son," Day repeated, raising her voice.

"But she didn't know that," Paul pointed out. "Besides, I had no other choice." He turned the gun toward Bram. "*He* gave me no other choice. Can you imagine how I felt when I found out? That my own father had been stolen from me by this street trash? That's all Bram was back then. I always had known I was destined for better things, that I wasn't really one of them. He was a nobody, just a little punk who was good at bluffing."

"He took you in," Day said. "You might have starved otherwise."

Paul didn't seem to hear her. "It was never fair. He was a nothing, but the other kids respected him. Even Father Tino liked him better, though I was the more obedient student. And Hilda called his insolence charming!" Paul almost spat the words. "He wasn't boring like I apparently was! It was bad enough then, but he can still do it. Even though you've heard all about his crime, you're still defending him!"

"What he did was wrong," Day said. "I agree it was very wrong. But apparently you didn't pay enough attention to Father Tino's teaching. You could have chosen to forgive. You didn't have to kill four people."

Paul looked at her as if she had taken leave of her senses. "Forgive? But he hadn't paid for what he had done."

"And you had to have your pound of flesh, Shylock?" Day asked.

He almost frothed at the mouth. "Don't quote that rubbish at me! All I wanted was justice."

"And you thought disfiguring him was just?"

Paul glanced with some satisfaction at Bram's puckered skin. "I would have accepted it as sufficient punishment. Except it didn't change anything. Everybody was still worrying about him, helping him, defending him. Even you, Ms. Day, for whom it was entirely illogical. I had seen to that."

"Yes. You killed my animals and poisoned my roses, didn't you?"

"Of course. I only moved up here from Florida for one reason. I am a patient man. I waited my chance for years, and the feud between you and Bram played right into my hands. I just exacerbated it a little in hopes you might execute justice for me. But you did nothing."

"I suppose Bram saw the light on in the barn," Day mused, "and being drunk, came down to have things out with me. That's when he saw the dead animals and dropped his ring."

Paul just looked at her blankly and said, "Hilda and Regan suspected that he might kill himself. That was unendurable. He had taken everything that should have been mine, and suddenly he was scorning it? I couldn't let him take the easy way out."

Bram himself had remained silent, offering no defense. He watched Paul alertly, as if waiting for some wavering of attention on the other man's part. It would not work, Day was sure. Seated on the floor as he was, it would take too long for Bram to get up. Unless he was planning some kind of tackle. She could hear the filly pacing uneasily in the riding ring outside, but the hawk above was very quiet.

Day felt a stirring in her hair. She had forgotten the possum again! This time he apparently had been buried deeply enough that neither of the men had spotted him. But Day could almost feel the sharp eyes of the bird above boring down through the shadows. She doubted if Paul was aware of it.

"Don't you have anything to say?" Paul had turned his attention to Bram. Day reached up, as if to scratch her head, and palmed the little creature, dropped her hand casually to the edge of the bale and let him slide away from her down the straw. The trouble was that, when frightened, possums generally curled themselves into a ball and didn't move. And she desperately wanted this one to move. *I'm sorry to have to do this to you, but go, please go!*

She thought Bram had caught her movement out of the corner of his eye because his hand squeezed her ankle briefly.

"What can I say? Day is right. What I did was wrong, and I'm sorry. But no punishment is going to be enough for you, is it? Even though I killed nobody, and your count is already up to four? Frankly, I wouldn't have believed you capable of shooting somebody directly as you did Hilda."

Paul's handsome face turned sulky. "As I told Regan, that shouldn't have happened. I liked Hilda. And I was satisfied with my punishment of you at that point. But over breakfast the morning after your accident, I happened to use a description of you that was almost word for word what was said at the rectory the afternoon you were chosen. I didn't even realize that myself until Hilda confronted me with it. She had looked it up in her diary or something. She insisted I must have been there, as of course I was. Actually, I rather welcomed the opportunity to point out to her that her favorite was a fake. That didn't turn out the way I had planned though. She didn't seem very surprised. She said that, having never seen any resemblance in you to either of your supposed parents, she always had doubts you were Royce's son. And something Regan had just told her about genetics had clinched it. Royce and Calida could not have had a brown-eyed child. But as, it seems, with all other females, it made no difference in her feelings for you. She said that you would remain her heir and that, all in all, she thought they had made the right choice that day at the rectory. It's just like it has always been," Paul concluded almost wearily. "You can do anything you want and get away with it, but she was going to turn me in for trying to kill you."

"So that's what the rose meant," Bram said. "*El Niño*. The child. The original child. I should have got that. Just as when Kurt mentioned a child, he wasn't talking about me, but the one in the road."

"The rose didn't mean anything of the sort," Paul responded impatiently. "I put it in Hilda's hand myself. It was supposed to point to Day here. As to any rational mind it did."

Day felt the possum moving around her feet. It seemed impossible that Paul hadn't seen the animal, but all of the killer's attention was fixed on Bram's face. The animal put its tiny paw on her ankle as if to climb up. She was, after all, the only mother it knew. She moved her foot casually, shaking it off. Having eaten and slept, it seemed willing enough to explore and began to pad slowly forward, stopping frequently to sniff. A rustling noise came from above, and Day coughed loudly to cover it up. The cough turned Paul's attention back to her.

"You have really brought this on yourself, Ms. Day. If you had only reacted like a reasonable person and sought revenge on Bram—or at least stayed away from him—you would have been all right."

"You're just like my father," Day said. "You refuse to take responsibility for anything yourself. Only, in your case, you're quite willing to hold everybody else responsible. You're like your mother too. Everything was done to her. Nothing was her fault."

"You're entitled to let off some steam," Paul said. "Though I think it would be more to the point to direct your anger toward the man beside you."

Though he was still watching Paul, Bram's head was set in a tense, listening attitude. A slight *skirtch, skirtch* came from above, as though the hawk were edging along its perch. Day kept her gaze up from the floor.

"Maybe you're like my father as well," Bram said to Paul. "Too much pride. Royce couldn't forgive himself even when God would have. That implied he was making himself, not God, the judge. Just as you are. Only Royce was judging himself, and you don't seem willing to do that."

Everything depended on whether the hawk was hungry enough to attempt a catch with humans present and whether he still remembered how. He had had his food brought to him, already dead, for weeks.

Paul made no response to Bram's words beyond a tolerant smile. "Well, this chat has been very pleasant, but I really do have to be going. So, if it's to be a murder-suicide, who wants to play the murderer?"

Bram had quietly released his hold on Day's ankle. She knew he would jump soon, whether the hawk came down or not.

Paul seemed to know it too. His face was pale, and sweat stood out on his forehead. "I'm afraid you're going to have to be the triggerman, Ms. Day," he said from between set teeth as he leveled the gun at Bram, "since I have no intention of moving close enough to Falco to make his death look like a plausible suicide."

"Hold it, Sedgwick!" barked a voice.

Hope leaped in Day, but she couldn't see anyone. The voice had seemed to come from one of the box stalls on the side. A long shudder ran through Paul's frame, but he didn't turn or drop the gun. Then something like a huge shadow swooped down from the other shadows above and fell on them. At least, it seemed that it was going to fall on them. Day heard the whoosh of spread wings and ducked automatically. Bram didn't duck at all; he simply threw himself forward toward Paul's feet. At the same time, Paul's head snapped up. He saw a hawk coming full at him, screamed, and jumped backward.

The bird was not, of course, aiming for Paul, but for the possum several feet behind him. Had he remained still, its trajectory would have missed him altogether. As it was, the hawk flapped frantically to gain altitude again. Its talons grazed Paul's head, and then it was up and out the door, the powerful surges of its wings carrying it high into the still sunlit sky.

Newpax burst out of the box stall. The possum stood frozen, face turned upward. Possums were, Day thought dispassionately, not very intelligent creatures. Bram had caught hold of Paul's wrist and was bending it back. Paul seemed to give, to let the barrel of the gun turn back toward his own face. But then his finger moved on the trigger.

Day jerked her head aside at the gun's retort and then walked out of the barn to meet Regan, who was hurrying in. After one glance at the man on the floor, Regan turned back outside too, and stood with Day looking up at the hawk that made ever-widening circles above them.

"When I think how close I came to being like Paul…"

Day said. "I thought it wasn't fair, too, so I cheated in retaliation by planting that arsenic. I suppose you knew that."

"I suspected it. People most often turn to God when they are fed up with themselves."

"I wasn't really turning to God. That started out as a pretense too."

"But did it stay that way?"

Day shook her head slowly. "He kind of…pulls you in, doesn't he?"

"There was a big difference between you and Paul. You felt sorry for what you had done, and he didn't. The only people who can't be forgiven are those who see no need for it."

# CHAPTER 15

■ ■ ■

*And then, as we have ta'en the sacrament,*
*We will unite the white rose and the red:*
*Smile heaven upon this fair conjunction,*
*That long have frown'd upon their enmity!*

The next evening the rose society gathered for a dinner at Bram's house. This time some were missing. Hilda and Paul were dead, and Millie had declined to come.

"I offered to tell her about Francis, but she didn't want to hear it," Regan explained. "She said we would just tell her lies."

"Wouldn't be surprised if she turns strange," Newpax said. "Once you start setting your mind against reality to make up your own version of it, a cog slips. Seen it happen." He and Inez had been invited to fill up some of the empty spaces.

"I think it's just as well that Sedgwick decided to kill himself," the police chief continued. "I know his type, quite common in the criminal element. It would have been a nasty trial. He would have made sure of that. You'll remember, Regan, that I had my eye on him from the start. And, like you, I realized he would have had the best chance of shooting Hilda. He could wear that gun around right under people's noses without anybody being the wiser. That reporter didn't seem to understand that the woman who saw Hilda working at the table after the battle started probably saw the dummy. At that distance, she wouldn't have been able to tell the difference. Of course, Hilda was shot just before the battle. I imagine he used a silencer of some sort. He could have had almost anything in that kit bag of his. It was tempting to assume the shooting must have happened during the battle, but a good cop never assumes anything.

"I'd been hiding in that stable keeping an eye on you two," Newpax concluded peevishly to Day. "So I had him covered the whole time. Your little trick with the hawk wasn't necessary, and it spoiled my clear shot. Frankly, though, I'm glad I didn't have to kill him. How's his wife taking it?"

"I don't think she was all that surprised," Regan said. "Day and I went to see her. She said Paul simply refused to be happy with whatever he had. She hoped he was at peace now, but she doubted it. I told her the whole story. I thought she deserved to know."

"I see you didn't though," Bram said to Newpax. "The newspapers just give the motive as jealousy—of me."

"Well, wasn't it?" Newpax tilted back in his chair. "If ever your right to your fortune was questioned, people would come out of the woodwork looking for their share. Eh, Gavin?"

Gavin looked affronted. "As far as I'm concerned, what belongs to my cousin still belongs to him. He was adopted legally."

"I'm going to turn the factory and the rest of what my father left over to Gavin," Bram said. "Royce bequeathed the house to my mother, though, and I inherited it from her. Since she did know what I was, I think I'm entitled to keep that and what Hilda left me."

"Legally, you could keep it all," Newpax said. "Even morally, it's what I would call problematic. But if it makes you feel better…From what I hear about the Graveston fortune, you won't be suffering anyway."

"You can almost see Paul's point," Tom commented. "Bram always lands on his feet, doesn't he?" The lazy grin with which he accompanied the statement freed it of any rancor. For once Tom appeared relaxed, content.

"You're forgetting my ugly mug," Bram pointed out.

"You'll make it work for you. I'm betting the ladies will find it romantic. Symptomatic of a dark, tortured past. Which," Tom added more seriously, "seems to be close to the truth. I'm through envying you. Maybe being poor isn't such a bad thing after all." He looked at his wife.

Inez nodded vigorously. "Poor is happier. More of a challenge."

"I might find out myself," Regan said, "if I don't get back home to keep an eye on my business. I'll be leaving tomorrow morning. I'll try to make it back for the fall conference."

"Please take our gratitude along," Day said, raising her glass. "To Regan. We would have been lost without you. And I mean that literally."

Murmurs of agreement and a clinking of glasses followed. Regan blushed rosily. "Thank you. But I think you would have found your way. I would like to add one thing."

She looked from Day to Bram. "Guilt is good up to the point it convinces you to repent and turn away from your wrongdoing. After that, it has served its purpose. You didn't make Paul what he was, Bram. His own choices did that. And it was his choice, not yours, that killed your brother."

"And a bad choice of my father's," Inez said. "He also thought that killing would make right. He was a hating man. But," she added practically, "I am not. So I do not think about it."

"I'm just wondering," Newpax said, "what would have happened if Javier had succeeded? In killing Royce Falco, I mean, and taking Bram here back to Mexico with him. Henry Day would have won the election, for one thing. Strange, isn't it, how one small move like a kid jumping into a road, can change so many lives?"

"Regan was saying something like that at the beginning," Gavin put in eagerly. "About how important your actions can really be. I didn't believe her at the time, but now I guess I do."

■　■　■

After the guests had left, Day, still in evening dress, was filling the sink to wash the china. From the living room, Bram, clumsily stacking cups from the after-dinner coffee, stopped to watch her. She had informed him earlier in the evening that she thought it time for her to quit working for him. "Frank is coming back tomorrow, and you won't have any trouble hiring another housekeeper now that this crisis is over. I've been offered my old job back, and I think I had better grab it while I can."

Bram turned his head to look into the mirror over the mantel. "You'll have to find yourself another identity," the therapist had said. And it was true. Now that he was no longer bound by his obligations to the dead, he didn't know who he was.

But he knew whom he wanted with him.

Would it be fair to ask her when she seemed to want to escape? And who wouldn't? He hadn't had to look at his ravaged face that much, but perhaps she had had her fill of it, her fill of him. Could she ever get beyond how his deception had led to her sister's death, to the blowing apart of her family? She had been very quiet since his confession in the stable the previous day. To add insult to injury, he had almost gotten her killed too.

He felt emotions that were unfamiliar to him: indecision, fear, reluctance to force the issue. *This isn't like you, Falco. You've always pushed your luck, and it's almost always worked for you. Give it one last run.*

Leaving the cups on the coffee table, Bram walked down the hall to his study to put an old record on the stereo. He flicked on the intercoms. When he returned to the kitchen, Day was smilingly listening to the strains of "Funny Face."

"Let's dance," he said, sweeping her into his arms and waltzing her out onto the terrace.

Below them, as on another night, flickered the flames lighting the rose-lined pathways. "You have a much better grip with that hand now," Day said.

"Haven't I? A much better grip on things in general, I think. I've never apologized to you for our last dance."

"Why should you? You made the right choice in the end."

"It was close," he said roughly. "It was very close."

"Besides, it was a lovely party. You've always given me lovely parties. Maybe I should apologize," she added impishly, "for costing you a prom queen twenty years ago."

"I didn't miss her. I did miss you though. As I said when we parted that time, it was the best night of my life."

Her head came up. "I don't remember that."

He laughed. "I said it in Spanish. I was a very cautious guy when it came to girls. I wanted to call you afterward, but I knew we had too much family baggage between us. Also I've always preferred my girlfriends to be vain and shallow."

"So you wouldn't feel bad about dumping them, I suppose."

"Bingo!"

"It's probably just as well that you didn't call then. Think what that would have said about me. I didn't expect you to, by the way."

"Think what that says about me. I didn't want to ruin a perfect memory. The reason I reacted so strongly about that arsenic was because after our prom you were something of an ideal to me, and I felt personally betrayed." She had her head down again so he couldn't read her expression. He laughed shakily. "Stupid, I know, after twenty years, but there you are. My reactions to you have never been exactly mild."

"So I've noticed. The truth is, I suppose, you've never trusted any woman since your real mother kicked you out into the streets. And Connie wouldn't have helped. You even kept poor Hilda at a distance, and she loved you like you were her son."

"I know. She could read me better than anyone else. I suppose that scared me."

"You're going to have to get over living like you're a fraud, you know. As if anyone who really finds you out won't like you."

"Now that you've found me out, what do you think?"

Her gaze slid only briefly upward before dropping away again. As if, he thought with a pang, she were avoiding his face.

"That doesn't matter, Bram. I told you, it's time for me to go and you to fly on your own. Now that you don't owe your parents anything, maybe you can decide what you really want."

"So you're setting me free as if I were one of your rehabilitated animals. Is that it?"

She smiled faintly. "That's the idea. I don't do this to make pets out of them, you know. I send them back out there to be what they were meant to be."

"I thought you said the natural animal was a tame animal."

"In an ideal world, maybe."

The music stopped, but he didn't remove his arm from her waist. "I know what I want."

Color crept up her face, and he felt a stiffening of resistance in her slender frame. "Don't say something you're going to regret, Bram. You just can't deal with a woman outside of a romantic relationship. Besides, I'm not Beauty, remember? I'm the bad fairy who really messed things up for you once."

"I don't know." He tilted her chin up to look at her face, but she kept her eyelids lowered. "Characters in fairy tales aren't always what they seem. Is there any reason the bad fairy can't turn into Beauty?"

"Because she's bad?"

"I don't think one mistake makes her bad. And the Beast could hardly talk, being so much worse. She might be sorry and come to nurse the poor guy. She might break her own spell. I like that story much better than the traditional one actually. That Beauty was just a little too ideal, if you know what I mean."

"I see." Her eyelashes flickered. "And how does she break this spell?"

"For that, I think the traditional way is fine. We mustn't improve too much on tradition, you know."

She smiled mechanically, but the resistance in her didn't relent. "I'm sorry, Bram. I don't think it's a good idea."

He released her, stepping away. "What is it?" he asked formally. "My face?"

"No, it isn't your face," she said crossly. "Don't be an idiot!"

"You still hate me?"

"I wish I could." She still refused to look at him.

"Are you sure it isn't you who is the distrustful one? You think I would run out on you like your father did?"

"Well, you haven't been exactly Mr. Dependability in the past, have you? You've deep-sixed a lot of women who were better looking than I am."

"Dame…" He stepped forward, but her fierce glare held him off.

"I am not going to be another one of your disposable doxies, Bram, and that's final!"

"So you don't believe I've changed."

Her expression softened. "I believe that you think you have. But at our age, change is very hard. You're right. I've never been good at trusting, and I don't know how to start now. I'm used to being poor and alone. I'll manage." She turned away toward the dishes remaining on the table.

At the same time, a dark-winged something launched itself down from the roof of the house, and she jumped back with a muffled shriek. Bram caught her from behind, wrapping both arms around her waist.

Ivan landed precariously on the back of a chair that teetered under his weight, leaned forward to snatch a half-finished steak from a plate, and launched himself upward again before the chair fell with a bang onto the tiles. "Oh no," Day said. "I forgot to put out any meat for him. You're supposed to do that for the first few days after they fly, until they get used to catching their own again."

"Face it," Bram murmured in her ear. "You've tamed two hawks, and you're going to have to decide what to do with us. Because Ivan and me, we're not going away."

For just an instant, she stiffened again, and his light tone deserted him. "Dame," he said hoarsely, urgently, "don't leave me! You're all I have!"

Resistance melted out of her, and she turned to look up at him. "Ivan will go," she whispered fiercely, "but you I'll keep.

I may be sorry, as the saying goes, but I'm quite sure I won't be bored."

Her brimming eyes were full of light and warmth that drew him irresistibly down to lips that yielded to the hungry demand of his twisted ones. Some distant part of his mind repeated its old cynical warning about the treacherous softness of women, but he was already too far gone to heed it.

When he finally raised his head to look down at her, he felt dazed. He put a tentative hand to her face and jerked the hand back again when he caught sight of his own misshapen fingers. She reached for them, raised them to her lips, and kissed them one by one and then stood on tiptoe to kiss the scars on his face. "I love you, my own personal Beast," she whispered. "And your wounds don't turn me off. Sometimes I wished they did, believe me."

He laughed huskily, turning his face against her hair. "Unconditional acceptance," he said. "The therapist said that was your duty, remember? I seem to recall that touching was required too. Lots of touching."

He could feel her responding laughter against his throat.

"You are outrageous, Bram. I knew you could have put that gel on yourself, if you really had wanted to."

"But it felt so much better when you did it. Will you marry me?"

Her laughter stopped, and her head came up.

"O ye of little faith," he mocked her gently. "I told you I was a changed character. Remember, unconditional acceptance."

"I think I should say that this has all been much too fast."

"Considering that our first date was twenty years ago, I would say we're a bit on the slow side myself. *Te amo, bella.*"

"You said that on our first date too. What does it mean?"

He lifted her hand to his lips. "I love you, beautiful one."

Her eyes welled up again. "You're just lucky I didn't know the language."

"Maybe deep down I hoped you did. Haven't we wasted too many years already?"

"To use the only Spanish I know, *si, señor,* I will marry you. But," she added provocatively as his hold tightened, "I have one stipulation. My animals must come with me."

"I'm sure I'll adapt to possums in the parlor eventually. Speaking of which…" He ran a hand deliberately through her hair. "Maybe I had better check that you're not hiding any excess baggage at the moment. No? Then kiss me again, Beauty. Maybe you can yet transform me into a prince."

If you would like to receive a complimentary subscription
to Thyme Will Tell,
Audrey Stallsmith's quarterly newsletter,
please write her at:

Audrey Stallsmith
Thyme Will Tell
P. O. Box 1136
Hadley, PA 16130

## Don't Miss the Other Thyme Will Tell Mysteries!

*Ask for these fine novels at your local bookstore!*

### Book One: Rosemary for Remembrance

When Regan Culver's beloved father is killed, she not only finds herself orphaned, but overwhelming evidence points to her as the murderer. Her only hope is to find the real killer herself—a quest that leads her from mysteries of the past into perils of the future in this thrilling gothic mystery of love, betrayal, and trust. (Available now; ISBN 1-57856-040-3)

"Stallsmith renders an enticing who-done-it mystery reminiscent of the popular *Murder She Wrote* TV series. Twists and turns will keep readers guessing the murderer's identity."
—*CBA Marketplace*

"This engrossing mystery has plenty of suspense, interesting characters, the requisite romance, and an added bonus of fascinating tidbits of herbal lore. It should appeal to women, who will identify with Regan as she struggles to allow her Christian faith to give her the strength she needs."
—*Church Libraries*

**BOOK TWO: MARIGOLDS FOR MOURNING**

When a popular high-school football star collapses into a coma on homecoming night, evidence indicates a heroin overdose. But did someone want the boy dead? Before garden designer/part-time sleuth Regan Culver and police chief Matt Olin can discover the truth and save the boy's life, they must make peace with each other. (Available now; ISBN 1-57856-054-3)